Maggody and the Moonbeams

An Arly Hanks Mystery

JOAN HESS

Simon & Schuster

New York London Toronto Sydney Singapore

SIMON & SCHUSTER
Rockefeller Center
1230 Avenue of the Americas
New York, NY 10020

Manufactured in the United States of America

1 3 5 7 9 10 8 6 4 2

Library of Congress Cataloging-in-Publication Data
Hess, Joan.
Maggody and the moonbeams : an Arly Hanks mystery /
Joan Hess.
p. cm.
1. Hanks, Arly (Fictitious character)—Fiction. 2. Maggody (Ark.
: Imaginary place)—Fiction. 3. Police—Arkansas—
Fiction. 4. Police chiefs—Fiction. 5. Policewomen—Fiction. 6.
Arkansas—Fiction. I. Title.

PS3558.E79785 M246 2001
813'.54—dc21   Library of Congress Control Number:
2001020208

ISBN 0-7432-0229-5

Maggody and the Moonbeams

1

To every thing, there is a season, be it football, baseball, Easter eggs, blushing brides, or professional bowling. This season in particular, heralded by the vernal equinox, had wafted in with honeysuckle-scented breezes, daffodils in starchy yellow tutus, belligerent thunderstorms, and the annual tsunami of hormones in the corridors of the high school—evidence of which could be found strewn along the banks of Boone Creek in the aftermath of moonlit nights. There may also have been a time to every purpose under the heaven, but it was hard to discern.

Especially for professional bowling.

I was in the front room (one of two, the other designated as the back room) of the red-bricked police department, situated catty-corner to the antiques store and with a clear view of the one stoplight in town, studying seed catalogues as if I might do something of a more botanical bent than planting my fanny in my cane-bottomed chair. Crime had skidded to a halt in Maggody, Arkansas, as far as I knew. The gingham curtains flapped sluggishly as I waged an internal debate: petunias versus marigolds, cucumbers versus zucchini. The possibilities were endless and the photographs lush. The tomatoes were worthy of excessive salivation when envisioned with four strips of crispy bacon and a generous slathering of mayonnaise between two slices of white bread. Only Yankees defile such perfection with lettuce.

My official title was Chief of Police Arly Hanks; defender of law, order, justice, the American way, and whatever else I'd been hired to do, having been the sole applicant with qualifications, or without, for that matter. My job mostly consisted of nailing speeders at the edge of town—I run a quality speed trap—and tracking down miscreants who failed to pay at the self-service pumps. Leaping over tall buildings in a single bound was not a challenge, since Maggody lacked them. Bank robberies were not a threat, the branch having burned to the ground a while back. Ditto the post office, as well as the Esso station out by the one-lane bridge. The block or so of what had been thriving businesses thirty years ago was now a stretch of hollow shells, the windows taped with bleached newspapers and flyers promoting events that had long since come and gone. Dunkin' Donuts and Burger King were not vying for the best location, and about all we could hope for was Toys Were Us.

There had been some bizarre moments, but these days we were reduced to Saturday night temper tantrums at the pool hall, a rare flareup on the bench outside the barbershop, and my dedicated (depending on the weather, anyway) attempts to find Raz Buchanon's moonshine operation up on Cotter's Ridge. For the most part, Maggody, Arkansas (population 755), was percolating just fine. Having come home to recuperate after a nasty divorce from a New York City advertising hotshot with silk boxers and a polyester mindset, I wanted nothing more than the opportunity to pull myself back together. And, well, a bacon and tomato sandwich, washed down with a cold beer and topped off with a slice of lemon meringue pie.

I was pondering where I might actually plant tomatoes when, to my deep dismay, the door burst open and Dahlia (nee O'Neil) Buchanon thundered into the PD. Three hundred plus pounds does thunder.

"Fire!" she shrieked.

"I don't smell smoke."

"At Ruby Bee's!"

Ruby Bee's Bar & Grill, for the unenlightened, is the establishment owned by my very own mother, whose nickname is short for Rubella Belinda, the family having an unfortunate tradition of choosing names for their melodic impact rather than pathology. The peculiar pink building is a hundred yards down the road from the PD, and the source for the majority of my carbohydrates, as well as all the local gossip, from Elsie's bunions to Mayor Jim Bob Buchanon's latest, but surely not last, excursion into infidelity.

"What do you mean?" I asked.

"I mean there's a fire, darn it! I was taking the babies for a walk, then I saw the smoke and—"

I stumbled to my feet. "A fire?"

"I swear," Dahlia said, wiping her cheeks with a tissue she'd pulled from a pocket hidden among the folds of her dress, "sometimes I wonder if you was huntin' wiffle birds when God passed out the brains. Smoke's pouring out of the bar. Bocaraton liked to run me over driving out of the parking lot, and Estelle is there, screeching to high heavens. It seems to me you might want to look into this, it being your mother and all."

Dahlia was far from being the tightest-wrapped Twinkie in the carton, but she had a point. I went around her and out to the edge of the road, sidestepping the double stroller constraining a pair of pensive, thumb-sucking passengers. Smoke was indeed pouring out of the bar, and an impromptu demolition derby was shaping up. Estelle Oppers, my mother's best friend and coconspirator in high crimes and misdemeanors, was flapping her arms like a woodpecker that had chanced upon a nest of plump termites.

"Did someone call the fire department in Hasty?" I asked Dahlia.

"How am I supposed to know that? I was a fire-drill monitor in sixth grade until Miz Myner caught me smoking in the girls' restroom. I was always real careful to put my butts in the toilet, but she still took away my badge and gave it to pimply ol' Himroyd Buchanon. He cackles about it to this day." She put her fists on what I supposed were her hips and stuck her face in mine; it was likely that one of us was on a sugar-high, and not from gazing at photographs of sweet potatoes. "Why doncha ask him if he called 'em, assuming you can lure him out of the root cellar behind his house? What's it been now—four years?"

I left her grumbling and hightailed it to the parking lot. There were no flames visible, but the smoke was hard to ignore, as well as the chaotic retreat of trucks, cars, and errant husbands who had no business guzzling beer at noon with their busty sweeties from the Pot O' Gold trailer park at the south end of town.

Estelle grabbed my arm. "You got to do something!"

"Is Ruby Bee in there?"

"She's in the kitchen with the fire extinguisher. I did my best to drag her out, but—"

I yanked myself free and barged inside. The fire seemed to be contained, but I could hear Ruby Bee howling, although in outrage rather than in pain. I snatched a thick wad of napkins from a dispenser, then took a deep breath, covered my mouth and nose, and opened the kitchen door. Smoke roiled at me, stinging my eyes and seeping through the napkins to scald my throat.

Ruby Bee was wielding the fire extinguisher with the confidence of a seasoned urban firefighter, swinging back and forth as she blasted the flames licking on the stove. If she were up against a dragon, I knew where I'd put my money.

"Git out of here!" she snarled without turning around. "I already said it's under control." She added a few comments that do not bear repeating, although I will admit I was impressed with her command of four-letter words. My fiftyish mother, with her rosy face, ruffled apron tied around a thick waist, pink eye shadow, and suspiciously blonde hair, could have matched any sailor in a bar in San Diego, hands down.

Forget I said that.

The fire was pretty much gasping its last. I opened the back door and the windows, then sat on a stool and waited until she set down the fire extinguisher. She and everything else, including me, were coated with a slimy film of yellowish powder.

"Grease fire, huh?" I said.

"Guess I don't have to call in a rocket scientist after all," she said as she used her apron to blot her eyes. "What happened was I was frying up some chicken when the phone rang. Duluth was carryin' on like circus elephants was putting up tents in his backyard, then Mrs. Jim Bob came in and started yacking at me about chaperoning a field trip. Before I could get free from her, Roy knocked over the pitcher of beer on his table, Bocaraton commenced to swinging at him, and I guess I flat-out forgot about the skillet of chicken right up until the smoke started pouring out of the kitchen like Satan had been loosed from hell."

I tried not to wrinkle my nose as I took in the stench. The ceiling was black, and the burners were crusted with charcoal and solidifying spew. The infamous skillet had been reduced to an artifact that would enthrall archeologists in a century or two, presuming it was buried in the nearest landfill. What remained of the chicken was decidedly extra-crispy. "Maybe he was."

"Don't go thinking this stove ain't cleaned on a regular basis," growled Ruby Bee. "Come rain or shine, every Tuesday morning I scour and scrub until my knuckles are raw. None of this would have happened if it hadn't been for Duluth, and Mrs. Jim Bob, and—"

"It doesn't matter."

"It does, too," she wailed, sinking down on the floor and covering her face. "The ventilators are clogged. I'm gonna have to find someone to scrape it all down. Insurance will most likely replace the stove, but the health department'll insist on inspecting everything and those folks are a sight slower than molasses in December. I might ought to just up and retire to Florida."

"And do what?" I asked as I sat down beside her. "Live off the proceeds of wet T-shirt contests?"

"I reckon I could find myself a rich old man with a hankering for cornbread and turnip greens."

I hugged her until she released a breath. "I hear the pickin's are slim. Besides, where would I have breakfast every morning and supper every evening? You wouldn't want me to subsist on chili dogs and onion rings from the Dairee Dee-Lishus, would you? Before too long, I'd be borrowing dresses from Dahlia to hide my thighs."

"What does it matter? You're not going to stay here forever, Arly. You're just biding your time before you leave again. It was real hard the first time, but I got through it 'cause I had no choice. Now I can see there's nothing for you here, nothing at all. All the young folk want to leave." She was right: the only ones that stay get married right out of high school, have babies, and scratch out a living like their folks, working at the poultry plant in Starley City and dreaming of nothing more than satellite dishes and a weekend at Branson once a year. Ruby Bee went on. "I almost understand why Diesel Buchanon went to live in a cave up on Cotter's Ridge. I'm not saying I share his affinity for squirrels and rabbits—they're gamey, no matter how you stew 'em—but this was all I had left, and—"

I swallowed a mouthful of guilt. "I'll be here for the time being, okay? You may have to close for a week or two, but there's no way Stump County can function without the daily blue plate specials at Ruby Bee's Bar & Grill. There'd be no happy hour for all the hard-working souls who deserve a beer and a basket of pretzels on Friday afternoon. No line-dancing on Saturday night, no telling what out back in the Flamingo Motel afterward. You don't want those randy couples driving all the way to Farberville."

"But you're gonna leave," she said flatly.

I licked my thumb and wiped a smudge of soot off her chin. "Yeah, eventually, but not before I'm ready to go back into battle." I looked up at the ceiling, which was dripping with foam stalactites. Another few gazillion years, and Ruby Bee's kitchen could compete with Carlsbad Cavern (ten intergalactic credits for general admission; discounts for senior citizens and children under twelve). The lemon-tinted stalagmites, on the other hand, were receding with odd little fizzles and wheezes.

Do not set off a fire extinguisher in the privacy of your own home to ascertain the accuracy of all this. You'll be sorry.

I was about to add something, although I wasn't quite sure what it might be, when Ruby Bee stood up.

"I can hear Estelle caterwauling out front like a possum in heat," she said gruffly. "Go tell her to stop it before the volunteer fire department shows up and starts squirting hoses. Once those boys have tracked mud on the dance floor and soaked all the staples in the pantry, they'll expect free beer. I can't face them and their smartass wisecracks just now."

"Why don't you call it a day? I'll run everybody off and lock the door."

To my surprise, she nodded. "I reckon so. Tell Estelle I'll call her in the morning. The rest of them can swill beer at the Dew Drop Inn or that bar in Hasty. I'm too tired to deal with the likes of Duluth and Mrs. Jim Bob."

"Go clean up, then make yourself a cup of tea and

spend the rest of the day watching soaps and talk shows on television. I'll call the insurance office."

"I feel so gosh darn stupid."

"You shouldn't," I said as I helped her to her feet.

"Sure, and Mrs. Jim Bob is gonna admit that she played fast and loose with the ballots for the last election at the Missionary Society. I heard tell Joyce Lambertino had quite a following, due in part to her tasty green tomato relish. She must have given me three quarts, and I ain't even a member." She forced a smile. "Guess I forgot to remind her of that."

"You need a bath and an aspirin." I regarded the damage, sighed, and added, "Don't worry. I'll track down a plumber and an electrician."

"And just what am I supposed to do in the meantime, missy? Do you think running a bar and grill is a pastime for when I get tired of trading stocks on the Internet and burying my profits in mayonnaise jars out in the pasture?"

I gave her a nudge. "Go on, Ruby Bee. I'll come by later."

She took a last look at the damage and went out the back door. I returned to the barroom, switched off all the pink and red neon beer signs, put the money from the cash register in the drawer beneath it, and locked the door on my way out.

"I can't imagine where the blasted fire department is," Estelle said, fuming as much as the fire extinguisher had. "Here Ruby Bee's being burnt to a cinder, and those ol' boys are sitting in a café somewheres, eating pie and flirting with the waitresses." Her voice rose several octaves. "There ought to be a law!"

I caught her shoulder and restrained her. "The fire is out and Ruby Bee's gone to her unit to lie down. She's not in the mood for company just now, but you can drop by in an hour. A bottle of sherry might be welcome." I handed her the one I'd filched from behind the bar.

"You sure? What if—"

"Real sure. I was in there, and the fire's out. It's hard to assess the extent of the damage to the kitchen, but Ruby Bee's unharmed. It's over."

"I tried to make her let me help her, but she wouldn't let me stay. You know I would have done whatever it took. I was filling pitchers with water when she shrieked at me to call the fire department and get everybody out of the barroom. That ain't to say anyone lingered to help."

"It's okay," I repeated.

"So how bad is it?"

"She'll be out of business for at least two weeks."

Estelle gnawed on her lip for a moment. "This is so awful, Arly. She's been real short of cash since she paid taxes, and everybody knows those insurance folks can be tighter'n bark on a tree. When my pipes burst a while back, you'd have thought it was my fault from the way they sniffed around and asked downright insultin' questions." She paused to make sure her towering beehive of red hair was firmly pinned; I saw no reason to point out that one of her false eyelashes was clinging to her chin like a suicidal spider. "I had to explain on more occasions than I care to remember that I wasn't in control of the temperature that particular night. When my power went out and—"

"We'll deal with it," I said. "Please wait until the volunteer fire department comes, and then send them away. My skin is crawling from the extinguisher residue. I'd really like to take a shower and change clothes."

I offered a few more words of reassurance, elicited her promise to wait in the parking lot, and headed for my so-called efficiency apartment above Roy Stiver's antiques store. Housing's limited in Maggody, and my only other option had been one of the units in the Flamingo Motel. Ruby Bee manages to look the other way, but everybody knows that the majority of customers would rent rooms by the hour if they could. Parchment-thin walls and squeaky beds might have left me counting things other than sheep.

I'd almost made it across the road when a muck-splattered pickup truck cut me off. It was, I regret to say, operated by our local moonshiner and purveyor of fetid stenches, Raz Buchanon. His beard was encrusted with the usual accumulation of crumbs and speckles of chewing tobacco, and his teeth were awaiting their semiannual encounter with a toothbrush. If that.

"Howdy, Arly," he said. "Ruby Bee okay?"

"She's fine, and thanks for asking, Raz. I'm on my way to clean up, so if you—"

"I could see the smoke all the way from my back porch. I dint know what to make of it at first. Marjorie got to frettin' sumphin' fierce, so I thought I'd better come see fer myself. Idalupino dun told me what happened."

"An accident," I said with a cursory grimace. "Now I'd like to—"

"Got sumphin' to ask you, Arly."

"Later, Raz."

He loosed a stream of tobacco juice that splattered on the pavement only a few inches from my foot, knowing damn well that I'd freeze. Seemingly oblivious to my scowl, he said, "A while back Marjorie and me was watchin' this show on the Discovery Channel about how racehorses have what they call companion animals to calm their jitters. They said how these horses are thoroughbreds, but so's Marjorie, ye know. Not ever' sow has a pedigree."

"And a very fine sow she is," I said evenly. "Enter her in the Kentucky Derby next month. Ruby Bee will undoubtedly offer a special on mint juleps, and Mayor Jim Bob can make book in the corner booth. Now, if you so much as look as though you're thinking about spitting on me, I will find a fire extinguisher and shove the nozzle where the sun don't shine. Do you understand?"

"You got no call to say that, Arly," he whined. "I was jest asking for your advice. You're the chief of police, ain't ye?"

"Thirty seconds, starting now."

"So like I said, Marjorie and me watched this show and she took to mopin' around the house, wishin' she had a companion animal like those fancy horses. I could tell right off what was ailing her, so I went into Farberville and bought her a gerbil. You know about gerbils, Arly? They look like—"

"I know what gerbils look like."

"Well," he said, puffing up his cheek and then wincing when I glowered, "ye might say it dint work out."

"Why not?"

His squinty eyes shifted away from me. "There ain't no reason to go into that. Lately I've been thinkin' about gittin' Marjorie a mule. Perkins owns one that ain't no good for much of anything, but he sez if I so much as drive onto his place, he'll greet me on his porch with a shotgun." He glanced at me, then spat on the floorboard of his truck. "Perkins got hisself a real bad attitude."

Sweat was beginning to dribble down my face, and I suspected it resembled tar. Every inch of my body itched so intensely that I wanted to rip off my clothes and attack myself with a toilet bowl brush.

"Raz," I said, "this is a terrible dilemma. If you'll tell me where your still is, I will personally intervene with Perkins so that Marjorie can have her very own pet mule."

"I ain't got a still, and there's no way of knowin' if Marjorie'll fancy Perkins's mule. They might not be compatible."

"You most certainly do have a still, you devious sumbitch, and one of these days I'll put you not only out of business, but also behind bars at the state pen. When that happens, Marjorie will find herself with a butcher for a companion—but not for long."

Raz gave me a deeply insulted look, slammed his truck
into gear, and took off with a squeal of rubber that almost,
but not quite, roused the nappers out in front of the barber
shop. Dahlia waved a fist at him and mouthed what most
likely were not endearments. Two boys on bicycles went
down in the gravel in front of the defunct New Age hardware store, but they undoubtedly were already dotted with
scabs and scratches. Growing up in Maggody will do that.

I hurried up the rickety wooden staircase on the side of
the antiques store and into my apartment. The cockroaches
skedaddled, the hot water heater obliged, and half an hour
later, I was feeling much better. I left my hair down until it
dried and I could pin it back up into a schoolmarmish bun
intended to discourage unwanted attention from good ol'
boys named Bubba, Bo, and Jellybelly.

I'd just started a fresh pot of coffee when Duluth
Buchanon came into the PD. He was short, thick-necked,
and cursed with the infamous Buchanon yellow eyes and
simian brow. We'd had a couple of encounters, once when
he'd driven his truck off the low-water bridge and I'd been
obliged to transport him to the county drunk tank, and another occasion at the supermarket when he'd tried to
shoplift a canned ham by stuffing it down his trousers, but
he did better than most of his kinfolk. Some members of the
clan, including the aforementioned Raz and Mayor Jim
Bob, can stare down bobcats and rattlesnakes. Others, such
as Dahlia's husband, lose the contest to bullfrogs, chip-
munks, and broken glass glinting in the weeds. Buchanons
run the gamut—if and when they can find it.

"Coffee?" I asked Duluth.

"Reckon so," he said as he dropped into the chair
across from my desk. "Ruby Bee all right?"

"She put out the fire in the kitchen, but not before a lot
of damage was done. It's a real mess."

"You want I should go by and take a look at it? I can

clean up, scrub the walls and ceiling, paint, replace cabinet doors, that kind of thing. I got no control over the cost of materials, but I'll give her a discount on labor."

I brought him a mug of coffee. "That'd be great, Duluth, and I know Ruby Bee will appreciate it. I was told you were upset earlier. Is there something you want to talk about?"

He took a thoughtful slurp. "Well, I suppose there is. My ex-wife, Norella, done run off."

"Norella's not from Maggody, is she?"

"Her family's mostly over in Splaid County. Her pa owned a feed store till he died of some sort of disease of a personal nature. Her and me was living at the Pot O' Gold in a real fine double-wide. Dishwasher, garbage-disposal, miniblinds, shag carpeting, everything I could give her. We had three boys in five years. I was still hoping for a little girl, but Norella went and had some operation after Jakob was born. I wasn't happy, but I sure as hell didn't make an effort to talk her out of it. When I came home from work, the trailer was always stinking of dirty diapers and vomit."

I tried to dredge up gossip that had been of minimal interest. "But you got divorced last year?"

"More like two years ago, come August. In the settlement, she was ordered to let me have the boys every other weekend and half the summer. Last fall she took to keeping them from me, saying they had doctor appointments or sleepovers with their cousins. I finally had to call my lawyer and have him file contempt charges. She countered with charges that I'd been hitting her and got a restraining order." He paused to swallow, and his eyes filled with tears from either the injustice of the accusation or the aftertaste of what I passed off as coffee. "I never laid a hand on her, Arly, not even when I found out she was sneaking around with her sister's husband. I just moved out and filed for divorce."

"This should be resolved in court."

"It would have been if she hadn't disappeared with my boys. Is there anything you can do?"

I opened a notebook and made a few notes. "Any idea what might have caused her to disappear like this?"

"Josie and me got married at Christmas. A month later, someone threw a rock through the living-room window. Two weeks back I found a pile of manure on the front porch. Right after that is when I learned she'd packed up everything and run off."

"Did you ask her family if anyone knows where they might be?"

He shook his head. "Her mother's called everybody she can think of, on account of she's as worried as I am about the boys. If you want to talk to her, she'll tell you same as I did, that I ain't ever done anything bad to Norella. I paid child support on the first of every month like the judge ordered, even when she wouldn't let me see the boys. I might not have been the best husband, but ain't nobody can accuse me of being a bad father."

"I understand, Duluth," I said, "but this is a family court matter. Norella has custody. She may have violated the visitation decree, but technically she hasn't kidnapped the boys."

"I suppose not," he said as he stood up and put the mug on the corner of my desk. "Thanks for hearing me out. Soon as I finish waiting around to talk to my lawyer in Farberville and trying to track down Norella, I'll go by Ruby Bee's and see what all I can do. I'm liable to be tied up for the time being, so you might ought to find somebody else."

I sprinted to the door. "Okay, Duluth, let me see what I can find out. Here's the key to the bar and grill. Assess the damage and get back to me."

"Norella's ma said she didn't think Norella had more than twenty or thirty dollars. None of the rest of the family's seen hide nor hair of her. I called the battered women's shelter in Farberville, but they were real tight-lipped. You might start there."

"I'll do my best," I vowed sincerely, "and talk to you later this afternoon."

His eyes may have been yellowish, but they were also shrewd as he nodded and left.

I was thumbing through the directory for the number of the shelter when yet another Buchanon intruded, confirming my view that there are entirely too many Buchanons in Stump County—or anywhere else on the planet.

"Arly," said Mrs. Jim Bob (aka Barbara Ann Buchanon Buchanon) as she came inside and sat down, making certain to smooth down her skirt and cross her ankles. Her white blouse was so brittle with starch that it crinkled like aluminum foil when she moved.

I propped my feet on the corner of my desk. "That's my name. Need my rank and serial number?"

"No, I need a favor."

"You want I should shoot Jim Bob? I'll have to bill you for the bullet, you know, but it will be worth it. Not one soul in Maggody will skip the funeral. Afterward, we can all enjoy Ruby Bee's green bean casserole and Estelle's special snowflake salad and—"

"Don't be impertinent, missy. We are going to need your assistance for the next . . . few days. I was under the impression that it was all under control, then Eula came down with a head cold and Elsie had the audacity to announce she was going to her niece's wedding in Texarkana. Millicent's rheumatism is flaring up and she can hardly be expected to come to our aid."

"As in?" I asked.

"The youth group at the Voice of the Almighty Lord Assembly Hall is scheduled to spend a week at Camp Pearly Gates down in the south part of the county, just past Dunkicker. I need a chaperon."

My feet hit the floor so abruptly that I came damn close to falling out of my chair. "What does that have to do with me?"

"The group is going the day after tomorrow. Six girls, four boys. It is imperative that they have constant supervision to prevent any sort of immoral interaction. I assume you know what *that* means. I'd hoped Lottie would accompany us, but she's barricaded herself in her house and refuses to answer the door. To think she calls herself a good Christian!"

"Cancel it."

"Camp Pearly Gates used to be a summer camp for children with asthma, cancer, and the like. Now church congregations all across the state have agreed to pitch in and restore it. Our youth group voted to go there instead of Branson for their spring break. I fell to my knees and thanked the Lord that all those years of Sunday school finally paid off and they're willing to make the sacrifice and utilize their youthful energy to help the less fortunate."

I really, truly hated it when she had the moral high ground. "But I don't see why you should need a second chaperon. Your presence ought to be more than adequate to keep them in line. Take hymnals and lots of marshmallows."

"Brother Verber will be accompanying us, naturally, but he and I will stay in the lodge, where we can supervise the work assignments, monitor supplies, see that kitchen chores are carried out, and lead nightly gatherings of a spiritual nature. Larry Joe Lambertino will be staying in the boys' cabin. You'll be with the girls. Between the four of us, we ought to be able to maintain discipline and prevent rampant promiscuity." She gave me the sharp look of a crow perched on a mound of putrefying flesh. "You of all people should know what wickedness these teenagers get into around here. This very morning I found whiskey bottles in the ditch in front of my driveway, and Jim Bob swears they steal so many packs of cigarettes from the supermarket that he can barely keep the shelves stocked. Just imagine what they'd do without someone to ride herd on them. I feel faint thinking about it."

She did look a bit pale, but it might have been caused by her girdle rather than the vision of couples behaving with abandon under the whispering pines.

"You'll have to find someone else," I said. "I already have a full-time job making sure the inmates don't take over the institution. If Larry Joe's agreed, why not ask Joyce to go, too?"

"I suppose she might, as long as you're willing to baby-sit their children. I happened to see them at the supermarket the other day, and it was all I could do not to rip open a box of tissue and wipe their disgusting noses. I'd be real surprised if they don't all have head lice. Joyce has never struck me as the sort to pay much attention to hygiene or personal appearance. Larry Joe's shirts look like he sleeps in them. I shudder to think what kind of example he's setting for the impressionable youth in his shop classes. I was fully expecting the whole town to come down with food poisoning after Joyce passed out jars of that repulsive green slime."

I stared at the water stain on the ceiling. "What about Ruby Bee? She might enjoy a restful week at this camp."

"And go prowling in the woods with a flashlight? How are you going to feel when she's bitten by a snake and dies? Why don't you start writing the eulogy about how you sent your own mother to her death because you couldn't be bothered? What kind of message will that send to our young people, who have volunteered to pass up waterslides and corndogs to help sick children deserving of a carefree week at camp? Some of those little children won't be with us a year from now, you know. I don't know if Jesus runs a summer camp up in heaven, but—"

"I can't take off for a week."

Her lips curled upward. "Yes, you can. The town council voted last night."

"In a secret meeting?"

"As you well know, I am married to the mayor of Maggody, and I saw to it that you were given permission to take a week of vacation time to accompany us to Camp Pearly Gates. We're meeting at the Voice of the Almighty Lord Assembly Hall on Saturday morning at six o'clock sharp. You'll need clothing, personal items, a sleeping bag, insect repellent, and a reliable flashlight. The teenagers will be bringing their Bibles, but since everybody knows you're an atheist, we won't ask that of you."

I did not ask if it might be more expedient to bring a case of condoms.

2

Once Mrs. Jim Bob had swept out in an acidic haze of self-righteousness, I sat back and wondered how difficult it might be to provoke an appendicitis that would allow me the better part of a week of TLC in the Farberville hospital, where I could indulge in pudding, overcooked broccoli, and cable television.

The specific organ failed to twinge.

I did not give up hope of anything short of spontaneous combustion, but resigned myself to deal with the matters at hand. I found the number of the battered women's shelter, dialed it, and was informed that no one named Norella Buchanon had been or currently was in residence. End of conversation, as in dial tone.

With reluctance, I called the sheriff's office. The dispatcher, LaBelle, always interprets my calls as a threat to her despotic rule, but eventually transferred me to Sheriff Harve Dorfer, who presents himself as a good ol' boy but can outwit the majority of the vermin in the county. Outwit them, but not necessarily outrun them; Harve's never met a chicken-fried steak or cheap cigar not to his liking.

"Coincidence you called," he said genially. "We got this ol' boy out in DeWatt, name of Ebie Whitebread, who's convinced communists are stealing his sheep."

"I'm not in the mood for sheep, Harve," I said. I told him what Duluth had told me. "Any chance to track her down? She's violating the court-ordered visitation."

"Norella Buchanon," he mumbled under his breath.

"Name's ringing a bell. Hang on a minute; I reckon there's more to the story." Wheezing, he shuffled papers, then scritched a match to light a cigar and said, "Yep, she's on the list of folks we'd like to talk to about a meth lab out in Emmett. We didn't issue a warrant, but she was told to show up here ten days ago."

"And she didn't."

"Hard to pull the wool over your eyes, ain't it? Let me see what I can find out, then I'll call you back."

I replaced the receiver, called Ruby Bee's insurance agent and set all that in motion, then spent some time fooling with my hair. Thus far I had resisted Estelle's offers to frost it, cut it, layer it, crimp it, curl it, or tint it auburn. I'd also resisted discounts on mascara, eyeliner, and lipstick. Beauty pageants in Branson were not on my agenda.

Harve called back the next day to say that the shelter had referred Norella to a community outreach service in Farberville, and that they had been unable to help her beyond a fifteen-dollar voucher for gas and a few coupons for a fast-food chain. After some not especially subtle prodding from me, he agreed there might be something in the file on the meth lab bust that might persuade the county prosecutor to put out a warrant for her. Law enforcement agencies across the state would not be searching for her, but if an officer pulled her over and checked the license plate, we might hear about it.

I found Duluth, bless his soul, in the kitchen at Ruby Bee's Bar & Grill and told him what little I'd learned. I lamely added that I'd spend more time on it when I returned from a week at Camp Pearly Gates. His surly look implied that I might as well remain there for all eternity, or at least a goodly portion of the thereafter.

And so I found myself shivering outside the Voice of the Almighty Lord Assembly Hall at six o'clock on Saturday morning, my essentials crammed in a duffel bag, my eyes grainy, my lips a shade of blue that not even Estelle could match had it been bewitching, which it wasn't. Various teenagers, including Darla Jean McIlhaney and Heather Riley, were deposited by parents who drove away with disturbingly gleeful expressions. The Dahlton twins were shoved out of a car that barely slowed down. Billy Dick MacNamara literally dove out of the back of a pickup truck as it raced past us.

"What are you doing here?" Darla Jean asked me, her teeth chattering either from the frost forming on her braces or the proximity to a law enforcement agent.

"I don't know," I answered sincerely.

Heather, the blonde who possibly was responsible for all the jokes, frowned. "You don't even attend this church. According to Brother Verber, you're destined for eternal damnation. He said you were going to sizzle in Satan's fiery furnace till the end of time."

"Did he?" I murmured as I glanced at the silver trailer that served as a rectory. "Sounds warm."

"Mrs. Jim Bob says you're an atheist," contributed one of the Dahlton twins.

"What's more," said Parwell Haggard, whose face was dotted with glossy pustules, "we heard tell you was a prostitute when you lived in New York City. You painted your face and walked the streets in short skirts and see-through blouses."

I wished I could see through him.

Larry Joe Lambertino arrived before I allowed myself to lapse into violence. He unfolded himself from the passenger's seat of the station wagon, said something I'm sure was meant to be heartening to his wife, Joyce, and managed to grab his suitcase and a sleeping bag out of the back before she drove away. I couldn't tell exactly how many children were crammed inside, but I had to agree with Mrs. Jim Bob's assessment of their noses.

"How'd you get talked into this?" he asked me, jamming his hands into his coat pockets. He was reedy, as if he could be blown over with less than half a huff and a puff, and had the unfortunate habit of scratching his head and appearing totally bewildered when tossed even the most innocuous question. No wonder; he wasn't all that much older than I, but he'd been teaching shop at the high school and moonlighting as a custodian when I'd contrived to escape. He'd undoubtedly spent more time with a mop than I had in line to use the ladies' room at Carnegie Hall during intermission; neither of us was the wiser for it.

"Same way you did, I suppose," I said.

"Ruby Bee doin' okay?"

It was a question I'd answered several dozen times in the previous two days, but I smiled and said, "Duluth is handling the repairs. His second cousin's an electrician, and his nephew's father-in-law is a plumber. The insurance appraiser promised to come out Monday and start the paperwork. Ruby Bee's pretty much staying in her unit."

"Down in the mouth, huh?"

My smile faded. "She'll be fine once she's back to baking biscuits and apple pies."

"Joyce is gonna take by some cookies later today and invite her over for supper. Maybe getting out will cheer her up."

"I hope so, Larry Joe," I said as I turned away, thinking about a certain condo in Manhattan. I wouldn't have recognized a neighbor if we'd jostled each other for position in the deli. Some of us had shared a view, but never a meal or even a conversation about anything more personal than the sluggishness of the elevator.

A few minutes later Brother Verber staggered out of his trailer, dragging a suitcase that must have contained enough clothes to hold him until the Judgment Day and a few millenniums thereafter. His nose was no rosier than usual, but what tufts of hair remained on his head stuck out like bolls of cotton. I didn't have the heart to tell him that his socks were mismatched, but I could tell from giggles behind me that it had not gone unnoticed.

We were milling about when Mrs. Jim Bob drove up in what had been a pint-size school bus but was now painted pastel blue and emblazoned with lettering that proclaimed it to be FLY BY NIGHT DRY CLEANING: YOUR STAIN IS OUR PAIN.

"It's going to be a tight squeeze," she announced as she climbed out, "but the rent was cheap and we're on a mission for the Almighty Lord. The twelve disciples relied on faith, not seatbelts. Put your gear in the back."

Although I knew there was a flaw in the sentiment, I was too groggy to figure it out. Within twenty minutes or so, the remainder of the designated do-gooders arrived and threw duffel bags, bedrolls, and backpacks into the bus, which was already jammed with boxes of food, tools, and a canvas bag of softball equipment. Brother Verber offered a brief prayer for our safety, tucked what looked suspiciously like a pint bottle in his coat pocket, and waved us into the bus.

Us, as in ten teenagers and four adults, in a space designed for half that number and reeking of whatever chemicals are used to eliminate grape juice stains. I was more concerned about potential bloodstains.

"Git your hand off of me, Billy Dick," hissed Darla Jean.

Mrs. Jim Bob glanced in the rearview mirror. "We will have none of that! Our mission is to follow through on our work assignment so that sickly children can spend a week in the fresh air before they join Jesus. Brother Verber, would you like to lead us in a hymn?"

"The Old Rugged Cross" lasted for a mile or so, and we had subsequently worked our way down from a hundred bottles of beer (nonalcoholic, of course) on the wall to sev-

enteen before we rattled across a cattle guard and under a
blistered sign proclaiming the entrance to Camp Pearly
Gates. Heather, who'd been moaning the entire time, made
good on her threat and threw up on my shoe. Big Mac
Buchanon made one final attempt to stick his head between
my legs, then sat up and said, "You reckon this is it?"

"Abandon all hope," I muttered, wishing I'd brought a
second pair of shoes.

Mrs. Jim Bob slammed on the brakes, sending Darla
Jean into the front seat and both Dahlton twins on top of
Jarvis Kennistern, who'd been napping on the floor and
woke up with a yelp. Larry Joe, whose head had been rest-
ing on Amy Dee's ample bosom, sat upright as though he'd
been jabbed with a dull needle. Various knees and elbows
collided.

Our commander-in-chief ignored the squeals and
squeaks behind her. "Brother Verber, get out the map we
were sent by the caretaker. The lodge is up ahead, but we
need to find the cabins. I do believe the girls will be up on
the hill and the boys down by the lake."

"Ain't this a pretty place?" Brother Verber said as he
rummaged through his pockets. "I can just see all the little
children frolicking happily, unawares of their limited time.
Once the dock is fixed up, they'll be paddlin' canoes and—"
He broke off abruptly.

"And what?" she said.

He looked back at me. "Did you see something in those
trees?"

"Like a squirrel?" I said as I slapped at Big Mac, who
was gnawing on my neck with adolescent fervor. I looked
out the dust-streaked window at the oak trees, scruffy
pines, and thickets of brambles leading down the hill to a
large lake. Dogwoods were still in bloom, as were redbuds
and varied wildflowers. What had once been a ball field
was overgrown with contentious clumps of weeds; the

bleachers we'd been sent to repair were rusted skeletons. A concrete pit, presumably the swimming pool, was now likely to be the breeding grounds for algae, tadpoles, water moccasins, and typhoid fever.

I felt no regret that I'd left my bathing suit at home.

Mrs. Jim Bob sighed. "We did not drive all this way to observe nature, Brother Verber."

He found a folded paper, studied it for a long moment, and said, "I ain't right sure, but it looks like Larry Joe and the boys can get out here and make their way to their cabin, then come to the lodge to unload supplies."

I grabbed a handful of Big Mac's hair and jerked him away before he could progress to my earlobe. "An excellent idea."

The sperm bank was deposited at the end of what one hoped was a path. We drove past an impressive stone lodge, replete with a broad veranda and weathered wicker furniture, and bounced along the road to a concrete-block building with a sagging roof.

"Eeew," said Darla Jean. "I can already feel the spiders crawling up my back. I wanna go home."

"Snakes," Heather added, hissing in an appropriately reptilian fashion.

Amy Dee gulped loudly. "Snakes? What kind of snakes?"

"We hate snakes!" the Dahlton twins shrieked in unison.

Reminding myself that we were on a worthy mission, I opened the door of the bus and dragged the most vocal of the group out onto the pine needles. "I will make sure that there are no spiders or snakes in the cabin. Once we're established, I doubt so much as a tree frog will risk crossing the threshold."

Tough talk. I opened the warped door and paused to allow whatever critters might have been in residence to beat a timely retreat. The structure was a good thirty feet long, lined on both sides with rickety iron bunk beds and a decor that seemed to consist of cobwebs and balls of dust—or possibly fur. What screens there were on the windows hung in tatters. The concrete floor was littered with what appeared to be rodent droppings, some distressingly fresh.

"It's fine," I announced as I went outside.

Brother Verber was at the back of the bus, pulling out sleeping bags and backpacks. He pulled me aside and, in a moist whisper, said, "I swear I saw something, Arly."

"Like what?"

"I don't know," he said, mopping his face with a handkerchief. "A fluttery white figure with a face like a skull. You don't think this place is haunted, do you?"

"If the staff was nondenominational, you might have spotted a Methodist from the netherworld. They can be pesky, or so I'm told."

He stepped away as Mrs. Jim Bob approached. "Get the girls settled," she said to me, "and then bring them down to the lodge. The pastor from the Baptist church over in Dunkicker assured me that the kitchen is acceptable, but knowing what I do about Baptists, I have misgivings. What's more, a group of Unitarians last stayed here, and we simply cannot trust them to have left the kitchen in a sanitary condition."

"Unitarians?" said Brother Verber, gazing nervously at the thick barrier of brush. "Do we know for sure that they went home?"

I left the two of them to sort it out and went into the cabin. The girls had spread their sleeping bags on the bunks, set out plastic bottles of shampoo and conditioners along the windowsills, and were busily fixing each other's hair, applying lipstick, and giggling as if nitrous oxide was seeping through the cracks in the concrete floor.

"Five minutes," I said, then stopped as Darla Jean pranced out from the bathroom at the back, dressed in a bikini that covered very little of her significant areas.

"Did anyone bring sunblock?" she asked.

I glared at her. "It's my understanding that we're here to renovate the campgrounds."

"Yeah, right," drawled Heather, "like we're gonna spend our spring break building bleachers at the softball field. It's a good thing I brought my algebra book so I can stay up every night and study."

"And floss," said one of the Dahlton twins. "Just imagine a whole week of flossing."

"I'm gonna floss from dusk till dawn," said the other.

Amy Dee squatted on the end of a bunk. "I'm thinking I might use this week to memorize the books of the Bible so I can get a ribbon at Sunday school. Genius, Exit Us, Levitation, Numbers—"

"You couldn't memorize your telephone number," said a girl with greasy black hair and wire-rimmed glasses, who'd been introduced as Amy Dee's cousin from Paris (Arkansas). "I hear Billy Dick sure did, though."

Darla Jean spun around. "What's that supposed to mean, bitch?"

"How would I know, whore?"

The squabble might have escalated into hair-pulling had Mrs. Jim Bob not come into the cabin. "I think we'd better get a few things straight right now," she said with all the warmth of a prison matron on death row. "As you were warned, alcohol and tobacco are prohibited. No bare midriffs or unseemly dress of any nature. Profanity will result in extra kitchen duty. We will gather at seven sharp each morning for the raising of the flag and the recitation of the Pledge of Allegiance. Breakfast will be served at seven-fifteen, lunch at noon, and supper at six. Gatherings of an appropriately inspirational nature will be held at seven, with lights out at ten o'clock and not a second later. Two of you will be assigned to prepare each meal; the boys will clean up afterward." She waggled a finger at each of them in turn. "What there will not be, under any circumstances, is hanky-panky. We are here to do God's work, which, in this case, happens to be rebuilding the bleachers and repairing the dock."

"Why don't the boys have to cook?" asked Darla Jean.

Mrs. Jim Bob chewed on this for a moment. "Because a woman's place is in the kitchen, but if you'd prefer to hose down the garbage cans, it can be arranged."

"I'm sure she would," I said, winning Darla Jean's dedicated animosity for the next seven days, and possibly until she moved away from Maggody to get a job eviscerating chickens in Starley City.

"Well, then," said Mrs. Jim Bob, "I shall expect all of you at the lodge shortly. We need to unload supplies. Brother Verber will be in charge."

Heather snickered. "You and Brother Verber are staying there by yourselves, right? Arly's going to keep track of us, and Mr. Lambertino will be watching the boys, but what's to stop you and Brother Verber from . . . ?"

Mrs. Jim Bob's lips tightened. "From what, Heather? Feel free to finish your sentence."

"It's just that everybody knows, or they think they do, that you and he . . ."

"Go on," she said coldly.

"Well, ever since you all were caught up at the cave by Raz's still, you know, the both of you wearing lacy lingerie—"

"There is an explanation, Heather. Perhaps you would care to come to the lodge and scrub the kitchen floor on your hands and knees while I share it with you?"

Heather did what I would have done, which was to start mumbling like crazy as she backed into the bathroom at the far end of the cabin. Mrs. Jim Bob shot her a final beady look, then reminded us that we were due at the lodge in ten minutes and drove away in the blue bus.

I clapped my hands until I had their attention. "Okay, ladies, you agreed to this. No one was hogtied and tossed onto the bus. You will have the chance to sunbathe, roast marshmallows, and sing camp songs, but you will not—and I repeat, will not—go wandering down the road to meet with someone of the opposite sex. One week consists of a mere seven days. We'll get up at six-thirty and be in our bunks at ten o'clock. We will stay in our respective bunks for the rest of the night. Questions?"

"Did you notice that Mr. Lambertino has a dimple?" drawled a Dahlton twin.

"And a cute butt?" said the other.

Darla Jean fell back on a bunk. "Give me a break! Next thing you're gonna say is the dimple's on his butt."

It may have taken ten minutes for the giggles and increasingly ribald remarks to subside, but eventually I calmed them down and escorted them to the lodge. Mr. Dimpled Butt was supervising the boys as they carried boxes into the lodge, Brother Verber seemingly having excused himself.

The main room of the lodge was dominated by a stone fireplace and broad windows with a view of the lake. Had it been crowded with leather sofas and easy chairs, it might have been charming. A dozen or so corroded folding chairs failed to provide the ambiance. The dining room resembled a mess hall, appropriately enough, and the kitchen had been scoured into shape by the Unitarians or the Baptists.

"Are you planning to feed these kids any time soon?" I asked Mrs. Jim Bob, who was waving her arms and issuing orders as if she fancied herself to be the director of a movie set.

"Did you not hear what I said earlier? Lunch will be provided at noon."

"They might be getting hungry."

"Or they might be filled with the glory that comes with doing the Almighty's work. As soon as we're unloaded, Larry Joe will take half of them to the softball field to start work on the bleachers. The rest, under your supervision, will get busy on the dock. Their rewards will not come from self-indulgence, but in knowing they are humble servants of the Lord. I hope you'll share that, too, Arly. I shudder every time I envision you in Satan's claws for all eternity. Look at this as your opportunity to—"

"That wasn't part of the deal," I interrupted. "I approve of what the kids have volunteered to do, and applaud them. On the other hand, I did not agree to be bombarded with pieties for a week. Don't think for a second that I can't walk back to the highway and hitch a ride home. Try for a lower bunk near the bathroom and keep an eye out for bats. The rafters may be a prime habitat for the Almighty's nocturnal rodents."

"Your attitude does not surprise me."

"What's more," I said, really heating up, "I am not going to head a work crew. My idea of a tool is a nail file. Larry Joe's in charge."

We were eyeballing each other when Brother Verber appeared, his demeanor a bit wobbly, his grin suspiciously genial. "The Unitarians did a right dandy job cleaning up the lodge," he announced. "The bedrooms upstairs ain't as nice as motel rooms, but they're clean. There's toilet paper in the bathrooms, jars with dried flowers, and crayon drawings taped on some of the walls. It made me think of when Jesus said, 'Let those li'l children come unto me.'" He pulled out a handkerchief and blew his nose. "It wrenched my heart, just imagining them with their disfigured limbs and withered lungs. I reckon a lot of them was orphans, locked away all year except for the one week they were allowed to frolic in the sunshine and—"

"What an appropriate topic for your evening homily," said Mrs. Jim Bob, grabbing Jarvis as he attempted to sidle behind her with a package of cookies half-hidden under his shirt. "I'm sure this young man would be honored to participate with a personal interpretation of one of the Ten Commandments." She tightened her grip on his wrist. "You may go to your cabin and contemplate the meaning of 'Thou shalt not steal.' If this concept confuses you, we can discuss it further."

"It's been a long while since breakfast," he said sullenly.

"There is no justification for breaking a commandment," she countered. "I do believe you need to spend the remainder of the day reading your Bible and praying for forgiveness. Should you and the Lord reach an accord, you may come to supper."

Although he was bulky enough to be drafted by an NFL team, he hung his head. "Yes, ma'am."

I felt the need to intervene. "That's unreasonable, Mrs. Jim Bob, and what's more, we need his help with the bleachers. Why don't you allow him to apologize and let it go?"

Brother Verber fell to his knees and clasped his hands together. "Lord, I sense we have a sinner about to repent his wicked ways and come back into the fold. Listen to the words of this prodigal son, then throw open Your arms and absolve him. It's gonna happen, Lord, and then we can all exalt in Thy mercy. Say it, boy! Let it ring out so that every squirrel and songbird can hear it!"

Jarvis handed Mrs. Jim Bob the package of cookies, then took a deep breath and said, "I'm real sorry and I'll never steal anything again as long as I live."

"Hallelujah!" boomed Brother Verber. "Let us all kneel and give thanks for this miracle on our very first day at Camp Pearly Gates!"

Mrs. Jim Bob remained standing. "Or at least an admission of guilt. All right, Jarvis, you may help with the bleachers this morning and have lunch with the others. I do hope we won't have any other problems with you this week. Your parents will not be pleased if I have to call them to fetch you. I understand your father's been laid off and your mother's cancer has come back. It would only add to their troubles if they found out you were nothing but a common thief and they had to drive all this way. You wouldn't want that, would you?"

"No ma'am."

"And that is exactly what I'll do if I catch any of you behaving in an ungodly fashion," she added to the kids hovering nearby. "You are here on a mission, not to paint your toenails and put ribbons in your hair."

Brother Verber staggered to his feet and clung to the back of a folding chair as if it were his pulpit. "'Vanity of vanities; all is vanity. What profit hath a man of all his labor which he taketh under the sun? One generation passeth away, and another generation cometh, but the earth abideth for ever.'"

Darla Jean stared at him. "So it doesn't much matter, since we're all gonna die anyway?"

"That ain't precisely what I was getting at," he said nervously. "It's just that vanity's a sin, same as stealing cookies."

"If I'm going to die this week, it ain't gonna be because I got a splinter in my toe repairing up some goddamn rotten bleachers!"

Mrs. Jim Bob's jaw dropped. "Darla Jean McIlhaney, I will not tolerate blasphemy! You go back to your cabin and stay there until I have a chance to decide how to deal with this unseemly outburst. Once you've simmered down, I hope you'll take the opportunity to pray for forgiveness."

"Don't bet the farm on it," she said as she spun around and banged out the door. I caught her partway down the stairs to the lawn. "Calm down," I said. "Go on back to the cabin, and rather than pray, get the broom in the bathroom and sweep the floor. I'll bring you a sandwich as soon as lunch is over."

"Just leave me alone. I brought some chips and candy bars, so it's not like I'll starve or anything."

"You sure?"

"Yeah."

"And you're not going to run away?" I persisted. "We're a good three miles from the highway, and more than seventy-five miles from Maggody."

"Have I ever lied to you?" she said defiantly.

Well, yes.

3

"So what now?" Heather whispered at me as I came back inside the lodge. She wasn't spitting out the words, but I sensed dampness on my face. "I can't believe you'd let Darla Jean run off like that! Her and Billy Dick came real near breaking up last week. She's liable to—well, do something!"

"And I'm supposed to know that?" I whispered back at her. "Do I look like my name's Ann Landers?"

Mrs. Jim Bob glared at Brother Verber, who was hiccuping in a corner, and said, "Mr. Lambertino will take the crew to the baseball field, with Arly as second-in-command. The Dahlton twins will remain here in order to start preparing lunch. We'll be having tomato soup and cheese sandwiches, so work up your appetites."

"Cheese sandwiches?" echoed Billy Dick.

"And tomato soup," she said. "Our menu for the week is both nutritious and filling. Tonight, if I remember correctly, we'll have spaghetti, along with lima beans and applesauce for dessert."

"Applesauce?" I said, my expression as appalled as those of the teenagers. I dislike applesauce, and lima beans make me think of diseased kidneys harvested from lab animals.

Mrs. Jim Bob held her ground, despite the very real threat of a rebellion. "Yes, applesauce. You may not be aware of it, but excessive sugar and sodium cause unseemly urges in adolescents, and I must say this group in particular

can profit from a lesson in self-control. Our meals will consist of nothing but wholesome foods that will cleanse our
systems and help us focus on our goal. At the end of the
week, if we have met the Lord's challenge, we'll have a
campfire with marshmallows."

"Whoop-dee-do," muttered one of the Dahlton twins.

I grabbed Larry Joe's arm and shook it until he stopped
blinking at Mrs. Jim Bob and gave me his attention. "Okay,
boss, let's go chop us some cotton."

He gestured at the teenagers. "Yesterday I dropped off a
load of lumber next to the field. Jarvis, you and Big Mac get
busy knocking together some sawhorses. Billy Dick and
Parwell, grab those toolboxes out by the bus. I don't know
what you girls are gonna do, but I'll come up with something."

The Dahlton twins were seething as we trooped across
the living room, but I presumed they'd survive and slap together some really yummy cheese sandwiches. The rest of
us hiked up to the field.

None of the existing planks beneath the bleachers were
salvageable. Larry Joe managed to keep everyone busy cart-
ing away the debris, hammering the metal frames back into
shape, and measuring the spans for fresh planks. The boys,
if not the girls, were all accustomed to taking directions
from him, and we'd made significant progress by noon.

I took in their sweaty faces and dirt-caked fingernails.
"Go to your cabins to wash up, then hustle to the lodge.
Lunch should be ready when you get there."

"Yeah, cheese sandwiches," said Billy Dick. "I can
hardly wait."

"Don't forget the applesauce tonight," Amy Dee said
with a smirk. "Maybe Mrs. Jim Bob will give you an extra
scoop if you're mannersome." She began to chant, "Billy
Dick, he makes us sick; we all think he's such a prick."

Cousin Lynette from Paris and Heather found this most

amusing, but Billy Dick did not. Once Larry Joe had tackled him and I'd come damn close to whacking the girls upside the head, I said, "Clean up and be at the lodge in ten minutes for lunch. Eat the cheese sandwiches or not—it doesn't matter to me. Getting through this week does, however. I'm going to close my eyes and count to ten. Anyone left will be scrubbing garbage cans with a toothbrush!"

I grabbed Larry Joe before he could dash away with the others. "Not you," I said wearily. "We have a problem. These kids aren't going to work every day for eight or nine hours and then sing hymns until bedtime. If they don't get decent meals and some organized recreation, they'll find ways to have some of an entirely different sort. Neither of us can stay awake all night for a week."

"Like I ain't been teaching high school for fourteen years? What say we work from eight till eleven in the morning, then play softball before lunch? In the afternoons, we'll knock off at three or so and go down to the lake. I'm not sure there's much we can do after the lights are out, but I guess we can try."

I shrugged. "What about the food? By tomorrow, they'll be adopting Diesel's diet."

Larry Joe pulled out a worn leather wallet. "All I've got's a twenty. Add that to what you've got and tell Mrs. Jim Bob you need to drive into town to buy a four-inch drill bit at the hardware store. We can feed 'em hamburgers this afternoon. Maybe some of them brought a few dollars, but after that, I dunno what we can do."

"Me, neither," I said as I took his bill and tucked it into my shirt pocket.

Larry Joe trudged down the hill toward the lodge, leaving me alone on what would have been home plate had there been anything whatsoever pounded into the dirt. A rabbit bounded into the infield, eyed me, and scampered into the woods. Unless Larry Joe and I fed the kids, the rabbit's life expectancy was less than nature dictated. Flopsy and Mopsy might find their way onto the menu by Monday; Cottontail and Peter would be history by Wednesday.

Mrs. Jim Bob was not impressed with the urgency of my request, but grudgingly gave me the key to the bus. Feeling as though I were driving away from a refugee camp, I kept my face averted as I drove under the camp sign and headed for the nearest outpost of civilization.

Dunkicker was twice as ugly as Maggody, but only because it was twice as big. We had one block of abandoned stores; Dunkicker had two. It did have a public library housed in a trailer, as well as a feed store and an establishment called Buttons and Bows. A building with metal siding purported to contain city hall, municipal court, the post office, and the police department. There were no jaunty gingham curtains in the windows or cars parked out front to indicate the offices were currently occupied.

It was impossible to slide into town unobtrusively in a blue bus with a vaguely sinister message painted on its sides. I parked in front of the Welcome Y'all Café and went inside.

The dozen tables were occupied, but conversation stopped cold. Feeling as though I'd stepped in a meadow muffin, I made my way to the counter, sat down on a stool, and studied a menu.

"You ready to order?" said a voice.

I looked up, then tried not to goggle. The waitress, or whatever she was, had dark hair chopped off to a length more commonly seen in the first week of boot camp. Her eyebrows had been shaved, and her mouth was heavily coated with magenta lipstick. Beneath her stained apron was a polyester pink dress and a name tag that identified her as Rachael. Dunkicker was either a movie site or a very bad dream.

"Yes, I guess so," I squeaked, aware that I had everyone's

attention. "I need eighteen cheeseburgers to go. Hold the onions, and toss in some packets of mustard and catsup."

"Eighteen?"

"That's right."

"To go?"

I forced a weak laugh. "It's going to take me a while to eat them, and I don't want to tie up the stool all day."

"You're gonna eat eighteen cheeseburgers?" she said incredulously.

"Could you please just put in the order?" I asked, hoping my back was not being permanently scarred by the hostility radiating from all corners of the room. "And some napkins, if you don't mind."

"How many napkins?" said this fiancée, if not bride, of Dracula. "Eighteen?"

"That would be great." I focused on the menu until she drifted away, and eventually a low babble of voices resumed behind me.

"Don't mind ol' Rach," said a uniformed cop as he sat down on the stool beside me. "She looks kinda funny, but she's got a good heart. When Miz Gillespie was dying last winter, Rach was there every evening, making vegetable soup, bathing her, seeing to her animals, even splitting firewood. Miz Gillespie's brother tried to make Rach accept a few dollars for helping, but she wouldn't take a penny."

I eased my badge out and flashed it at him. "Chief of Police Arly Hanks, from Maggody. I'm not here in any professional capacity. A group of local kids are staying at Camp Pearly Gates for a week."

"I'm Corporal Robarts," he said. "Panknine's the chief. You'd usually find him here on a Saturday afternoon, having pie and coffee, but he's got back trouble and is in a contraption over at the hospital in Fort Smith."

"Traction," I suggested.

"Yeah, that's what they called it. He got to where he couldn't hardly get out of bed in the morning. His wife got sick of waiting on him and hauled him over to see a specialist."

Corporal Robarts was possibly a few years older than Kevin Buchanon, but no brighter. His hair was slicked back with what may well have been bacon grease, and his face was slack, as though he'd just awakened and needed a jolt of caffeine. I doubted it would help.

"Anything else I can do for you?" I asked politely.

"We don't get a lot of visitors. Chief Panknine sez we got to keep our fingers on the pulse of Dunkicker."

"There's a pulse?"

He stood up. "We don't want any trouble, Miz Hanks. We all get along just fine, no matter our differences. Rach and the others make their contribution to the community, same as everybody else. They may not look like the folks back in your town, but that's not any of your business. Leah went door-to-door to collect clothes and eyeglasses for the county nursing home. Judith helps the old folks get their gardens ready for spring planting. Sarah runs the hot meal program down the road at the Baptist church. Don't go rockin' the boat."

I regarded him evenly. "I came in here to buy cheeseburgers, Corporal Robarts. I've got ten hungry teenagers willing to devote a week to making repairs at Camp Pearly Gates. That's all I'm doing."

The waitress named Rach appeared with two bulging bags stained with grease. I paid at the cash register, smiled at those watching me with deep suspicion, and went outside to the hideous blue bus.

The needle on the gas gauge was quivering just above the empty mark. I was down to four dollars, but that would at least allow me to buy enough gas to let Mrs. Jim Bob and

Brother Verber worry about the possibility we might be stranded in our bucolic labor camp.

Resisting the urge to eat a couple of the cheeseburgers, I drove to the convenience store and was unscrewing the gas cap when a disturbingly familiar station wagon pulled up beside me.

"Why, ain't this a coincidence!" squealed Estelle as she poked her head out of the window. "I was all set to go inside and ask for directions to Camp Pearly Gates, but here you are."

I looked at the somewhat less enthusiastic passenger in the front seat. "What are you all doing here?"

Estelle got out of the car and dragged me behind the gas pumps. "Your mother is mightily depressed," she said. "She wouldn't hardly eat a piece of pizza last night, and this morning she couldn't find the energy to go to the flea market on the other side of Hasty. We go there most every other week, you know, and just last month she found a real nice cookie jar."

"And you think rebuilding bleachers will make her feel better?" I asked.

Ruby Bee gave Estelle an icy look as she joined us. "What's going on is that the electrician came and said he had no choice but to cut off the power to the bar for four or five days. That meant everything in the freezer would spoil. The stove's ruined, so there's no way I could cook it all up. I was gonna get some trash bags when Estelle suggested we pack up all the food in ice chests and come down here for a few days. If nobody wants catfish and chicken fried steaks, I can dump it in the garbage bin, same as I would have done in Maggody."

Estelle stared at me, perhaps thinking we were in the midst of some sort of mute communication. "What's more," she said with a shrill laugh, "we brought bedrolls, fishing poles, and suntan lotion. When Ruby Bee's not cooking, we'll be sitting on the dock in our shorts, gazing at the clouds and dabbling our toes. You reckon there's room for us?"

"There most certainly is," I said, worried by my mother's demeanor. "I haven't seen much of the lodge, but I was told there are bedrooms on the second floor. I can assure you that anything you're willing to cook will be met with glee; Mrs. Jim Bob's proposed menu for this evening consists of spaghetti, lima beans, and applesauce."

"You never had a taste for applesauce," Ruby Bee said, brightening a bit. "I've got ten pounds of catfish steaks, along with enough cornmeal for hushpuppies."

"And a quart of Joyce's green tomato relish," added Estelle. "Just watching Mrs. Jim Bob's face when you serve it ought to make every mile of the drive worthwhile."

Ruby Bee struggled, with marginal success, not to gloat. "We drove by a produce stand on the edge of town. If Arly here can tell us how to find this campground, we can go back to buy some new potatoes."

I found a scrap of paper on the floor of the bus and drew them a map, relatively uncomplicated since only one road went through Dunkicker. "I've got a couple of bags of cheeseburgers for the kids," I said, "but I can assure you they'll all be waiting to unload everything when you get there. You'll have whatever help you need in the kitchen."

Ruby Bee stiffened. "I'll have you know I've been feeding folks at the bar and grill for thirty-odd years, with no help from anyone, including the likes of you."

"Of course not," I said.

"So don't go thinking I need help these days. I may not cook fancy food like they do in Noow Yark City, but nobody's ever left my bar and grill with an empty stomach or a complaint about the black-eyed peas."

I stared helplessly at Estelle, who could only gnaw on her lower lip. "Nobody, Ruby Bee. Why don't you pick up potatoes at the produce stand and come on to the camp? I'll have some of the kids haul the ice chests to the kitchen and carry your suitcases upstairs. I can't promise the fishing is any good, but—"

"It ain't like I can fix crepes," Ruby Bee said, getting testier with every word. "I hope you all can handle buttermilk pancakes and sausages for breakfast."

"Sounds great," I said as Estelle hustled Ruby Bee back into the station wagon, gave me a grim look, and drove away. I toyed briefly with the idea that Ruby Bee might be persuaded to see a doctor in Farberville, but I knew it was a ridiculous premise. There was no way on God's earth that I could hint that she might be in the throes of menopause, or even suffering from depression as a result of the fire in the kitchen. She'd raised me on her own, with help from no one. She would accept none now.

I put four dollars' worth of gas into the guzzler, went inside to pay, and drove back to Camp Pearly Gates with eighteen cold cheeseburgers and a premonition that I was in for a rough week.

◗

Dahlia Buchanon had never been one to keep her feelings bottled up like orange soda pop. When Kevin came in the door, she hauled him over to the kitchen table.

"Look at this!" she said, breathing heavily, as she almost always did. "Kevvie Junior and Rose Marie are gonna be famous! We ain't gonna haft to worry about the high cost of braces and piano lessons and college!"

"We ain't?" said Kevin as he sat down at the table and fluttered his fingers at the babies, who were drooling on plastic toys in the playpen. "That's good to hear, my sweetums, 'specially now that we have another little angel on the way. Jim Bob ain't likely to give me a raise afore Christmas."

Dahlia sat down across from him and thrust a folded

newspaper at him. "See this, Kevin? It sez that Hollywood is on the lookout for babies to model in advertisements. They'll earn so much money that you can quit your job at the supermarket. It's gonna break your ma's heart when we move to California, but maybe she and Pa can come visit ever' now and then. Why, we can afford to send a limousine to pick 'em up at the airport and bring 'em right to the front door of our mansion."

Kevin tried to imagine his pa riding in anything but a pickup truck, then gave up and took a closer look at the newspaper ad. "It sez they're looking for babies and children. Why do you reckon they'd pick Kevvie Junior and Rose Marie?"

"Think, Kevin."

He rubbed his chin. "Well, there's no questioning that they're cute as a pair of junebugs."

Dahlia glowered at him. "And . . . ?"

"Rose Marie has the sweetest grin I've ever laid eyes on. Kevvie Junior's gonna be a fine football player; his little arms are just twitching to throw a pass down the field. I always thought I could be a quarterback, but then—"

"Your nose got broke on the first day of practice," Dahlia said, "if you recollect."

Kevin most certainly did recollect. Shirelle Pomfritte had been on the sidelines, practicing a routine with the pep squad. Instead of dashing to his aid with a lacy hanky or even an ice pack, she'd outright brayed while he staggered around the field, bleeding like a stuck pig. Remembering the moment brought tears to his eyes.

He blinked and peered at the small ad. "It doesn't promise a million dollars."

"Kevvie Junior and Rose Marie are twins. They'd probably earn more if they was triplets, but there's not anything we can do about that." Dahlia smiled at her five-month-old cash cows, or calves, anyway. "Can't you just see 'em in one of those commercials on television? There they'd be, smiling at the camera and winning ever'body's hearts." Her expression abruptly darkened with a menace that rivaled a thunderstorm gathering over Cotter's Ridge. "You got to promise me one thing, Kevin Fitzgerald Buchanon, and I mean it."

"You know I'd hang the moon for you," he said, meaning it but not real clear where this was going.

Dahlia sat down in his lap and wrapped her arms around him. "If we get all-fired rich and live in a mansion in Beverly Hills, you won't go running after some skinny little actress in a bikini. I know I'll be all swollen like last time, with my ankles thick as stumps and my belly so big it could be mistaken for a ten-pound sack of turnips. If I was to lose you to a starlet, I don't know what I'd do. Swear you won't leave me, Kevin."

"Leave you?" he said, squirming as his legs became increasingly numb. "You are the light of my life, my dandelion wine princess. You are the mother of my fine, sturdy children, and the only thing I think about all day while I mop the floor at the SuperSaver and restock the shelves. Ain't no sickly actress ever gonna catch my eye, much less steal my heart away."

"Well, then," Dahlia said as she stood up, "I'm gonna call this number on Monday morning. We got the two cutest babies in the country. Not even Brother Verber could say it's a sin to take advantage of that."

Kevin was kinda glad Brother Verber had rolled out on the bus, along with Mrs. Jim Bob. He didn't want to think about what his parents would say over Sunday breakfast, but he had a good twenty-four hours to consider it. With any luck, about the time the scrambled eggs and grits were set on the table, the babies would commence to wail, Dahlia and his ma would get all flustered, and his pa might not hafta hear about the limousine just yet.

✖

"Don't go fingering those cupcakes," said Jim Bob, glaring at the scruffy boy who'd been lingering by the checkout display. "Shoplifters go straight to the state penitentiary, where they're locked up in cells with murderers and rapists. You won't last twenty minutes with the likes of them. A little pissant like you'd be someone's girlie about the time you took your first shower."

"I ain't dun nothing."

Jim Bob was feeling pretty good, what with his wife gone for a week. Brother Verber was gone as well, meaning there'd be no tedious church service in the morning or one of those goddamn awful potluck suppers in the evening. Without green bean casseroles and raw carrot salads facing him in the immediate future, he figured to take home some tamales and beer, put his muddy shoes on the coffee table, and watch wrasslin' on the television. He'd burp and belch so loud the windows would rattle clear across the county. His farts would scare off any skunk that dared come across the yard. He'd sleep naked and put on dirty underwear in the morning. It was unfortunate that Cherry Lucinda was peeved at him, but she might relent by the middle of the week if he showed up on her doorstep with a handful of daffodils from the garden out back and a pint bottle of peppermint schnapps.

It wasn't all that bad being single, Jim Bob thought as he continued to glare at the kid. "Get your sorry ass out of here. I'm giving you a break this time, but if you ever set foot in here again, you'll end up being a princess at the prison prom."

"Fuck you," the kid said succinctly.

"Haven't I seen you before? Seems to me you're one of Robin Buchanon's bushcolts. Hammet's your name, right? You and the rest of the runts did some serious damage to

my house. All of you should have been hauled off to the
pound and been put out of my misery, if not yours."

"Want I should spell it this time?"

Jim Bob thought about smacking the kid, but he was in
too good a mood to bother. "Go on now, and don't come
back. All the checkout girls are gonna be on the watch for
you. Set foot in here again and I'll whip your sorry butt,
then have you arrested."

"Like you could," the miscreant said as he backed toward the door. "Like you could fuck your way out of a
gunny sack." His further parting remarks were obscene,
implying without subtlety that Jim Bob's mother had found
satisfying sexual relationships with immediate family members and farm animals. Some of the combinations were
highly improbable, but they were enough to cause Eula
Lemoy to clutch her bosom and Constantinople Buchanon
to clack his dentures as if they were castanets.

"What you gaping at?" Jim Bob snarled at the checkout
girls, then went back to his office and pulled out the bottle
of bourbon he kept in his desk drawer. Somebody ought to
come up with a bigger fly swatter, he thought as he took a
pull on the bottle. Little shits like the one up front needed
to be slapped flatter'n a red flour beetle.

He amused himself with the scenario as he finished off
the bourbon and sat back. Cherry Lucinda could stew in
her own juices for a few days. In the meantime, there was
no telling what pretty things might be at the Dew Drop Inn
on a Saturday night.

While the cat's away, he thought, rubbing his hands together, the mice got no choice but to play.

✖

Hammet hunkered by the Dumpster behind the supermarket, greedily gnawing on a discolored head of lettuce.
He would have preferred a sandwich, but at least he'd

made it out the door with a candy bar in one coat pocket and a package of cheese in the other. He hadn't had more than a few crackers in the last twenty-four hours, and he forced himself to eat as much lettuce as he could.

When his gut growled ominously, he tossed aside the lettuce and prowled through the vehicles parked alongside the building. All of them were locked. He supposed he could bust out a windshield with a rock, but it wasn't gonna do him much good to steal CDs or magazines. It wasn't gonna do him much good if he saw a key in an ignition switch, for that matter, since he didn't know how to drive.

One truck caught his attention. It was parked nearest the steps leading up to the delivery dock, and a spray-painted sign on the wall indicated that the space was reserved for Jim Bob. Slashing the tires would have been entertaining, but required a knife or a screwdriver. He found a sharp rock and scratched lines across the doors and hood.

The problem was, he thought as he threw the rock into the trees at the back of the parking lot, Arly weren't nowhere to be found. Ruby Bee's Bar & Grill was darker than the inside of a cow, and all the motel units were locked.

There weren't no way of knowing if the shack was still standing up on Cotter's Ridge. Even if it was, the only food he might hope to find there would be scraggly carrots and maybe a few ears of corn in the garden. Catchin' critters was harder than it sounded, and it wasn't like he had matches or anything to make a fire.

The church was likely to be empty on a Saturday afternoon, he reckoned. He could at least stretch out on a pew and get some sleep.

Running away was damn hard work, even harder than memorizing multiplication tables and state capitals.

✄

When I returned, Estelle's station wagon was parked in front of the lodge. Jarvis and Billy Dick were unloading it, while Heather, Amy Dee, and Lynette watched from the veranda.

"Finished with lunch?" I asked them.

"Was that what you'd call it?" said Heather. "My pa's hogs eat better than that."

"And we had grapes for dessert," Lynette added.

I tried to look encouraging. "Grapes are good. Were they green or red?"

"Brown and mushy," muttered Jarvis as he went past me, bedding under his arms.

I found Larry Joe in the living room and told him about the two sacks of cheeseburgers in the bus. Once he'd rounded up the kids and led them toward the ball field, I went into the kitchen, where Big Mac and Parwell were washing dishes under Mrs. Jim Bob's unwavering supervision.

"I assume you bought the bit," she said to me.

I had no idea what she was talking about. Bought the bit? Bit the bullet? Bought the farm?

"The four-inch bit for the drill," she continued. "That is why you took the bus into Dunkicker, isn't it? I'd like to think you weren't looking for an establishment that sells alcoholic beverages."

I slapped my forehead. "Oh, the bit! The hardware had one, in a box on a shelf in the back corner. The Lord's looking after us, Mrs. Jim Bob."

"I will not tolerate blasphemy!"

Ruby Bee came into the kitchen. "Where's the skillets and the mixing bowls?"

Mrs. Jim Bob sucked up a breath. "Although it is kind of you to offer to assist, Ruby Bee, I think it's better that the teenagers take responsibility for meals. They tend to assume that food simply appears on their plates."

"Fine," said Ruby Bee. "You just make sure they understand whose decision it was to have spaghetti and lima beans, instead of fried catfish and hushpuppies."

"Hushpuppies?" said Brother Verber, joining us. "Those moist, delicious morsels of cornbread and a delicate flavoring of onions, crisped to perfection and just beggin' for a dollop of butter? The Good Lord created hushpuppies, Mrs. Jim Bob."

"As He did lima beans," she responded tartly.

Tears welled in Brother Verber's eyes. "I'm gonna go upstairs and study my Bible, but I have a feeling that the Good Lord didn't have much to say about lima beans."

"Nobody has much to say about lima beans," inserted Estelle. "Not Matthew, Mark, Luke, or John, if I recollect. Loaves and fishes, on the other hand, were on the menu on one occasion."

I left them to battle it out, grabbed the last sandwich off a tray, and went to make sure Darla Jean had not made good on her implicit threat to leave.

Which she had.

4

I walked to the cabin, collected my sleeping bag and duffel bag from the ditch beside the road, and went into the cabin. Darla Jean was not there—surprise, surprise. I dumped my gear on a bottom bunk, checked the stalls in the bathroom, and wandered around, trying to figure out where Darla Jean might have chosen to deposit her shampoo, mousse, conditioner, hair dryer, rollers, makeup kit, stuffed animals, lurid magazines, candy bars, and cigarettes. In that all six girls seemed to have brought identical survival kits, I couldn't tell.

However, it looked as though all six remained fully equipped for any crises of a cosmic—or cosmetic—nature. Being a trained professional and all, I concluded that Darla Jean would not put herself in a situation that might lead to bad hair, and therefore was more likely to have headed for the lake instead of the highway.

I ambled down the road. The songbirds were out in full force, trilling, warbling, and screeching. Foliage was lacy enough to permit glimpses of cabins identical to ours scattered higher on the hillside. The insects, both butterflies and less engaging species, had determined they were safely past the final frost and were on the lookout for blossoms and blood. Critters rustled in the leaves, but I'd grown up in the pastures and woods surrounding Maggody, and nothing short of a skunk was worth worrying about.

Music, however, was. Rattlesnakes rattled, but they did

not harmonize. Crows did not form string quartets, replete with violins, cello, and bass—if that's what I was hearing. I wasn't sure. I pushed through some brush and squinted at the lake as sunshine hit my face. Two flat-bottomed fishing boats were visible, but both were at a distance and did not look like the source of what was increasingly sounding like an adulation of springtime, courtesy of Vivaldi.

The New York Philharmonic, if present, was deftly hidden. The only potential conductor in view stood at the edge of the lake, leading his invisible orchestra with a pliant plastic rod. Rather than a tux, he was wearing a flannel shirt, a torn khaki vest, baggy pants, sneakers, and a canvas hat adorned with those weird little feather doodads beloved by fishermen.

"Hello," I called as I thrashed my way toward him with all the stealth of a backhoe.

He looked back. "Yeah?"

I came through the final barrier of briars. "I hope I'm not interrupting."

"I hope you're delivering a pizza," he said, his face creasing genially. "Otherwise, it looks as though I'll have bologna sandwiches for supper again. A couple more days of this, and I'll be out of mustard."

He was not unpleasant looking, despite the stubble on his cheeks and the stains on his clothing. Nice chin, clear blue eyes, only a hint of gray in the hair visible beneath his hat. I could easily imagine him (after an overnight stay at the Fly By Night dry cleaner's, anyway) striding down Wall Street to his corner office with a window overlooking the East River. His receptionist would have a gelatinous English accent, and his private secretary would be named Kaitlin. Men called Brett and Bart would bring him coffee and simper. Senior partners would propose him for membership in politically incorrect clubs.

So maybe I was making a bit of a leap. "No pizza," I said, wishing I'd stayed in the cabin long enough to wash my face. "You camping here?"

He put down the rod. "Well, that's my tent."

"Mr. Vivaldi hiding in there?"

"I'm not trespassing, am I? I have a fishing license, and I thought this area was—"

"I'm not from the fish and game commission, and I don't think anyone cares if you are trespassing. I certainly don't."

"How kind of you." He came across the muddy expanse and studied me. "Jacko."

"Arly," I said, mentally kicking myself for the blush heating my face. There's something about tall, blue-eyed, slightly ungroomed guys that reduces me to a middle-school mindset. A Peter O'Toole fantasy from my childhood, perhaps. "I'm here with a bunch of teenagers, and one of them's missing. I'm looking for her."

"Short brown hair, braces, bikini, transparent white shirt knotted around her waist, mesh bag hanging on her shoulder?"

"You've seen her?" I instinctively stared at his tent, which was zipped. Music wafted out, but unaccompanied by whimpers.

Jacko gave me a disappointed look. "Do I look like the type to detain some backwoods Lolita and have my way with her?"

I struggled not to imagine what his way might be.

"But you did see her, right?"

"About an hour ago, she came stumbling down here like you did. She took one look at me, screeched, and then dashed back up to the road. I will admit I haven't shaved or done more than bathe out of a basin for the last four days, and my wardrobe's not from a pricey catalogue. What's more, not everyone likes Vivaldi—or even Bach, which I believe was on the tape player at the time."

"She didn't say anything?"

"She screeched," he said patiently. "I was so unnerved that I had no choice but to pour myself a shot of bourbon. Would you care for one?"

"I'd better keep looking for her." I began to back away. "Good luck with your fishing, Jacko."

"And you with your hunting, Arly."

Vivaldi failed to produce any appropriately impassioned strains that might send thwarted lovers dashing across a muddy expanse to fling themselves into each other's arms. Damn.

"If you run out of mustard, come up to the lodge," I said. "We're having fried catfish and hushpuppies."

"I'll keep that in mind."

"You haven't seen anything else, have you?"

"Like what?"

I'd had more poise at the ninth-grade mixer. "Anything that might have seemed odd."

"Odder than a voluptuous teenaged girl in a bikini, goggling as though I'd just reeled in a kissin' cousin of the Loch Ness monster?"

"Just asking," I said, barely stopping myself from scuffling my shoe in the dirt. "If she shows up, tell her I'm looking for her."

He did not reply. I fought my way back to the road and went on, noticing for the first time a battered black hatchback pulled well off the road and partially hidden by scrub pines. I wasn't much interested in whether he was trespassing. If he was, it was Corporal Robarts's problem.

Half a mile farther, the road fizzled out at the remains of a concrete boat ramp leading into the lake. Darla Jean was not sunning herself, paddling in the water, constructing a canoe from birch bark, or doing much of anything that I could see. I sat down on a stump and munched on the cheese sandwich as I regarded the brown water.

So where was Darla Jean? It seemed likely that she'd deliberately provoked Mrs. Jim Bob in order to be banished to the cabin for the remainder of the day, thus avoiding physical labor and supervision. Jacko had mentioned she was wearing a bikini when she'd skittered into his campsite.

I wasn't worried, exactly. Darla Jean most likely had come this far. There were no sandy beaches fringed with palm trees along the shore, but a few scattered plastic toys and gnawed apple cores suggested it might be a picnic area for folks in the area. The only background noise came from the birds and squirrels. I considered shouting her name, then decided against it. Later in the day, if she hadn't returned, I would feel obliged to take action—presuming I had a clue how to go about it. Larry Joe and I might have to organize a search party, but I wasn't sure if we could do so without tipping off Mrs. Jim Bob.

I peered at the two boats, wondering if there were any possibility that Darla Jean had been bound with duct tape and was floundering atop empty beer cans, Ding Dong wrappers, and bait buckets. Monet might not have opted to capture the scene (it was sadly lacking in water lilies), but it seemed tranquil.

I went back to the cabin. Darla Jean had not returned in my absence, as far as I could tell. I continued to the lodge, not at all sure what I ought to do. Estelle's station wagon was parked next to the bus, and next to it, a monstrous, mud-splattered SUV. I could hear shouts and laughter from the softball field. Brother Verber was sitting on the end of the dock, either rehearsing his evening homily or plotting a watery demise. Whatever.

"Here's Arly," Mrs. Jim Bob said as I came into the front room. "She's here to keep an eye on the girls."

An unfamiliar woman seated on a folding chair nodded at me. "It was very admirable of you to agree to chaperon these youthful Christian soldiers."

"I do my best to be admirable, if not admired by one and all," I said. Although the woman was lean in areas where Mrs. Jim Bob was plump, she had an uncanny resemblance to her. I finally realized it was the smirk tugging at the corners of her mouth, as though she'd judged me on first sight and found me sadly lacking. Her hair had been lacquered into unwavering obedience; not even a gust from the lake would have dislodged a single strand. She was dressed in a floral dress as though she'd dropped by on her way to a tea dance at the local country club, although I suspected the only golf played in Dunkicker was of the putt-putt variety.

Mrs. Jim Bob was not amused. "This is Willetta Robarts, Arly. She is a member of the Camp Pearly Gates Foundation."

"My son mentioned that your group arrived earlier today," murmured Willetta. "I wanted to stop in and make sure you found the accommodations sufficient for your needs."

"Everything seems fine," I said, uneasy about what else Corporal Robarts had seen fit to mention.

She smiled at Mrs. Jim Bob. "And the lodge? Charming, isn't it? We're doing our best to raise money for appropriate furnishing, but this is the best we can do for the time being. It's stark, I'm sorry to say. This time next year we'll have comfortable furniture, and the dining room will be much cheerier. Several organizations have already inquired about the possibility of holding conferences and retreats. It will be a way for us to raise money to provide summer sessions for our little campers. Many of them come from impoverished backgrounds, and therefore scholarship funds are invaluable."

Mrs. Jim Bob almost purred. "It's a blessing for our youth to contribute to the restoration, Mrs. Robarts. Perhaps our local missionary society can spend a few days communing with the glories of the Almighty's handiwork."

"What a lovely idea," Willetta said, "although you may be a bit daunted by our fees. Liability coverage and all, you know." She paused to allow Mrs. Jim Bob to blink several times, then went on. "My great-great-grandfather purchased several thousand acres when he moved here from North Carolina after the war. The mountains reminded him of home, he wrote in his journal. Much of the land was used for cattle and farming, but he never allowed any development surrounding the lake. He would have been proud of what's been done here. Four of his eleven children died before reaching school age. Now, even with the advances of modern medicine, so many little ones—"

"I'd better see if Larry Joe needs help," I said before she worked herself up any further. "The little ones are going to need a place to play softball this summer."

Mrs. Jim Bob glowered at me. "I should think you might show some respect for the generosity of the Robarts family, Arly. Her family donated all this out of Christian charity, of which not everyone in this room has an overabundance."

"What shreds I have are itching to build bleachers," I said. "Are Ruby Bee and Estelle settled in?"

"Ruby Bee is poking through the kitchen cabinets and I believe Estelle went for a walk." Her eyes narrowed. "And what have you been doing?"

"I went to the cabin to make sure Darla Jean was okay."

"And?"

"And what? Isn't it a little late in the game for you to concern yourself with her well-being?"

Willetta Robarts stood up. "I need to be on my way. If you have any problems, feel free to call Anthony. He's the caretaker these days. Up until last fall, we had a caretaker in residence, but the poor man finally drank himself to death. We didn't realize it for several months, since he was a bit of a recluse who hiked into town only two or three times a year to buy necessities. When Anthony discovered the body . . . well, it was far from pleasant. To this day, Anthony refuses to eat chocolate chip ice cream."

"How tragic," said Mrs. Jim Bob.

"He has no problem with vanilla and strawberry," she said, "or even butterscotch swirl."

I glanced at Mrs. Jim Bob, who was visibly unnerved, and went through the dining room to the kitchen. Ruby Bee might have last been seen poking through cabinets, but she'd moved on. All the dishes from lunch had been washed and were propped in racks to dry. A dish towel, neatly folded, hung from the refrigerator door. A vase containing dogs' tooth violets sat on the window sill above the sink.

If I'd had any hope that Darla Jean was cutting planks for the bleachers, it would have been relatively idyllic. The evening's menu had been revised, and I had no doubt the contents of Ruby Bee's freezer would keep us happy for a few days. Mrs. Jim Bob had seemed to accept my limited role in all of this. Larry Joe's wattage was a bit brighter than usual. Corporal Robarts's avowed preferences in ice cream flavors did not concern me.

I went out the back door, intending to go to the ball field to help out as best I could. When I'd attended the high school in Maggody, all the girls had been required to take home ec classes under the benign and befuddled tutelage of Lottie Estes, while the boys had been shunted to Larry Joe's shop classes. Given equal opportunity, I could have been a fine welder in a chop shop in Starley City.

Someone, possibly a Methodist or Unitarian, had planted a vegetable garden. I immediately recognized the row of tomato plants, as well as several tidy lines of nascent carrots and radishes. If I'd had my catalogue, I could have identified the rest of it, but all I could do was nod approvingly at the mulch and such. Could zucchini and cucumbers be far behind?

I was visualizing a garden behind the PD when Ruby Bee came puffing down the hillside. "Out for a walk?" I said.

"Reckon so," she gasped, clutching her chest and coming damn close to sprawling into my arms. Her face was whiter than any batch of rolls she'd set out to rise.

I helped her to a metal bench. "You don't look so good, Ruby Bee. How about a glass of water?"

"Water ain't about to help. There's a bottle of sherry under the sink."

"Coming right up," I said, then hurried inside and rummaged behind detergent bottles until I found her stash. I poured a couple of inches into a glass and went back to the patio. "What's wrong with you?"

She drained the glass. "Nothing."

"Don't give me that," I said as calmly as possible, considering I was hoping that this part of the county had emergency ambulance services. "Why are you upset?"

"Who says I'm upset?"

"I polled everyone on the patio and the consensus is that you're upset. It wasn't a large poll, mind you, but there were no dissenting votes."

Ruby Bee shoved the glass into my hand. "Don't get smart with me, missy. You may think you're all growed up, but I can still take you over my knee and whup your behind till you whimper for mercy."

"Hold that thought," I said as I went into the kitchen and splashed more sherry into the glass. I took a gulp from the bottle, then went back outside with what might have been a somewhat strained expression.

She was staring at the hillside. "You believe in ghosts?"

"No, but the Tooth Fairy owes me three dollars."

"That ain't funny."

"I suppose not," I admitted. "You think you saw a ghost?"

"I know I saw something."

"Okay, that's a beginning. What did you see?"

She sighed. "I don't know. Maybe it was nothing more than a piece of cloth caught on a bush. It seems like everything's crazy these days, Arly. I don't know if I'm coming or going, or if I already came and went. You might ought to pack me off to a nursing home afore you leave."

"What's wrong with you? Have I done something?"

"No, of course not. You got your life to lead, and I got mine. Our paths are gonna stray."

"That's probably true," I said. "I've never pretended from the day I came back to Maggody that I was there to do anything other than recuperate from the divorce. I'm biding my time until I can trust myself to flounder back into the real world. I could go to law school, you know, or become a vet or a nuclear physicist. The Marines are looking for a few good men. With hefty doses of testosterone—"

"You still ain't funny."

"I suppose not. Did you see a ghost?"

"I suppose not." She clutched my hand and we silently watched the light rippling across the garden.

✦

Hammet Buchanon's nap in a pew at the Voice of the Almighty Lord Assembly Hall had been worth every minute of it, although the pew was hard and the sunlight through the dusty windows was peskier'n a swarm of skeeters.

He weren't one to complain, however, having spent the first ten years of his life in a squalid cabin without indoor plumbing or electricity. After his ma'd been killed, he and the others had been farmed out to foster care. Which hadn't been downright awful, although it seemed like he was spending most of his wakin' hours at school or church.

It weren't natural, he'd decided three nights ago as he

shimmied down the drainpipe and headed for Maggody. Arly'd understand and let him stay, even iff'n she hadn't been real keen on it before. Why, he could fix a place to sleep under the table in the back of the PD, and git up ever' morning to sweep and turn on the coffeepot. They'd have doughnuts for breakfast, just like in all the cops shows on TV.

Thing was, Arly weren't nowhere to be found. Her car was out in front of the PD, meanin' she hadn't gone off to track down cold-blooded killers and tell the shitheels how they had the right to remain silent. Hisself, he'd just shoot 'em in the gut and toss their bodies in the river. Serve 'em right.

He was thinking how to suggest this enlightened approach to Arly when he heard the front door of the church open. He slithered off the pew and rolled underneath it, then curled up tighter than a sickly armadillo.

"Let me carry one of those sacks, Millicent," a woman said.

"Mighty kind of you, Eula, but I got a grip on them. I'm just going to set them behind the pulpit until Brother Verber gets back and unlocks the storage room."

"Been doing some spring cleaning for the rummage sale?"

"I've been telling Darla Jean to clean out her drawers and closet. She kept whining that she was too busy, so I decided to do it for her while she's gone with the church group. Some of the clothes the girls wear these days are disgraceful, and the music they listen to is enough to make my stomach turn. Darla Jean thinks I can't hear the lyrics long as her bedroom door is closed, but let me tell you, Eula, you've never heard such filth in all your born days!"

Their voices receded as they went toward the pulpit, but Hammet stayed where he was, sensing he might learn something to his advantage.

"I won't argue with you, Millicent. Most of the young

folk have been spared the rod and spoiled rotten. Did you hear what happened in the supermarket earlier?" After a pause during which Millicent either mutely shook her head or shrugged, she continued. "Jim Bob spotted one of those vile children that Robin Buchanon was raising up on Cotter's Ridge. He was stealing food, if you can imagine. Jim Bob would have had him arrested on the spot if Arly was in town."

"Better yet," Millicent said with a snicker, "Jim Bob could have called in Brother Verber to save his twisted soul. After all, we got a fine baptismal font, and Mrs. Jim Bob's likely to have more than one bar of lye soap in her bathroom cabinet for when Jim Bob comes staggering in with whiskey on his breath and lipstick smeared on his collar. I hate to think what kind of mischief he's gonna get up to while she and Brother Verber are gone this week."

Their voices grew louder as they came up the aisle.

"All I can say," said Eula, "was if I was that particular bushcolt, I'd eat whatever food I found setting on the piano bench by the pulpit and then skedaddle back where I came from."

"What on earth does that mean, Eula?"

Her response was cut off as the door closed. Hammet sucked in his breath as long as he could, then wiggled out from under the pew. He stayed on the floor, though, making sure no one was lurking in the vestibule in hopes of pouncing on him and trying to drown him in some tub of holy water. His foster ma'd tried to have him baptized a year ago, but it'd taken four full-growed men to hold him under the water and he'd come up cussin' something awful. The preacher had called it off then and there.

He finally stood up. When nothing happened, he went down to the piano bench and rooted through a box of ham sandwiches, apples, and a piece of pecan pie in plastic wrap. It was enough to hold him for the rest of the day, but it sounded like Arly wouldn't be back for awhiles. Breaking into her apartment might not sit well with her, 'specially when he was going to try to sweet-talk her into letting him stay on. Ruby Bee and Estelle wouldn't take it well, neither. He couldn't tell where Brother Verber was for the time being, but breaking into his trailer might result in a lengthy stay in the place Jim Bob had been sputtering about.

He took the box and let himself out, and then found a shadowy hollow between the shrubs alongside the church. As he licked the mustard off a slice of ham, he considered the possibilities.

5

Having endured a prickly lecture in which it'd been made clearer than spring water that my assistance was neither required nor desired, I left Ruby Bee yanking out measuring spoons and utensils. Willetta Robarts had driven away, and Mrs. Jim Bob must have retreated upstairs to pray for my salvation, as futile as the cause may have been. Brother Verber remained slouched at the end of the dock, unmindful of the mosquitoes buzzing around him. Although we were a couple of hours away from sunset, the blue of the sky seemed to be intensifying in readiness for what might prove to be a gratifying presentation.

I walked up the hill to the softball field. Darla Jean was not present, but the other kids were working industriously under Larry Joe's practiced supervision.

Or so it seemed.

"Oh my gawd!" shrieked Heather, dropping one end of a freshly cut plank. "I've got a sliver under my fingernail. It's bleeding, too!"

Amy Dee, who'd instinctively dropped the other end, clutched one foot and began to hop around like a mutant frog. "You broke my toe! When I catch up with you, you'll see some real blood, you whore!"

"At least my initials ain't scratched in every locker in the boys' gym."

"How would you know?"

Larry Joe got between them before they could get hold

of each other's hair. Keeping them at arm's length and ignoring their threats, he said, "Parwell, you and Big Mac set this in place and start drilling holes for the bolts. Heather, you go on down to the lodge. The first-aid kit's got a pair of tweezers fit to pluck a pine tree off the mountainside."

"Tweezers?" gulped Heather. Her eyeballs rolled back and she crumpled to the ground.

Larry Joe stared down at her, mystified. "What'd I say?"

I may have overestimated his wattage. I knelt next to Heather and flopped her over so her face wasn't pressed in the dust. Her eyelids trembled but remained closed. "She'll be okay in a minute."

"That was awesome," said Big Mac as he loomed over my shoulder. "Reminds me of that faintin' goat my Uncle Bromide had for a spell. If you snuck up behind it and shouted, it keeled right over. Funniest damn thing I ever seen."

Parwell whacked him on the shoulder. "Bet it wasn't as funny as when you tried to get it up for Lanci Louise Ferncliff. She told me she tried so hard not to laugh that she near to peed in her pants." He began to sing, "My wiener's got a first name, it's L-I-M-P-Y . . ."

"Sumbitch!" Big Mac howled, his face turning redder than the tomatoes in the seed catalogue, pages twenty-nine through thirty-two.

I stood up and made it clear I was ready to smack both of them if they didn't back away. "Let me tell you of a lesser-known commandment: Thou shalt not piss me off. These six words need to haunt you every minute of your waking hours, from reveille to taps, presuming we have a bugler in our midst. You are welcome to settle this later, but for now, shut up and do whatever Larry Joe says—unless you'd like to participate in an anger management session led by Mrs. Jim Bob and Brother Verber." I glared at the rest of them. "That goes for all of you. Questions?"

"No, ma'am," Parwell and Big Mac muttered in unison. Heather had regained consciousness, if indeed she'd ever lost it, and was sitting up. I grabbed her wrist and pulled her to her feet. "I'll go down to the lodge with you."

"Yeah, okay," she said without enthusiasm.

Larry Joe clapped his hands. "It looks like we're gonna get a storm, so we'll call it a day. Jarvis, you and Big Mac move all the tools to the dugout and make sure they're covered with tarps. Parwell and Billy Dick, stack the lumber. You Dahlton gals need to gather up all the softball equipment and stuff it back in the bag. Amy Dee, you sit down over there and take off your shoe and sock. From the way you was carrying on, you'd better hope your toe looks like a ripe purple plum."

I glanced at the sky as I escorted Heather down the hill. Across the lake, dark clouds were massing. Whitecaps riffled the lake like peaks of seven-minute icing, and what had been a pleasant breeze now had a bite. I hoped Jacko had enough sense to move his gear to his car before the storm hit. Sodden sleeping bags smell worse than wet dogs, or even teenagers in heat.

"I'm sorry to be a bother," Heather said, sniveling just enough to annoy me. "When I was a little kid, I was barefoot and stepped hard on a thorn. My ma had to hold me down while my pa tried to dig it out with tweezers. When that didn't do any good, he made me drink a glass of whiskey so he could cut the thorn out with a knife. I thought I was gonna die right then and there."

"All we're gonna to do is soak your finger in warm salt water," I said soothingly. As we neared the lodge, I stopped her. "Look, Heather, I didn't find Darla Jean. She put on her bikini and walked down to the lake, where she was last seen about two hours ago, give or take. She wouldn't swim out too far, would she?"

"I don't think so. They made her learn how to swim at

camp four or five summers back, but she didn't like it. Whenever we go to the pool in Farberville, she'll sit on the side of the pool and dangle her feet, but I ain't ever seen her get in the water. She won't even wade in Boone Creek because of the minnows."

"Minnows?" I said.

"Darla Jean claims they're baby barracudas, and the crawdads hide under rocks till they're big as lobsters and able to pinch off your toes. She swears that house flies suck blood. She flunked biology two years in a row, and was going for a third when Ms. Mertzworth got kinda discouraged and gave her a passing grade for staying in the lines when we colored mimeographed handouts of amoebae."

"Do you have any idea where she might be?"

"Ms. Mertzworth? She went off to be a missionary in one of those African countries that nobody can spell."

"I meant Darla Jean."

Heather considered this as she chomped on a wad of gum. "Maybe she was hiding when you went to look for her. She wasn't real excited about hauling lumber and stuff, and the only reason she came was because of Billy Dick. Then they had such a big fight two nights ago that she threw his letter jacket in the lake outside Farberville. I hate to think what he'll do when he finds out."

"So she's doing this to get back at him?" I said blankly. "He doesn't even know she's missing."

"I reckon he will when Mrs. Jim Bob hears about it."

I grimaced. "You have a point. Let's get you settled with Ruby Bee in the kitchen. I'll go back to the cabin, but then I'm going to feel obliged to do something. Darla Jean can't spend the night in the woods, especially with a thunderstorm coming."

"Hold on a minute." Heather sat down on a log and plastered the gum on her finger, then removed it. "Okay, I got it out." She picked out the sliver of wood, tossed it over her shoulder, and put the gum back into her mouth. "It might be better for me to go to the cabin. If Darla Jean's hiding in the area, she's more likely to listen to me than someone like you."

"Like me?"

"Oh, you know, like old and everything. Can I tell her she's not in trouble?"

"She's not in trouble if she shows up for supper," I said, resisting the irrational urge to force her to examine my teeth as if I were a racehorse about to be retired to pasture. "I'm more than willing to tell Mrs. Jim Bob and Brother Verber that she spent the afternoon repenting on her knees."

"You'd lie? Isn't that kinda like bearing false witness?"

"Yes, Heather, I suppose it is. You have any better suggestions?"

She mumbled a response and hurried down the path. I gave her a minute's head start, then headed for the lodge as rain began to rustle the leaves.

✸

Jim Bob sat in his office at the back of the supermarket, scrolling through screen after screen of images of sweet young things baring their souls (and other things) for any and all to behold. The more innocent of the websites he'd found focused on hooters. Others were downright lewd, which isn't to imply he objected. Mrs. Jim Bob found her enlightenment in the Bible; he found his on the Internet.

He was downloading pictures from a site featuring pretty little cheerleaders that'd forgotten to put on their panties when Kevin Buchanon came into the office.

"Kin I ask you something, Jim Bob?"

Sighing, he deleted the image on the screen. "You just did."

Kevin sucked on his lip for a few seconds. "No, kin I really ask you something?"

"Two down, one to go."

"But, Jim Bob," Kevin said, lapsing into a whine that made Jim Bob's teeth ache, "I need some advice. I'd ask Arly, or even Ruby Bee, but they're gone for the week, in case you hadn't heard, along with Mrs. Jim Bob. Brother Verber is, too, but this ain't something I'd want to ask him about. I know he's the preacher, but—"

"Spit it out, Kevin."

"What?"

Jim Bob reminded himself that it was damn hard to find employees who were willing to work for minimum wage and had never heard of overtime pay. "You wanted to ask me something."

"I sure did, Jim Bob. Kin I sit down?"

"Does this look like a bus station? Just ask your question and then get back to work. I'm planning to leave in half an hour, and I'm gonna inspect all the aisles to make sure they've been mopped. Jim Bob's SuperSaver Buy 4 Less has a reputation in this community, boy, and I aim to make sure the floors are shiny and the shelves are neat and the produce is mostly fresh. Did you spray the fruit?"

Kevin tried to remember how all this had started. He'd had a question, but now Jim Bob had so many questions that it was murkier than a mess of collard greens. "Well, I guess it ain't a bus station," he said real carefully, "since the only buses that come through town are heading for Branson and they don't stop here. I was spraying the fruit when Idalupino startled me and . . . well, she grabbed the hose right out of my hand and said she'd finish up. I thought I'd wait till closing time and then wax the floors. I always wax the floors on Saturday night so they'll be nice and bright on Sunday."

"Is this conversation going anywhere?"

Kevin pondered this. "You got somewhere in mind, Jim Bob?"

"You had a question, Kevin," Jim Bob said, barely getting out the words. "Ask it."

"Well," Kevin said, wishing he could sit down but staying where he was, "it has to do with Kevvie Junior and Rose Marie being models in Hollywood."

"Say what?"

"Dahlia's convinced they can be in commercials on account of how cute they is. The thing is, as cute as they is, and ain't nobody better say otherwise, this ad—"

Jim Bob cut him off. "Do I look like somebody who gives a shit?"

"But I was wondering—"

"I get real irritated when I have to repeat myself. When I come in tomorrow, I'd better be able to see my reflection on every square foot of the floor. The oranges and apples had better be glistening like they'd been plucked straight from the orchards. The paper towels on sale better be stacked in a pyramid that damn near bumps the ceiling. Got that, boy?"

Kevin nodded, then left the office and retrieved his mop from a bucket of scummy water. He knew it'd been dumb to go to Jim Bob for advice, but he shore wasn't about to ask Idalupino after the way she'd cussed at him. She should have known better than to creep up behind him when he had the hose in his hand.

✶

Estelle and I were seated at the kitchen table, peeling potatoes and trying to ignore Ruby Bee's grumbles, when the first crack of thunder shook the lodge from the chimney to the basement. Estelle's paring knife clattered on the floor.

"Goodness gracious," she said.

"It's a thunderstorm, for pity's sake," said Ruby Bee. "You plannin' to go upstairs and crawl under the covers?"

"You're a fine one to talk. You've been on pins and needles since we left this morning."

"Mostly because of your driving. I liked to have a heart attack when you passed that chicken truck outside Starley City." She glared at me as though I'd been driving the vehicle under discussion. "There we were, going up a mountainside, no guard rails or nothing, and—"

"I'm just glad you all made it," I said, "and the kids are, too. Do you want the potatoes sliced or quartered?"

Said kids erupted into the front room of the lodge seconds after rain began to pound down with such intensity that I found myself wondering if the lodge might shudder and slide into the lake. I went into the living room, where they were whimpering and shivering like puppies.

"There's firewood on the back porch," I said to Larry Joe. "Amy Dee, you and Lynette can help me make tea for everybody. Ruby Bee hasn't started frying the catfish yet, but we should be able to eat in an hour or so."

Mrs. Jim Bob came down the staircase like Gloria Swanson in *Sunset Boulevard*. "I can only hope you made satisfactory progress this afternoon," she said as she peered sternly at them. "We only have a week, and the Robarts Foundation is counting on us to do our best."

She undoubtedly would have continued had not lightning hit so close to the lodge that I could feel the hair on my arms quiver. Thunder resounded almost immediately. The light bulbs snapped, crackled, and popped. Dimness of the most dismal sort enveloped us as though someone had thrown a moth-eaten blanket over the building.

"Armageddon is upon us," intoned Brother Verber as he stumbled into the room like a poorly constructed patchwork monster. "Fall to your knees and pray with me, children. 'Yea, though I walk through the valley of the shadow of death, I shall fear no evil; for Thou art—'"

Although it was far from pitch black, the Dahlton twins began to shriek. Mrs. Jim Bob commenced a lecture that could not be heard over the continual outbursts of thunder. Big Mac fell to the floor and began to roll around, begging forgiveness for everything from stealing hooch from Raz to filching candy from the supermarket and putting a dead fish under the hood of my car. Lynette and Amy Dee clutched each other and sobbed hysterically. Larry Joe was paralyzed with either fear or revulsion.

"Stop this!" I said between claps of thunder. "This is a typical spring storm, not an assault from a SWAT team. We're perfectly safe here. Once the storm passes, we'll replace the bulbs and have supper. The range is gas, so we may end up eating by candlelight, but we will eat. Now let's get some wood and start a fire." I did not add that the dead fish incident would be discussed at a later date, but I figured I had a likely candidate to till my garden patch and keep it weeded for the season.

One of the Dahlton twins pointed at Brother Verber. "But he said—"

"He was testing you," I countered obscurely. "Everybody needs to get an armload of wood. Scoot!"

The kids didn't exactly scoot, but they trooped through the dining room to the back porch. Eight of them, anyway; Darla Jean and Heather were noticeably absent. Hoping Mrs. Jim Bob wasn't counting noses, I said to her, "I think I saw extra light bulbs in the pantry."

"I'm sure Mrs. Robarts has seen that we are well-supplied with necessities. She was quite wounded when you walked out so abruptly."

"Is there any other way to walk out? I suppose I might

have hopped and skipped to the door, but somehow—"

"One of these days, young lady, you're going to be sorry for that sassy mouth of yours."

Thunder drowned out her ensuing remarks, none of which were apt to be novel. I watched her jaw waggle for a moment, then went to the kitchen and assured Ruby Bee and Estelle that all the bulbs would be replaced in a few minutes. They seemed to have resolved their differences for the moment, and had retrieved the sherry bottle from under the sink.

I started a kettle of water, took out a dozen mugs, and found teabags and a sugar bowl in a cabinet. Dishes clinked as thunder once again resounded.

"I hope you ain't thinking I can cook in the dark," Ruby Bee said as I counted out spoons from a drawer. "Estelle and me might just go back to Maggody. Maybe I'm a magnet for bad luck."

Estelle snorted. "And who appointed you the center of the universe? We get storms like this every spring, and they happen whether or not Rubella Belinda Hanks is in the vicinity. You got no call to say it's your doing. Mrs. Jim Bob would say it's blasphemous. I might agree."

"I never said such a thing, and I resent you saying I did."

I felt like the captain on the bridge of an ocean liner, spotting an iceberg and incapable of halting headway. "Nobody said anything, okay? The storm will pass. Stay here if you like, or come sit by the fire and have a cup of tea. Mrs. Jim Bob may try to get the kids to belt out a few hymns, but I don't think she'll have much luck. Call me when the kettle begins to whistle."

When I returned to the living room, Larry Joe had coaxed a tentative fire in the fireplace. The kids had moved the metal chairs and were sprawled on the floor, grousing but in a more amiable fashion. Rain continued to pound down, but the outbursts of lightning and thunder were beginning to lessen, and the seconds between them indicated the storm was moving on to expend its remaining savagery on Dunkicker and towns eastward.

All I needed to complete the cozy picture were Darla Jean and Heather. Surely they were at the cabin, experimenting with eye shadow and discussing Billy Dick in descriptions that dripped with venom. Surely.

Ruby Bee appeared in the doorway with a tray. "How about some nice hot tea?" she said as if she'd planned it herself. "I just happen to have brought some oatmeal-raisin cookies along. Anybody interested?"

As the kids crowded around her, I kept an eye on Mrs. Jim Bob. She was eyeballing Brother Verber, who had pulled off his shoes and was baking his socks in front of the fire. So far, so good. I considered whether or not I could slide out the back door and go to the cabin without my absence being noticed. Probably not, I decided glumly. Mrs. Jim Bob's nose was already twitching with suspicion.

"How about a round of charades?" I said brightly.

"Give me a break," Jarvis muttered. "We gonna play spin-the-bottle next?"

"This will be fun," I continued. "Let's divide into teams and come up with clues. Larry Joe will take one team, and Ruby Bee the other."

"Charades?" said the Dahlton twins, sounding as though I'd suggested injecting ourselves with flesh-eating viruses to determine who survived to the bitter end.

"You'll love it. You can make up clues for the other team, and then we'll see who ends up with the best time."

"And then?" said Parwell. "Do the winners get to go home?"

Mrs. Jim Bob bristled. "I do not appreciate your attitude, Parwell, nor does the Almighty Lord. You knew exactly why you were coming here, and you should be grateful that Ruby Bee has arrived to provide meals that will be tasty, if not wholesome. Don't toy with your chances of salvation; one more smart remark and you might find yourself in the fiery furnaces next to Arly."

A timely clap of thunder drowned out Ruby Bee's remark, which might have been tart, to put it mildly. The girls squealed; the boys flinched. Brother Verber dropped to his knees and began to plead to be spared from being roasted, toasted, fried, or fricasseed.

I was about to duck out the back way when a heavy hand pounded on the door. Squealing and flinching were instantaneously replaced with gulping. For the record, adolescent gulping is less attractive, and, in fact, downright distasteful. After a moment, I said, "I'll get it."

No one argued.

So, yeah, we're talking frightened teenagers, isolated campground, thunderstorm, pouring rain, electricity disabled, no doubt telephone lines down and the road washed out. Had I seen this on late-night television, along with its seventeen sequels? Machete or chainsaw?

I looked at Mrs. Jim Bob, who, for the first time since I'd returned and assumed my job as chief of police, showed no inclination to overrule me. She, along with my very own mother, Brother Verber, Estelle, Larry Joe, and the kids, could have been participants in a garden store's display of statuary. Gnomes, elves, dwarfs, and toads; all were petrified as if the concrete fairy had waved her magic wand.

Knuckles rapped once again. I might have been a bit uneasy as I went to the door and opened it.

Jacko was carrying Darla Jean in his arms. Her legs were bare, but her upper body was covered with the flannel shirt he'd been wearing earlier. He'd buttoned the vest, but his arms, shoulders, and a significant amount of his chest glistened with rain in the minimal light. "This one's yours, right?" he said as he brushed past me. "Where shall I put her?"

Ruby Bee, who'd allowed me to open the door to a potential serial killer, leaped to her feet. "Just who do you think you are?" she demanded from a prudent distance.

"I think I'm the guy who found her lying in the road. I suppose I could have taken her to my campsite and chopped her up to make stew, but I was in the mood for bouillabaisse. She's cold and in shock. Is there a warm bed somewhere?"

"Upstairs," I said vaguely, having not yet been there.

Ruby Bee cut off Mrs. Jim Bob, who was sputtering. "Yes, indeed. No one's gotten around to explaining why this poor child, dressed in a slip of a bathing suit, should have been out on an evening like this, but I'm sure someone"—she stared at me—"is gonna explain afore too long. In the meantime, let's tuck her in bed and try to give her some hot liquids. Estelle, bring up a cup of tea with a dollop of . . . something medicinal."

Jacko followed us upstairs, staggering under his burden. Ruby Bee opened a door and stepped back. "Put her in here," she commanded, no doubt envisioning herself in a stiff white uniform and perky cap.

I pulled back the covers and tried not to allow my imagination to run wild as Jacko unceremoniously allowed Darla Jean to bounce on the mattress. She was shivering, but I could see no bruises or other indications of physical assault. I sat on the edge of the bed and pulled the blankets up to her chin.

"You're safe now," I said.

"Ain't none of us safe," she whispered, then buried her face in the pillow.

Our Lady of the Lamp glared at Jacko. "I assume you have an explanation for this."

"Not a good one," he said. "I found her whimpering under a bush and figured I ought to bring her here."

"And why would you think that, mister? Are you accustomed to finding young girls under bushes?"

"On a daily basis?"

I intervened. "He's set up camp down the road from the cabin where the girls and I are staying. I asked him earlier if he'd seen Darla Jean."

"And his reply?" said Mrs. Jim Bob, who must have been eavesdropping just outside the room. "If fornication has been a factor, then I have no choice but to call her parents to fetch her. They will be sorely disappointed, Darla Jean, as will I. This week has been dedicated to doing the Almighty Lord's work, not engaging in depravity."

Jacko gave me a disconcerted look, then left the room. I told Ruby Bee and Mrs. Jim Bob to do the same, then squeezed Darla Jean's shoulder until she rolled over.

"So where have you been and why are you so upset?" I asked.

"It's all crazy."

"That much is obvious."

Estelle attempted to slip into the room. I took the mug from her, thanked her, and eased her backward until I could close the door in her face.

"Go on, Darla Jean."

"Well," she said, sitting up in bed to slurp the tea, "I went for a walk."

"Wearing your bikini."

"Like there's something sinful about working on a tan? All I was gonna do was sit by the water for an hour, and then go back to the cabin to sweep the floors. I was even gonna scrub the toilet bowls just to prove I'd learned my lesson."

"And here I was thinking you might have orchestrated this whole thing to get out of the work detail. Maybe I ought to call Brother Verber up here so he can coach me while I pray for your forgiveness for all my evil thoughts."

"Do you wanna know what happened?"

I sat down on the foot of the bed. "Why don't you tell me?"

"I was walking down the road when I saw this little boy, not more than four or five years old. He ran into the bushes. I went after him to tell him I wasn't gonna hurt him, but then I saw this old guy with a fishing rod."

"And you screeched?"

"I wasn't expecting to see anybody," she admitted. "I went back up to the road, calling for him but in a low voice so's not to scare him. I mean, what was this kid doing by his lonesome? I went all the way down to the edge of the lake, hoping I'd find his family having a picnic or something. There wasn't anyone. I was thinking I'd come find you when I saw him scuttling up the hill."

I looked at the welts and scratches on her face. "So you went after him?"

Her eyes filled with tears. "What was I supposed to do? He wasn't any older than my little cousin Emory, and I'd like to think somebody'd help him if he got hisself lost in the woods."

"And?" I said encouragingly.

"Well, Emory has blond hair, and the little boy's hair was dark and flopping in his face, but—"

"You couldn't figure out why he was out in the woods by himself," I said.

"Emory lives in West Memphis, so I knew right off it wasn't him. Besides, he has a birthmark on his—"

"So you went after this child who was not Emory?"

"He was moving faster than a squirrel, and a 'course he could duck under branches that whacked me in the face. It was like I was in a movie, Arly. The storm clouds made everything dark. Lightning was flashing something awful, and all I could think was that this little boy was lost in the woods. Halfway up the hillside he disappeared. I stumbled around for a long while, begging him to come out of wherever he was hiding, then decided I'd better come back here so you could do something. That's when . . ."

"You found him?" I suggested, always in favor of a happy ending.

"I tripped over the body."

6

"Whose body?" I said.

"Like I should know?" Darla Jean finished off the tea and handed me the mug. "You know, this kinda rocked. Do you think I can have some more, maybe with extra sugar?"

"In a few minutes. Please tell me what you're talking about—and it had better not be a bloated squirrel."

Shivering, she pulled up the blankets. "Not hardly. The whole thing was really, really awful, Arly. I kept falling over stumps and rocks, but I just had to catch up with this poor little boy that shouldn't ought to have been there by hisself in the first place. I didn't mean to, but I guess I scared him, which was making me feel like crap. Maybe I should have come and found you. Thing was, I kept imagining Emory and—"

"Let's fast-forward to the point when you tripped over a body."

"You don't believe me, do you? You got that same look my ma always gets when I tell her I'm going to Heather's to study."

"I don't have enough information to decide, Darla Jean. Continue."

"It seemed like we were up and down the hillside. Every now and then I'd catch sight of him, but then he'd dart out of sight. Finally there came a time when I flatout lost him. I didn't know what to do, and I was sitting on a log, praying he'd show up again, when it got dark and rain commenced.

Lightning hit a tree not twenty feet from where I was and damn near barbecued my skin. I was picking myself up when it turned out I was sprawled in a creekbed that was filling up fast. I'm gonna be puking up tadpoles for the better part of a week."

"And so you got up and started back here," I prompted her.

Darla Jean began to tremble. "I was real scared. The sky was flashing and crashing, and water was gushing down the hill. I wasn't real sure how to find the lodge, but I figured the road was between me and the lake."

"The body, Darla Jean. Was it the child?"

"Gosh, no. I couldn't have left him out in the woods by hisself." She took a deep breath. "It was an alien. Did you ever see those photographs in the tabloids of what they called 'Grays'? Big round heads, with almond eyes and slits for mouths?"

"Those were not photographs," I said. "They were drawings. Could this have been a woman with a shaved head?"

"It was an alien," she insisted. "It makes as much sense as a woman with a shaved head, fer chrissake. I mean, some of the basketball players shave their heads, but ain't no woman's gonna do that, except maybe nuns, and I'm not thinking there's a convent anywhere nearby." She gave me a defiant glare. "Do you think we ought to call the television stations so they can interview me for the ten o'clock news?"

"Let's hold off for the time being. Are you sure this . . . creature was dead? Could he or she have been unconscious?"

"Golly gee, Arly, I forgot to ask. I didn't even say 'excuse me' when I caught my foot on its leg and went face down in the mud again."

"Can you tell me where you saw the body?"

She clutched a pillow to her chest and squeezed it so

tightly that tiny down feathers spewed out like snowflakes. "I don't know. When I was stumbling down to the road, I thought I saw the bleachers and the roof of the dugout over to my right. I was thinking I might be able to find the lodge when my foot came down the wrong way and I twisted my ankle something fierce. The pain was so awful that I couldn't hardly hobble, so I crawled as far as I could and then got under some bushes to wait until the rain stopped. I wasn't sure what I was going to do when that man came along and scooped me up. I was so panicky that I don't recollect much after that."

I pulled back the blankets and eased out her ankle, which was not only swollen, but also blotched with unsightly hues of green and purple. "It may be nothing more than a nasty sprain, Darla Jean, but you'll need an X-ray in the morning to make sure nothing's broken. As soon as we're finished talking, I'll ask Ruby Bee to bring up an ice pack."

"Do you think I can have something to eat?"

I felt a stab of guilt as I remembered the cheese sandwich I'd stuck into my pocket for her, and subsequently eaten while gazing at the lake. "Give me another minute or so, then I'll go downstairs and find something for you until Ruby Bee fries up the catfish and hushpuppies. How far were you from the field when you found this body?"

"Give me a break," she said as she buried her face in the pillow. "If I knew anything, I'd tell you. You need to be out finding that little boy instead of badgering me. He's still out there, unless he was running back to a spaceship. He's liable to be cold and scared. If he's anything like Emory, he'll be screaming so loud he can be heard all the way back to Maggody. I'm done talking to you, so let me be."

I looked at her for a moment, then gave up and went out into the hall. I'd expected to find a veritable horde of eavesdroppers, but no one appeared to be within earshot, which was for the best. I had a much better theory than aliens about whose body she'd encountered.

Billy Dick was hovering at the bottom of the stairs. "Is she okay?" he whispered.

"It's possible that she broke her ankle. I have a feeling she'd just as soon not see you now, so go back and join the others."

"It's all my fault."

"No, Billy Dick, as much as I hate to break it to you, your name did not come up in our conversation. If Darla Jean wants to see you tomorrow, I'll tell you."

The kids were subdued, the girls holding each other's hands and glancing nervously at the front door, the boys hanging their heads. I gestured for Larry Joe to join me in the dining room.

"Is Darla Jean hurt?" he asked.

"She's either sprained or broken her ankle. I'll ask Estelle to take her for an X-ray tomorrow. Mrs. Robarts can tell her the closest place to go."

"Then everything's okay."

"Not exactly. Darla Jean swears she came across a body in the woods."

He stiffened. "Whose?"

"It's hard to say. I guess we'd better take a look. Maybe there are some raincoats in a closet somewhere. Don't mention this to anybody."

"Mrs. Jim Bob'll want to know where we're going."

Bearing false witness (or lying through my teeth, anyway) was becoming easier by the second. "No problem; I'll tell her we're fetching our flashlights in case we need them later."

I detoured through the kitchen and asked Ruby Bee and Estelle to take Darla Jean a sandwich, an ice pack, a couple of aspirin, and another mug of tea. Ignoring their questions, I went back into the dining room.

Larry Joe had a couple of plastic ponchos draped over his arm. "Just let me handle this," I said to him as we pulled them over our heads and went into the living room.

Mrs. Jim Bob had been pacing in front of the fireplace, but she cut us off midway across the room.

"And where are you two going?" she demanded, her arms crossed and her eyes so beady they looked as if they'd been sucked into her skull. "I'd like to think you're not planning some sort of sexual interlude in one of the cabins. Arly, I'm sure you are aware that Larry Joe is a family man with obligations not only to his wife and children, but also to the community. He is a deacon in the church and an upstanding member of the school board. Furthermore, the seventh commandment specifically warns against the evils of adultery. Larry Joe, all I can say is that your conscience needs to be your guide, no matter how strong the temptation may be."

I bit my tongue until I'd allowed myself a few seconds to regain control. It was not the time to drag her outside and tie her to a tree in hopes Thor might be in the mood for target practice. I certainly was. "Jarvis, you and Parwell get some light bulbs from the pantry in the kitchen."

"It might just be the circuit breakers," said Jarvis. "I reckon we can find the box and see. If flipping the switches doesn't work, we'll start changing bulbs." He gave me a sly look. "So where are you and Mr. Lambertino going?"

"To bring back flashlights," I said briskly. "It should take us no more than ten or fifteen minutes."

I hustled Larry Joe out the door before he could blurt out something to further complicate the situation. The rain had eased up for the moment, but more lightning was flickering across the lake—and therefore heading this way, and the thunder, although muffled, sounded like a grizzly bear prematurely aroused from hibernation. The road was nearly invisible under elongated muddy puddles.

Larry Joe was far from an acquiescent Dr. Watson. "This is plum crazy, Arly. Camp Pearly Gates ain't no tidy little patch of woods; there're paths and roads all over the place. How are we supposed to find this body, if there is one?"

"Darla Jean thought she was behind the softball field," I said. "Let's go down the road and see if we can spot where Jacko might have left footprints when he found her."

"You know that guy?" said Larry Joe as he followed me, huffing like a solid community figure, a family man, a deacon and member of the school board, or someone with a beer belly and a penchant for puffing cigars with Hizzoner the Moron. "He didn't, well, do anything to her, did he?"

"All I know about him is that he's a lousy fisherman and a Good Samaritan. Darla Jean may be on crutches until graduation, but she's just frightened." Saying this reminded me of her story of chasing the child, which had taken a backseat in my mind when she'd told me about the body. She hadn't been lying about it, but how could any family have overlooked a small child when packing up the picnic basket and tossing the cooler into the back of the pickup truck?

I decided to hold off telling Larry Joe the full story. We slogged down the road, doing what we could to avoid the deeper puddles, until we were past the far edge of the softball field.

"Look here," Larry Joe said, pointing at some indentations in the bank above the road. "I can't tell if they're footprints, but I guess they might have been an hour ago."

"Very good," I said. The woods seemed to encroach as daylight faded; rain dripped off thorns as venom might drip off fangs. "I suppose we ought to go up that way and have a look. You want to go first?"

"Maybe you should, since you're a cop. The marks could be evidence."

I took a deep breath. "At the police academy, we made a lot of plaster casts of footprints and tire tracks, but that may not be a pertinent skill right now." I took two steps, and promptly slid back down into ankle-deep water. Managing to keep a long string of four-letter words to myself, I made a second attempt with even less success, then said, "Listen carefully, Larry Joe. Put your hands on my rear and shove me up until I can grab that sapling. This will remain between the two of us; Mrs. Jim Bob and Joyce will never know. Can you do this?"

Larry Joe looked as though he'd prefer to dive into the puddle and suffocate, but he nodded, and with reluctance, applied the requested pressure until I found my footing. I hung on to the sapling and offered him a hand, and after several unfortunate starts, he joined me.

"Now what?" he said, gazing unhappily at the mud seeping through the laces of his shoes.

"Darla Jean mentioned a creekbed that was filling up fast. Hear anything?"

He cocked his head. "Over that way, maybe. Before we go thrashing around like a couple of pie-eyed piglets, just what did Darla Jean think she saw?"

It still seemed premature to mention the dead alien and the potential presence of the mother ship. "She wasn't able to tell me much," I said. "Let's head up this way until it gets dark. If we don't find anything, then . . ."

"Aw, hell, come on."

Larry Joe took the lead, which meant he also took the brunt of wet branches and briars. I followed meekly. We slipped and slid, cussed under our respective breaths, and at last found a creek that was doing its best to cut a swath worthy of the Grand Canyon, given a few million years.

"There's something," he said, stopping abruptly.

I peered over his shoulder. The light was lessening with every minute, but the body, sprawled across the creek and draped in a white robe, was hard to miss. I swallowed, then said, "Let me go first. I don't think we can preserve the crime scene, but I might notice something." I picked my way over treacherously mossy rocks, bent down over the body, which was decidedly terrestrial in origin, and felt for a pulse in her neck. Her flesh was cold, her eyes dull. I presumed it was Rachael from the café, although there was something about her features that was unfamiliar.

"She's dead," I said, standing up.

Larry Joe's face was almost as pale as hers. "What happened to her? Why's she out here and dressed like that? Is she some kind of witch?"

I stared at the surrounding brush, hoping I'd see a small face watching us. This woman had not been Darla Jean's quarry. Where was the child?

"What's the matter?" said Larry Joe, his voice cracking. "Is somebody else here?"

I let him imagine the worst while I tried to figure out what to do. Moving the body to the road would be damn near impossible under the existing conditions. If there was any evidence indicating the cause of death, we would destroy it with unwieldy attempts to keep our footing while carrying what appeared to be a hundred and forty pounds of dead weight.

Very dead weight.

I held up my hand to hush Larry Joe, then kneeled down and pushed the woman's head to one side. I was immediately sorry that I had. I stumbled backward and sank down, battling nausea.

"What's wrong with you?" demanded Larry Joe.

"I'll be okay in a minute. We need to go back to the lodge and call the local police. Whoever this woman is, she didn't lose her balance and bang her head on a rock. The back of her head's caved in. Something really walloped her."

Lightning illuminated the object Larry Joe raised above his head. "Like maybe this bat?"

Had a movie production crew been present, the director would have shouted, "Cut!"

✹

Hammet offered a few choice words as the rain began to splatter. He was cold, tired, and still hungry, even after eating the sandwiches and pie. What's more, it was getting dark. He supposed he could sleep in the church, but folks would start coming in the morning and he might get caught. He sure as hell didn't want to get arrested and sent to the gawdawful place Jim Bob had described.

He couldn't quite figure out what had happened to everybody, but it seemed like Arly, Ruby Bee, Estelle, and Mrs. Jim Bob was all off for the time being. He finished the last apple, flung the core at the silver trailer, and got up. There was one other place in Maggody where he'd stayed before, and it was big enough that he ought to be able to keep out of sight, and at the same time stay warm and dry. He couldn't sleep in a bed or lie on the sofa watchin' television, but he reckoned there were all sorts of storage rooms and closets in such a fine house. With Mrs. Jim gone, it wasn't like Jim Bob would come looking for the vacuum cleaner. If he was careful about stealing food, he could most likely hide out there till Arly got back. It was kinda hard to guess what she'd do, but at least she wouldn't arrest him or anything like that. More than likely, she'd just sigh and send him back to the foster home. It never hurt to try.

He set off across the pasture behind the row of abandoned buildings, trying to remember the layout of the house where he and his brothers and sisters had been dumped while Arly figured out what shitheel had killed their mama. At the back of the garage was a room with what he'd later learned was a washing machine and dryer.

The floor was concrete, though, and likely to be clammy as a cave. He couldn't recollect if there was a basement or an attic. He stopped in the knee-deep weeds and tried to think. Between the kitchen and the living room was a closet crammed with winter coats where he'd hid during a game of hide-and-seek. Not even his dumbshit brother had found him in there. It hadn't smelled real good, but it didn't stink near as bad as the dirty quilt he'd slept on in the cabin up on the ridge.

He figured it'd do.

✕

Jim Bob had meant to shut down his computer and go home, but messages in the chat room were coming fast and furious. Most of 'em were from pissant teenagers with screen names like Vaginalee and Studboy. He'd fired off his share of responses, just to amuse himself by trying to see if he could make them squirm. It was about as tough as shooting fish in a barrel.

Then a new presence popped up in the chat room, one making more sense than the brain-dead morons with nothing better to write than, "Yo, dudes." Jim Bob waited for a while, reading the messages from a poster using the name "Love-Pussy." Clearly she was older than the pimply assholes in the chat room, and she was making veiled suggestions that would send most of them under their beds to jerk off.

Jim Bob continued reading for a few minutes, enjoying the specter of the fourteen-year-old boys utilizing their impaired vocabularies and geeky emotions to impress this mysterious LovePussy. She wasn't buying, but she was teasing the living hell out of them.

He finally decided to put the litter out of their misery and posted a message to LovePussy that claimed she was all talk and no action. An instant message came up on his screen, offering to prove otherwise.

Jim Bob damn near fell out of his chair. Once he'd pulled himself together, he replied, asking how LovePussy thought she might make good on her promise. Her response had chilled him: "See you at the Dew Drop Inn in half an hour."

Jim Bob turned off his computer and swept all the papers, including such irrelevancies as the payroll and the current invoices, into a desk drawer. As he blotted his face with his handkerchief, he wondered if he had time to swing by his house and take a shower.

Probably not, he concluded. If "LovePussy" actually showed up at the Dew Drop, she might not be the kind to wait around. He locked his office and went to the registers.

"Idalupino, close up at nine. Kevin's fixing to wax the floors, but he's got a key so's to let himself out when he's done."

"I'm supposed to be off at seven," she protested. "Me and some of my girlfriends are gonna have us a night out. We've been planning it for weeks."

"So go at nine. Big fuckin' deal."

"The schedule says you're closing tonight. Besides, I need to wash my hair and do my nails. I even bought an outfit 'specially for tonight."

"Maybe you ought to save it for going on job interviews next week, 'cause that's what you'll be doing after I fire you. If I was you, I'd start at the poultry plant in Starley City. I hear they're always looking for workers to yank the guts out of chickens. Kinda messy, but you get to go to the company picnic on the Fourth of July. Oh, and you get a fruitcake at Christmas."

Idalupino stared at him. "You're a real sumbitch, Jim Bob."

"So they say." He went back through the store and out the loading dock door to his truck. He ran a comb through his stubby hair and splashed on some cologne from the bottle he kept in the glove compartment.

The Dew Drop Inn was twenty minutes away. He wasn't sure if she'd even show up, but if she did, he figured he was in for one helluva night.

✹

When Larry Joe and I made it back to the road, I piled up a few rocks as a marker, then walked back to the lodge, oblivious to his demands for an explanation. As we reached the porch, I turned around. "There is a telephone, isn't there?"

"Yeah, back in the little office, but it doesn't work. While you were upstairs with Darla Jean, I tried to call Joyce to make sure she was okay. Lightning must have hit a transformer somewhere."

This was not good, but I was encouraged to see the lights were back on inside.

"Wait here," I said to Larry Joe, then went over to Estelle's station wagon. As I'd hoped, the key was in the ignition, which was standard behavior in Maggody. "I'm going into Dunkicker to tell the deputy what we found. Let's hope he can get some backup from the sheriff's department. What I need you to do is go inside and see if Heather's there. If not, go down to the girls' cabin and tell her that we found Darla Jean."

"Wouldn't it be better if one of the other girls went?"

"I don't want any of them setting foot out of the lodge until we know for sure that . . ." I dribbled off, unable to think of a tactful way to finish the sentence.

Larry Joe grunted. "That there's not a crazy killer hiding in the woods, spying on us and waiting to attack somebody else? Is that what you mean?" I shrugged. "What am I supposed to tell Mrs. Jim Bob this time? You decided to do some night fishin' and stole Estelle's station wagon to go into Dunkicker and buy bait?"

"As good as anything else," I said. "Just make sure

everybody stays inside until I get back. It's liable to be several hours."

I left him standing on the porch and drove away, desperately hoping I wouldn't go through a puddle deep enough to stall out the engine. There I'd be, sitting in the station wagon, lightning and thunder all around me, twiddling my thumbs and waiting for the guy in the hockey mask (or, in this case, perhaps a catcher's mask).

I kept a death grip on the steering wheel and my mind on the road until I arrived on pavement. Letting out the breath I'd held for at least five minutes, I turned toward Dunkicker. Surely someone at the Welcome Y'all Café could help me find Corporal Robarts.

Parking places were not at a premium, in that one lone pickup dominated the gravel expanse. Cold bullets of rain chased me inside the building. I pulled off the poncho and left it by the door, then brushed ineffectually at the mud caked on my pants. "Some storm," I murmured inanely.

"I'd say. Want a cup of coffee?"

I looked up and saw Rachael behind the counter, somewhat friendlier than she'd been earlier and clearly alive and kicking. "That'd be great." I sat down on a stool and wrapped my hands around the ceramic mug she put down on the counter. "I'll have to pay you tomorrow."

"You look like you might ought to be drinking it right now. Something to eat?"

"No, thank you," I said, obediently sipping. I glanced around. All the tables were vacant, with the exception of the three toothless wonders to be found at every café in the South, cackling, drooling, and arguing about their dawgs. Now that I had seen Rachael, I was even more bewildered. It did not, however, seem appropriate to discuss it. "I'm looking for Corporal Robarts."

"Anthony usually has his supper at home on Saturday night." Rachael refilled my mug. "You sure you don't want another eighteen cheeseburgers? Scrawny girl like you needs her calories."

"As do ten teenagers," I said, and told her about the group. "We have a situation at Camp Pearly Gates, and the telephone's out because of the storm. Can you tell me how to find Corporal Robarts?"

"You want I should call him and tell him to get over here?"

"Please."

Rachael went around the corner to a short hallway and fed a coin into a pay phone. I sat on the stool, drinking coffee and doing my best not to listen to the conversation from the booth, which was now centered on professional wrasslin' and the remote possibility that it might just be rigged. I tuned it out as best I could. The ghastliness of what Larry Joe and I had found came flooding over me as both my body and brain began to thaw. The body had not been who I had assumed her to be. But a second woman with a shaved head and magenta lipstick, dressed in a white robe? And the child? Had there been one, or had Darla Jean conjured up the spectral presence of Cousin Emory for some reason?

Rachael came back and told me that Corporal Robarts was on his way, then went to the corner table to top off coffee and ask if anyone wanted another piece of pecan pie.

I simply sat, trying to assimilate what I'd seen, what I'd done, what I should have done, what I needed to do. Back at the ranch, so to speak, I was short one teenager. Both Brother Verber and Ruby Bee claimed to have seen something disturbing, although it seemed possible that they had seen the now deceased woman hiding in the woods. The woman with Rachael's sense of style. That woman, yeah.

A few minutes later Corporal Robarts came in and sat down on the stool beside me. "Heard you're looking for me," he said. "Just as well you came into town, saving me from driving all the way out to the camp in weather like this. I got one of yours locked up at the police department. I was gonna hunt you up soon as I had my supper. Ma always has pork chops and gravy on Saturday. Warm apple pie with vanilla ice cream for dessert. It just doesn't get any better than that."

I hated to break it to Corporal Robarts, but his evening was destined to go downhill.

Like a bobsled.

7

"One of mine?" I said, surprised. I would have argued that I wasn't missing one, but I was. However, Heather had shown no inclination to hoof it into Dunkicker, much less get herself arrested.

Corporal Robarts grinned, allowing me a view of clumps of pork stuck between his teeth. "A good ol' boy, name of Duluth Buchanon—funny yellow eyes, forehead like somebody'd squashed his head. I picked him up about an hour ago and left him to sleep it off over at the police department."

I damn near rocked off the stool. "Duluth Buchanon, here? What was he doing?"

"Crawling alongside the road and braying like a jackass. I would have let him be, but it was rainin' and I figured he'd be better off in a cell than facedown in a ditch. I couldn't find his vehicle, but he must have left it somewhere. The municipal judge'll be here Tuesday, fine him fifty dollars for public drunkenness, and let him go."

"Duluth Buchanon?"

"That's what it said on the driver's license in his pocket. I reckon that's not why you was looking for me."

"No," I said, smiling gratefully at Rachael as she refilled my mug and left a couple of cookies on the edge of the saucer. I waited until she had moved away, then said, "I found a dead body in the woods at Camp Pearly Gates. A woman. She had the same shaved head and makeup as Rachael, but she was dressed in some sort of white robe."

"You sure she was dead?"

Rachael made a small noise. It was impossible to determine if she'd turned white, considering that she already had the complexion of someone who'd been chipped out of a glacier after a few thousand years.

I turned back to Corporal Robarts. "Real sure. I went to take a look after one of the girls in our group claimed to have stumbled over the body a few minutes after the storm came in."

"What was the girl doing out there by herself?"

"It's pretty complicated. Why don't you call the sheriff's department and request backup? While we're waiting, I'll tell you what I know."

"I ain't about to call the sheriff's department or anybody else on account of what you think you may have seen. For all I know, you brought a dozen bottles of field whiskey in the back of that blue bus of yours. Was Duluth Buchanon your driver? That might explain why he's drunker'n a skunk." He shook his head resolutely. "I'll call Chief Panknine in the morning and see what he sez."

I resisted the impulse to fling coffee in his smug face. "I saw the body, dammit! Somebody shattered the back of her head with a softball bat. You are not equipped to handle this investigation on your own. We need a forensics team from the sheriff's department, and"—I forced myself to add—"a couple of dogs. There may be a lost child."

"Anything else? How about a stinky, nine-foot-tall hulk with an excess of body hair and real big feet?"

All eyes were on me as I went to the pay phone in the hallway, punched buttons, and made a collect call to the sheriff's department. When LaBelle answered, I told her to accept the call or spend the remainder of her life being stalked by whatever sexual deviants I could recruit from the state prison. Having sent a few there myself, I was sincere in my threat.

"I am not permitted to accept collect calls," she said as soon as the operator had reluctantly exited the connection, which was undoubtedly the highlight of her shift. "The quorum court recently hired an auditor to make sure—"

"Let me speak to Harve."

"He's over at his sister's house, it being her twentieth wedding anniversary. You could have slapped me silly with a pom-pom when he told me they'd been married that long. I was in school with Jerrilynda, you know, and I always figured she'd take off with some roustabout from a carnival. She had a thing about tattoos and what she referred to as manly odors."

"Listen carefully, LaBelle," I said. "I'm going to give you a telephone number. Track down Harve and tell him to call me back immediately. Understand?"

"His budget's—"

"Remember Siffalus Buchanon, the guy with the glass eye and fondness for barbed wire? He should be getting out on parole any day now."

She spat back the number after I gave it to her, then slammed down the receiver. I sat down on the end stool and waited for the pay phone to ring, refusing to look at the trio of troglodytes, Rachael, or Corporal Robarts.

Corporal Robarts finally found the courage to approach me. "You called Sheriff Dorfer, right?"

"This cannot wait until you speak to your chief in the morning. There is a corpse in the woods, and quite possibly a child cowering underneath a ledge."

"This ain't your jurisdiction."

"No, it's not," I said. "It is, however, Sheriff Dorfer's, especially with your police chief out of commission. He's not going to like it, but he'll send some backup to retrieve the body and start the investigation. So why don't you run along back to your mama's and have your apple pie and ice cream?"

"Chief Panknine's gonna be real pissed."

"So's Sheriff Dorfer when he's obliged to leave the festivities and call me. You have three options here: tuck your tail and run, take the call and behave like the acting law enforcement agent, or sit down on that stool and allow me to take charge. I really don't care."

Sweat dotted his forehead as it must have done a very few years ago when he'd faced an exam in high-school algebra. "Are you sure you saw this body?"

"Tell you what," I said, "let's drive out to the campground and you can see for yourself. I can't draw you a map, but I can point you in the right direction."

"What about the child?"

"I don't know, but if we're still here when the phone rings, I'm going to tell Sheriff Dorfer about your blatant ineptitude and request that his department take charge of the investigation. You won't even get your name in the local newspaper—if there is one."

"Go on," said Rachael from behind the counter. "I'll make your excuses when the sheriff calls."

He gave me a mulish look. "I can't just go off on your say-so. I got a prisoner over at the police department."

I glanced at the pay phone. "LaBelle's talking to Sheriff Dorfer as we speak. He'll harrumph for a few minutes, then get rid of her and call me back. When he does, he'll be about as happy as a boar with ticks on its balls. You're going to have to deal with him sooner or later, but you'd better have your act together when you do. He's got a temper, and he doesn't suffer fools."

"You saying I'm a fool?"

I would have felt sorry for him if I hadn't been so frustrated, as well as wet, hungry, covered with scratches, and splattered with mud. "It's up to you."

"All right," he said with the bravado of John Wayne eying the Apache warriors on the crest of the mountain. "We can drive out and take a look. Rach, if Sheriff Dorfer calls, get his number and tell him I'll report when I know more. If there's a body like she says, I most likely will need assistance. If there's not, he can call her over at the police department, 'cause she's gonna be in the cell with her neighbor from back home in Maggody."

"Got a flashlight?" I asked as we headed for the door.

"Hold on." He went back to the counter and had a whispered conversation with Rachael. Eventually she slammed a flashlight into his hand and suggested, loudly enough to be heard not only by me but also by the rapt audience in the corner, that he'd better haul his sorry ass out the door before the phone rang.

He gestured for me to climb into his car, which lacked an insignia or a blue bubble on its roof. "Chief Panknine's wife is driving the official vehicle," he explained as we drove toward Camp Pearly Gates. "Hers is in the shop, and what with her needing to go to the hospital every day, I couldn't see asking her to turn it over. The town council's considering the purchase of a second vehicle."

"I can't even get new pencils out of mine," I said, relaxing a bit. I'd been rough with him, but I figured I'd need his help. "Tell me something, Corporal Robarts. When I talked to you earlier today, you said something about Rachael and others like her. I can't recollect the names, but I had the impression that she's not here on her own. You have to admit she's got an odd sense of style. What's the deal?"

"I think we got us enough to deal with right now. Here's the gate."

"Go on down the road. I left a pile of stones as a marker."

"Like that place in England?"

"No, I lacked the energy to construct a scale model of Stonehenge. Maybe next time." I watched the road carefully. "Stop here."

The rain had slackened, and the thunderstorm had finally gone on its way. It was getting dark, however, and neither of us could rally much enthusiasm as we got out of his car and regarded the ditch filled with what I knew from personal experience was cold water.

"Up this way?" he said.

I nodded. "Not too far."

As much as I would have preferred to send him on his own, I scrambled up the bank, grabbed the same sapling that had served me well earlier, and offered him my hand. He took it with obvious reluctance. Once I yanked him alongside of me, with perhaps a tad more vigor than required, we set off up the hill. Larry Joe and I had not blazed a trail, but I followed the sound of water and we eventually saw the white-clad figure.

"You left her like this?" he said.

"She wasn't in danger of drowning. Do you recognize her?"

He squatted and studied her face, then stood up. "Yeah, she went by the name of Ruth, and was helping Sarah at the church. I don't know her real name, though."

"I have a feeling she doesn't have a driver's license in her pocket." I pointed at the softball bat. "That's liable to be the weapon. We brought some equipment to the field earlier today; it's possible that this was in the bag."

"So," Corporal Robarts said, switching from John Wayne to Columbo, "you brought the weapon and your driver's been arrested. Is this a church group or a street gang?"

I considered the pleasure I would have if I coerced him into asking Mrs. Jim Bob that very question, then let it go and said, "I need to stop by the lodge before we go back to call Sheriff Dorfer."

"To make sure they have alibis?"

"To make sure everybody's okay." I headed toward the road, and after a moment, he stumbled along behind me.

We did not speak as he drove to the lodge, and I told him to wait in the car while I went inside.

The members of the gang were sitting on the floor, cheerfully wolfing down catfish, hushpuppies, fried potatoes, and Joyce's green tomato relish. The redolence made me dizzy, but I stoically continued and found Larry Joe in the dining room with Mrs. Jim Bob, Brother Verber, and Estelle.

I grabbed his arm and pulled him into a corner. "Is Heather here?" I whispered.

"Yeah, she's upstairs with Darla Jean, but she's not doing so well. I found her in the bathroom at your cabin, choking like she had a chicken bone caught in her throat. I was about to pound her on the back when she got hold of herself and told me what was wrong. Seems she went to the cabin like you told her to do, but when she didn't find Darla Jean, she decided to take a shower. She'd just finished washing her hair when she saw somebody watching her through a window. She grabbed her clothes and ducked into a toilet stall."

"Did she say how old this person was?"

Larry Joe looked at the others, who were watching us, then dropped his voice to a barely audible mutter. "She says it was an alien."

I was getting real tired of alien sightings. "So she's upstairs now, presumably eating supper and keeping Darla Jean company. I'm probably going to be out most of the night, dealing with the body. I think it'll be best if the rest of the kids get their sleeping bags and stay here on the living-room floor. Mrs. Jim Bob can arrange a barrier of folding chairs and sit up till dawn, if she wishes. Arm her with a wet towel so she can snap them if they get any ideas."

Larry Joe scratched his head. "She won't agree unless I tell her why. What am I supposed to say?"

"Tell her that I'm investigating a report of trespassers on the campgrounds. The cabin doors don't lock. If I'm not back in the morning, she can escort the girls to their cabin to shower and change clothes, or persuade Ruby Bee and Estelle to do it. I want all of them under constant supervision until this is cleared up."

"What the hell's going on, Arly? This place is scaring the bejeezus outta me. I mean, I get nervous going to the high school at night to mop the halls and clean the restrooms. I've never found a dead body, though. The only body I'd ever seen before was at my great-aunt Ursala's funeral. I was only six or seven, and my parents made me lean over the coffin and kiss her cheek. I had nightmares for years afterward."

"I don't know what's going on, Larry Joe, but I'll keep you posted. Now go sit down and finish your supper before Mrs. Jim Bob gets more suspicious than she already is."

I left him gawking at me and went into the kitchen. Ruby Bee was flipping another batch of catfish steaks out of a skillet.

"Just where have you been, missy?" she demanded without turning around.

"And where's my station wagon?" said Estelle as she joined us. "I disremember giving you permission to take it. Now there's a strange man out front, seemingly waiting for you." Her artfully drawn eyebrows furrowed. "This is all very peculiar."

"It's complicated," I said with heartfelt sincerity. "I apologize for taking your station wagon, and I'll have it back at some point tonight. The man out front is from the police department in Dunkicker. There seem to be unauthorized people on the campgrounds, and we're looking into it. I've told Larry Joe that I want all of the kids to stay at the lodge until I get this straightened out."

"What's going on?" asked Ruby Bee. "Here we are, aiming to do a few good deeds, and all of a sudden, it seems like . . ."

I kissed her cheek, and Estelle's, for good measure. "I can't explain now."

"Seems to me we're entitled," huffed Estelle.

"In the morning," I said, then hurried through the living room before Mrs. Jim Bob could catch up with me. Corporal Robarts was sulking behind the steering wheel.

"Drive," I said.

Mrs. Jim Bob came skittering to the bottom of the porch steps as we made our escape up the road. I doubted I'd have my job when we got back to Maggody, but unemployment might just be the catalyst to send me back into battle with those of a more polysyllabic bent. Being a cop in a small town wasn't all that pleasant, as I was sure Corporal Robarts realized. Museum security at the Louvre, I thought, or even a desk job at the FBI.

"So what about the child?"

I shook myself into the present. "I don't know. Darla Jean spotted him down by the lake. She went to find him, chased him all over the place, and had lost him when the storm hit. She said he was perhaps four or five years old. Has anyone reported a missing child?"

"And I'd be having supper at my mama's house if a child was lost, planning to have a look-see after I finished my pie? What do you take me for, Miz Hanks?"

"I apologize, Corporal Robarts. I had no business even implying you'd ignore such a report. I doubt we're going to be close friends, but I hope we can work together on this case. It's your jurisdiction, and you're in charge. I'll make sure the sheriff's team understands that."

"Only had my badge for a month," he muttered. "The police academy turned me down on account of my juvenile record, and Chief Panknine gave me the job 'cause my mama owns most of the town. Busting drunks is one thing. Murder's something else."

"I can't argue with that," I said, wishing I'd borrowed a

sweater from Ruby Bee. I was soaked to the bone and I could barely remember when I'd last eaten more than the cheese sandwich. I wasn't hungry; I was hollow. "When we get to Dunkicker, drop me off at the café. I'll fetch my car and meet you at the police department."

"Wanting to interrogate Rachael?"

"I was dreaming of a hamburger, but I do need to know what's going on here. She and the woman in the creek obviously have ties. Brother Verber, Ruby Bee, and Heather all saw what they interpreted as apparitions, but I don't buy into that shit. What's the deal? Is Camp Pearly Gates an alien airfield? If so, I have a moral obligation to get Darla Jean on the ten o'clock news. Television cameras, vans, helicopters, whatever."

He did not look at me, but his eyelid was twitching so madly that I wanted to slap a patch over it. "We don't need no news teams up here. These women aren't hurting anybody. They've got some goofy beliefs, but we let them be."

"These women? Are you talking about a cult?"

"Reckon so. Daughters of the Moon, they say. They call themselves Moonbeams. Folks in town call 'em Beamers."

"You're making this up—right?" I said weakly.

"Suit yourself." He turned onto the highway and accelerated toward Dunkicker.

✖

Jim Bob pulled into the garage, then hurried back into the driveway and waited with a grin as Tonya and Sonya got out of their car. Identical twins, blonde, tall, slender, dressed in halters and miniskirts, giggly as all get out and acting like he was the cutest little ol' thing they'd ever laid eyes on. He knew he wasn't, but when one of them had breathed "LovePussy" into his left ear and the other had done the same into his right, both sides of his brain had melted like a popsicle on the pavement in August. Being a gentleman, he'd bought them several drinks and attempted to make conversation, but their cleavage kept distracting him, the halters doing nothing to restrain their very conspicuous nipples. That, and the way they wiggled on the barstools, like something needed to be scratched.

Jim Bob was willing and, at least for the moment, able. He'd never taken on two women before. Maybe they'd all end up together, or maybe they preferred a tag team sort of thing. He just hoped he could rise to the challenge.

But first he wanted to ask them about a couple of things that'd been puzzling him on the drive home. "How'd you girls know I was close to the Dew Drop Inn—instead of in Alaska or Florida?"

Tonya smiled. "Why, we recognized your screen name, honey, and you've been known to brag in chat rooms about being the mayor of Maggody. We were interested, seeing how we live in Farberville. Sonya even found the town's website and a picture of you. Quite the handsome devil, aren't you?"

"Why ain't I ever seen you two at the Dew Drop before?"

It was Sonya's turn to smile. "Oh, I think you have, but you must not have noticed us, what with all the women fawning over you." She paused. "You live all by yourself in this big fancy house?"

"My wife's out of town this week," he admitted.

"Well, then," Tonya said brightly, "We can make ourselves at home. You got more bourbon, honey? My throat's parched after the drive, and I sure could stand to kick off my shoes, put on some music, and sip a little something. Sonya, get the CDs out of the glove compartment. I feel a party comin' on."

"So do I, sister," said Sonya as she ducked back into their car and reappeared with a handful of CDs. "We are gonna have ourselves one wild night."

Jim Bob's eyes welled with tears as the thanked the

Almighty for providing heaven on earth. His wife and Brother Verber might see it differently, but they were fifty miles away in some forsaken camp. He had wine, women, and song, along with food and booze and not a chance anybody'd ever find out. Sonya and Tonya, surely sent from above. He certainly intended to be touched by an angel, and in more ways than one.

Tonya, who seemed a bit more forward, took his hand. "I hope you got something to eat, Mr. Mayor. My stomach's rumbling and grumbling like the New Madrid fault. I sure could do with a bit of supper before the earth starts shakin' under our feet."

"Oh, yeah," Jim Bob said, drawing her toward the door. "My wife left all kinds of casseroles. You want some lasagna or maybe meatloaf? All we have to do is heat it up."

"And then heat you up? You're already approaching medium-high. Don't go boiling just yet, honey."

Sonya caught up with them and tweaked his butt. "But we'll save you for dessert, Mr. Mayor. I just adore a man with a title."

Jim Bob was grinning so hard his cheeks ached as he led them into the kitchen and opened the refrigerator. "That's funny," he said. "I could have sworn the lasagna was right here on the top shelf. Meatloaf sound okay?"

Sonya and Tonya nodded, then went off to explore the house while he put the pan into the oven, took out plates and cutlery, and hunted through drawers for napkins. It was gonna be worth it, he thought as he listened to them shriek with hilarity over the newly upholstered sofa and fringed fuchsia and lavender throw pillows, all of which had set him back a pretty penny only a month ago. It hadn't seemed all that hilarious to him. He couldn't quite make out what they were saying as they went upstairs, but they seemed to find the flocked wallpaper equally hilarious.

It got real quiet for a spell, but he was way too caught

up in his fantasies to think much about it. He was setting the meatloaf on the stove when they reappeared.

"Oh, Mr. Mayor," said Tonya, or maybe Sonya, "the most terriblest thing has happened. While we were freshening up in your bathroom, we had a call on my cellphone. Our poor granny fell and broke her hip. Mama wants us to meet her at the hospital."

"You're leaving?" squeaked Jim Bob.

Sonya, or maybe Tonya, licked his earlobe. "You know we wouldn't if we didn't have to, but our mama hasn't been herself since she lost her leg in a car wreck, and our papa's so fat that he hasn't left his bedroom in seventeen years. Our brother Ivan is doing time for rape, and sweet little Smirnoff keeps insisting he's a frog, so he lives down at the pond. We got no choice but to help our mama. It's a family thing, you know."

"A frog?" said Jim Bob.

"He's making progress in therapy," said Tonya, or maybe Sonya. "Last year he thought he was a polliwog. Do you mind if we make ourselves sandwiches?"

They sounded so matter-of-fact that Jim Bob couldn't gauge their sincerity. "If he believed he was a polliwog . . . what did he do?"

Sonya, or maybe Tonya, put out a loaf of bread and a bottle of catsup. "Lived in the bathtub most of the time. Ever' now and then he'd let us drain off the water and then refill it. You would not believe the shit we had to put up with from social workers and truancy officers. They'd come pounding on the door night and day. Whenever we saw them driving up, we'd put on Tina Turner tapes and play 'em at full volume. You like Tina, Mr. Mayor?"

Mr. Mayor was having a helluva hard time thinking of anything to say. Here he'd been imagining a night of lust and abandonment, and now he was being forced to entertain the most unsavory images. "Tina, yeah, I like her," he managed to say, having no idea who she was.

"Tell you what, then. We gotta go to the hospital, but we'll come back here tonight if we can. If not, maybe we can come tomorrow night—presuming your wife will still be gone. A threesome is okay, but we don't much care for a foursome unless we're playing bridge. Then again, there's nothing I'd rather do than make a grand slam. That takes all thirteen tricks, and we just happen to know them all."

✖

"I was thinking," Dahlia said as she flopped over in bed, "that we ought not have a swimming pool just yet."

Kevin was mystified. "In the backyard?"

"No, silly, behind our mansion. Kevvie Junior and Rose Marie will be toddling afore too long. We could, I suppose, hire a lifeguard, but even then I wouldn't be comfortable knowing there was a swimming pool where our cherished darlings might be in danger. No pool."

"We ain't got a mansion."

"But we will soon, and we have to think about these things."

Kevin resisted the impulse to pull the covers over his head and pray that the lack of air might cause him to pass out. "We do not have a mansion, my petunia of passion. If we was to buy a plastic wading pool at Wal-Mart, I can't see that we need a lifeguard. You can keep an eye on them."

"I am talking about Hollywood," Dahlia said testily. "When we get there, we might ought to find a mansion without a pool. Most of them have 'em, but we should at least insist there's a fence. Kevvie Junior and Rose Marie can take swimming lessons, but this new one's gonna be too little."

"We do not have a mansion," repeated Kevin, speaking slowly and very, very carefully. "We don't even have a backyard, except for that patch of crabgrass by the vegetable garden. This ad you saw doesn't promise that our little darlings will earn enough so's we can have a mansion in Hollywood."

"So you don't think Kevvie Junior and Rose Marie will have modeling careers?"

Kevin wished he was waxing floors at the supermarket, but, sadly enough, he wasn't. "Of course I do," he murmured meekly. "It's just that, well, it may take some time. I don't think we ought to be packing our bags just yet."

"What do you think?"

Thinking was not one of his skills. He made an attempt to distract her, but she slapped him off and rolled away. He listened to her grumbles as she sank into her pillow, clueless as to what to say or do to win her heart once again. Maybe she was right, he thought. The twins were the cutest li'l things he'd ever laid eyes on, but he had doubts they'd all be loading up the car and heading for Beverly Hills and a mansion with or without a swimming pool.

But that didn't mean his pa would cotton to ridin' in a limo, 'specially if the chauffeur was a pansy. His pa hated pansies.

8

The homecoming parade, or so it seemed, marched into the cabin at some insanely early hour when not even the birds were stirring. The girls were trying to be quiet, but the snickers, giggles, and whispers composed a full woodwind section.

Estelle shook my shoulder. "Are you all right?"

"I was doing just fine," I said as I sat up. "What time is it?"

"Seven-fifteen. Ruby Bee's fixing breakfast, and Mrs. Jim Bob wasn't feeling charitable enough to escort the girls down here. We fretted about you most of the night. Larry Joe clammed up, but it was obvious he was worried sick. He seemed to think you'd come back to the lodge, but then you didn't and Ruby Bee was pacing and peering out the window till dawn. Darla Jean took to moaning about her ankle, so I spent the night keeping it packed with ice and holding her hand. Poor little thing finally fell asleep three hours ago."

"Which is about when I got back here." I rubbed my eyes. "Nothing happened after I left, then?"

"I ain't the person to answer that, am I, missy? I didn't steal a station wagon and go driving off, or come back with a strange man and make all sorts of discombobulated remarks. You'd have thought we were at that hotel in Noow Yark City, with headlights flashing all night long."

The girls (minus Darla Jean and Heather) began to appear from the bathroom, dressed in robes, their hair wrapped in towels. None of them had the nerve to speak to me, however, which was for the best. I had no idea what might be going through their adolescent minds.

"There was a problem last evening," I announced. "A woman's body was found behind the softball field. Did any of you see anything that seemed odd?"

"Well," said Amy Dee as she took a cigarette from her purse, glanced at me, and then defiantly lit it, "when Mr. Lambertino got all riled up on account of Jarvis cutting a board too short, Parwell and me sort of wandered behind the dugout." She paused until the giggles died down. "I could have sworn I saw a couple of brats hunkered under a bush on the hill. Parwell didn't believe me, but I saw 'em."

"Brats?" I repeated. "How old?"

"Fifth, maybe sixth grade. Soon as they saw I was looking at them, they scampered away."

One of the Dahlton twins flung herself down on a lower bunk. "They must have been children who came to this place and then died. Now their spirits roam the woods, watching us, waiting for us to leave them in peace. This woman Arly found must have been their mother, coming to fetch them back to their graves."

"I wanna go home," wailed the other twin, flopping on the mattress next to her sister. "This is like so unbelievably weird."

I stood up. "No, the woman was alive and well as of yesterday afternoon. There are some other people currently living at Camp Pearly Gates. When the church groups began to arrive, they moved to the more remote cabins."

"There are?" gasped Estelle.

"You sure they ain't dead?" asked Lynette, as helpful as ever. "I saw this movie once where—"

"Very sure," I said firmly. "Now get dressed and go back to the lodge for breakfast. You can enjoy Ruby Bee's biscuits and gravy, or Mrs. Jim Bob's oatmeal and prunes. Afterward, Mr. Lambertino will go with you to the softball field and put you to work. If you prefer not to participate, I'm sure Brother Verber will be happy to counsel you the rest of the morning on the joys of godliness, celibacy, and sobriety."

"He doesn't know much about that last thing you said," Estelle muttered. "He spent the night under the dining-room table. Mrs. Jim Bob tried to convince Ruby Bee and me to help her drag him out and carry him upstairs. We refused and sat on the porch, sipping sherry, watching the moonlight on the lake—and waiting on you."

"Let me take a quick shower, then I'll come to the lodge and explain," I said. "In the meantime, stay with the girls."

"You aimin' to return my station wagon any time soon?"

"I think I'd better hang on to it for the time being. I've got to go back into Dunkicker this morning, and I'd rather not stick out like a high-school graduate at a Buchanon family reunion."

"I reckon that's okay, but we deserve to know what all's going on."

"I'll be there in fifteen minutes."

She herded out her hastily dressed flock, allowing me a few minutes of peace. I cradled my face as I tried to digest all that had taken place through the long, wet, bone-chilling night. After Corporal Robarts and I had returned to Dunkicker and calls were made, I sent him out to check on the other Beamers and warn them to be careful. Eventually two sheriff's deputies arrived and we headed back to the crime scene, followed by the county coroner, his assistant, and a hearse and driver, courtesy of the local mortuary. We waited while the scene was photographed, then collectively grimaced as the body was transported to the road. The bat had been tagged, but none of us thought it might offer much evidence. Footprints, fingerprints, and bloodstains had long since been washed away.

It had hardly been murder most foul in the conservatory, with a candlestick conveniently discarded on a loveseat.

The Welcome Y'all Café had been closed, preventing me from the ingestation of greasy sustenance or the opportunity to question Rachael. Corporal Robarts clearly regretted having mentioned this mysterious cult; he'd clammed up and refused to answer any more questions about them.

I looked at my watch and realized I was due at his office in an hour. Harve had been, as I'd anticipated, cantankerous, and had ordered me to call him when I had something to say that made a whit of sense. The deputies he'd sent, Les (with whom I'd worked on several occasions), and a muscular young woman named Bonita who kept muttering about law school, were camped out at a local motel. The body should have been at the state medical lab in Little Rock by now, but we'd all agreed that the cause of death was obvious and the time obscured by weather-related circumstances.

I dragged myself into the shower, put on clean clothes, brushed my teeth, slapped on several layers of mascara so I might look awake, and then drove Estelle's station wagon to the lodge.

The blue bus was not parked out front.

This was interesting, but hardly worthy of alarm. The aroma of pork sausages, pancakes, and freshly baked biscuits sucked me into the dining room (my stomach abhors a vacuum). The kids were sitting at the tables, squabbling cheerfully as they passed jars of jam and plastic bottles of maple-flavored syrup. Larry Joe was regarding them as he might a potential plague of locusts. Brother Verber had been relocated from underfoot, and Mrs. Jim Bob was nowhere to be seen.

Silence erupted when I entered the room. "Here's what I know," I said. "A woman was found murdered late yesterday afternoon, her body left in a creekbed behind the softball field. I've already asked the girls, but I'll repeat this: Did you see anything that might help us figure out what happened?"

Nobody had a contribution. I waved off Larry Joe, who was clearly itching to pull me aside, and went into the kitchen. "Any chance for scrambled eggs and a piece of toast?"

Ruby Bee bristled. "Make do with what's on the table."

"Where's Estelle?" I asked as I poured myself a cup of coffee.

"She and Heather took Darla Jean to some hospital to have her ankle X-rayed. Now I'm not one to expect a decent explanation of what all has been happening around here, so I just came in here and made breakfast for these kids. After all, why should I know what's going on? I'm nothing more than a short-order cook in some people's eyes. I don't have anything better to do, do I? Fry up sausages, put biscuits in the oven, wash dishes—"

"Nobody asked you to do all this."

"And just what am I supposed to do—let these kids waste away on lima beans and applesauce? It's not like I have an establishment back in Maggody, is it? No, I have a charbroiled kitchen and enough workmen to make up a baseball team. Duluth upped and vanished yesterday. All these slovenly men kept pounding on my door like I knew what was going on. The insurance man—"

"I will deal with it," I said, wondering if Duluth had come out of what had been a dedicated stupor. Why he would have followed us to Dunkicker was hard to imagine. The Daughters of the Moon would hardly have recruited him, even if he'd agreed to shave his head and wear lipstick. The only Buchanon to do so was Dunmoore, and he was doing time for unseemly behavior outside the fence at the school playground.

"You gonna eat something?" Ruby Bee asked gruffly.

"Oh, yes," I said, then went back to the dining room and took a chair between Jarvis and Big Mac. I skewered a couple of pancakes onto a plate and doused them with syrup. "You all sure you didn't see anything yesterday?"

"Like what?" asked Jarvis.

"People in the woods, that sort of thing. Pass the sausages, please."

Jarvis shook his head. Big Mac gave him a curious look, then passed me both the plate of sausages and a pitcher of orange juice. I was holding my first forkful of pancakes dripping with syrup when Lady Macbeth swept into the room.

"I'd like to speak to you," she said to me.

"I'd like to eat breakfast."

"Now."

"Can't this wait, Mrs. Jim Bob? I haven't had anything to eat since yesterday afternoon. I was up all night, and I have to go back into Dunkicker to—"

"Mrs. Robarts just parked out front. Something is going on, and I don't see how I can speak to her until I know what it is. I did not have a restful night, either. Ruby Bee and Estelle refused to monitor the sleeping arrangements in the lodge. There is a reason why I made sure the girls and the boys would be in cabins well separated, but then Larry Joe insisted that they all sleep in the very same room." She stared coldly at him. "That was, of course, begging for trouble. Ruby Bee's cherry cobbler contained so much sugar that—"

"Ruby Bee made cherry cobbler?" I said weakly. "Did she happen to bring ice cream?"

"No, and I found the crust to be less than flaky. Will you please stop slobbering and tell me what happened?"

I jabbed the bite into my mouth, wiped my chin, and trailed her into the living room as Willetta Robarts came through the front door.

"Anthony has told me," she said. "This is very distressing."

"Yes, we all think that," said Mrs. Jim Bob, glowering at me as she escorted Mrs. Robarts to a really comfy metal folding chair. "Arly and I were just discussing it."

Mrs. Robarts did not thaw. "According to Anthony, the murder weapon was brought by your group. Camp Pearly Gates has operated without violence for forty-seven years. Oh, we've had the occasional drownings in the lake and snakebites, but no one had ever been bludgeoned on the grounds. This will not do, Mrs. Buchanon."

"Bludgeoned?" echoed the aforementioned Mrs. Buchanon.

Despite the petty pleasure I took from watching her writhe, I felt enough pity to intervene. "She has no idea what took place, Mrs. Robarts, and neither do your son, the two deputies sent from Farberville, nor I. The victim had nothing to do with us. Were you aware of this cult?"

"Cult?" said Mrs. Jim Bob, sounding as though CPR might be in her immediate future.

"Don't be absurd!" snapped Mrs. Robarts.

"Why on earth am I being absurd? Your son admitted he had knowledge of their presence. I simply assumed that you did, too. What's really ridiculous is to accuse any of us of having a clue. We arrived yesterday to spend a week making repairs on the bleachers and the dock."

"But the weapon . . ."

"The canvas bag was left in the dugout when the storm blew in," I retorted. "Anyone could have taken the bat."

Mrs. Jim Bob began to hyperventilate. "Taken the bat and what?"

I looked at Mrs. Robarts. "So you were unaware of the cult living inside the campgrounds? Anthony never mentioned this small detail over supper?"

Willetta Robarts shrugged. "Of course I was aware of

them. They have been here for more than two years. They
are Christians, although somewhat overzealous in their ad-
herence to biblical canons. The money they earn working in
Dunkicker is pooled and used to buy whatever they cannot
produce themselves. The children are schooled in one of the
cabins. They perform a limited amount of community service in exchange for being allowed to stay here for free. It is
an arrangement that serves all of us."

If Mrs. Jim Bob's jaw had fallen any farther, she would
have tripped over it as she sat down next to Mrs. Robarts.
"I can't believe you'd allow these people on your property!
What if it's a cult where they murder the children and then
commit suicide? What if they have weapons and the federal
agents come and there's a standoff with tear gas and one of
us—"

"I stay in touch with their leader, Deborah, who is very
spiritual, yet level-headed in mundane matters. She comes
to me when they need medicine for one of the children, or
when they're being harassed by trailer park trash from
nearby towns."

"Why do the women shave their heads?" I asked.

"To humble themselves," she said as she rose. "I do
hope this can be handled discreetly, Arly. If the media catch
wind of this, they'll arrive like a flock of turkey buzzards
and completely destroy these devout Christian families and
their chosen lifestyle. They do not wish to be sensational-
ized in the same way the Amish have been."

"I'm going into town," I told Mrs. Jim Bob. "You look
as if you could use a little extra syrup on your pancakes."

"You mind your mouth, young lady. We have a guest."

I got into the station wagon and began what had become a familiar drive. The sky was back to blue, the foliage
robust after a hearty watering. The air was a bit nippy, but
once the sun had been up for a few hours, it would warm
up nicely. I would have preferred to be fishing off the dock

with Ruby Bee and Estelle, or even helping out at the soft-ball field.

I came around a bend and saw a figure shuffling down the middle of the road, oblivious to the puddles and uneven ridges of mud. For a brief moment, I thought it might be Jacko, but then realized that it was the pastor of the Voice of the Almighty Lord Assembly Hall.

"Running away from camp?" I asked as I pulled along-side him. "It's a long walk into town. Need a ride?"

He gave me the look of a bloodhound that had lost the scent and knew he deserved nothing but contempt from his handler. "I can't stay here any longer. I figure I can make my way back to Maggody somehow or other. If nobody will give me a ride, then I'll just walk. After all, the Jews wandered in the desert for forty years. I reckon I can wan-der down the highway for a few days."

I got out of the car and eyed him across the roof. "Why can't you stay here any longer, Brother Verber?"

"You recollect how I said I saw something yesterday when we first arrived? I prayed for the Lord to tell me what it was, and He finally got around to it. It was the ghost of my sister Daisy."

"Get in the front seat and let's talk about it."

He wiped his forehead, peered nervously at the sun-dap-pled trees and bushes, and did as I suggested. "Daisy was six years older'n me. By the time she turned fifteen, she was a wild one, kicking up her heels with every boy in town. She got herself throwed out of school at least once a month. No matter how often my papa whupped her and locked her in her room, she'd never even pretend to repent. My mama was so humiliated by the gossip that she all but stopped go-ing to church. The preacher used to give sermons about the Whore of Babylon and stare right at us the whole time, his eyes blazing and spittle flying all over the congregation members unfortunate enough to sit in the front pews. Folks took to comin' earlier and earlier every week, just to get a seat in the back of the church. Some of them said they'd just as soon sleep over Saturday night as risk a pious shower come Sunday morning."

"How did Daisy die?" I asked, aware I was due at the PD in less than fifteen minutes. Mindful of the state he was in, I couldn't shove him out of the station wagon and drive away, nor could I be sure that if I finally found a place to turn around (not all that easy) and took him back to the lodge he wouldn't take off again, mumbling to himself about Daisy and spittle and whatever other memories were fogging up his mind. "Did she come down with a terminal disease?"

"Mama would have handled that better," he said, snuffling. "One night, when she was just shy of seventeen, she climbed out her bedroom window and down a sycamore tree by the house. I was out in the yard catching lightning bugs, and she didn't see me at first. I asked her what she was doing. She said it was none of my business, but if I told anyone, she'd come back, rip out my tongue, and nail it to the door of the tool shed. She said some other things, too, then ran down the road." He stopped and blew his nose. "'Long about midnight, there was pounding on the front door. I hid at the top of the stairs. A state policeman had come to tell Mama and Papa how Daisy and her boyfriend had been out drinking and driving, and had a wreck. I knew right then it was my fault. If I'd hollered for Papa when Daisy started to leave, he would have caught her and none of it would have happened. She would have hurt me real bad, but at least she'd have been alive."

"You were only ten years old."

"But I knew what she was doin' was sinful. I just let her go because I was afraid of her. Now I'm afraid of her again. She's here for retribution on account of she knows that I should have saved her life that night."

"And the Lord told you all this?"

"That's right, and I got to get back to Maggody and take sanctuary in the Assembly Hall. Not even a ghost as vicious as Daisy would have the audacity to come in there."

I was still ten minutes from Dunkicker. "We need to talk about this some more," I said. "You can ride into town with me while I tell you what you really saw."

"I know what I saw, Arly. I don't reckon it'll hurt to let you get me to the highway, then we'll part ways."

As we bumped down the road, I told him about the body in the creek and the peculiar women and children living on the hillside above the lodge. "They must wear white robes unless they're working in town. What with their shaved heads and dark lipstick, they're pretty spooky, especially from a distance."

"If you think you can make up a preposterous tale to keep me from leaving—"

"I'm not making this up."

"The Lord told me I saw Daisy," he insisted, his lower lip protruding.

"The Lord did no such thing," I said. "Maybe you'd better come with me when we confront the members of the cult. You can see for yourself."

Snuffling ripened into blubbering. "If I was to come face-to-face with Daisy, I'd have a heart attack. That'd suit her just fine. She used to poke me with pins just to make me cry."

Great. I had one dead body, one menopausal mother, ten frightened teenagers, and now this pudgy baby who was likely to wipe his nose on my shirt if I didn't keep an eye on him.

At least he didn't leap out of the station wagon as I reached the highway and turned toward Dunkicker. By the time I pulled into the parking lot outside the municipal building, he'd subsided, although I remained leery.

"Pull yourself together," I said. "There's a member of your flock inside who's in dire need of guidance. Did you bring your Bible?"

"Someone needs my guidance?"

"Duluth Buchanon was arrested yesterday for public drunkenness. I have no idea what he's doing here. Maybe you can talk to him, being his spiritual leader and all."

Brother Verber brightened at the thought of sermonizing to a sinner, particularly one behind bars and unable to escape the pieties and scathing appraisals of his proximity to damnation. "Why, I think the Lord would approve of me trying to help this strayed member of the flock. Once I have won his confidence, I'm right sure he'll confide in me."

"Me, too," I said as we went into the brick building. Corporal Robarts was on the telephone, whining. Les and Bonita were drinking coffee and sharing a newspaper.

"You're late," Les said.

I shrugged. "Yeah, I know. Have you heard anything from the lab?"

"Only that they'll send the fingerprints to the FBI. We'll be shooting off fireworks before we hear anything."

"What about the drunk?"

"He's stirring, but as ornery as a polecat. When Bonita here offered him coffee, he swore at her. I think he'll be pissing in a can and eating granola bars for the rest of the day."

Brother Verber licked his finger, and held it up as if to calculate which way the wind was blowing. "I sense there is a troubled soul in need of the comfort only a man of the cloth can bring. Prayer can bring him back on the path of righteousness. If you'll just show me to his cell . . ."

"Down the hallway," said Bonita, who had sharp eyes and short, wiry red hair. "He's all yours, honey."

He clasped his hands together. "'The Lord is my shepherd; I shall not want.'"

"I can assure you all he wants is to get out, but you do your best." Bonita gave him a shove, then turned around and grinned at us. "Guess I didn't mention that the prisoner spent the night barfing all over himself and soiling his pants. It smells real nasty down there."

Corporal Robarts muttered an expletive, then stuck the receiver at me. "Sheriff Dorfer wants to talk to you."

"Lucky me." I took the receiver. "What, Harve? Got a hangover from the party?"

Harve growled. "Maybe I do, but it ain't as bad as the headache you're gonna get. Panknine's not bad, but he's out of the picture and this Robarts boy can't tie his shoes. You're in charge of the investigation."

"I most certainly am not."

"I am authorized by the county prosecutor to appoint anyone I damn well choose to run an investigation. Les is a good man, but he ain't the next General Patton. Bonita's a bright girl, and once she gets some experience, she'll be coming after my job. If it weren't for my back acting up, I'd do it myself."

I swiped the discarded newspaper sections off the desk and rested my fanny on it. "Has your back ever acted up just before a fishing trip, Harve? Has it ever prevented you from playing poker in the back room at city hall or kept you from putting a case of whiskey in the trunk of your car?"

"Now, Arly," he said in that patronizing tone that always infuriates me, "you know how I hate to stick you with this, but it's not all that complicated. You get a bunch of women living in the woods, one of them's liable to go crazy and turn on another one. You ask 'em a few questions, pull out the tissues when they start crying, and before you know it, you'll have a confession. Les and Bonita will transport her here and do the paperwork, and you can go right back to whatever the hell you're doing down there."

"I'm not supposed to be doing anything beyond being a chaperon, Harve."

"So go collect this murderer, then have yourself a nice afternoon at the lake. Be sure to wear a hat and use plenty of sunblock."

He hung up before I could respond. I replaced the receiver, then looked at Corporal Robarts, who was fuming, and at Les and Bonita, who could not have cared less what Harve said, what the deputy thought, or how Brother Verber was faring down the hall.

"Guess I'm in charge," I said.

Corporal Robarts pulled off his hat and slammed it down. "You said last night that this was my jurisdiction!"

"And you said you'd had your badge for all of one month. Have you ever investigated anything?"

"Milton Higgleton called the other day and said he was hearing voices in his attic. I investigated that. Chief Panknine said I did real fine."

"International drug smugglers or squirrels?"

He looked away. "Squirrels."

"This may be more complicated," I said tactfully. "You, Les, and I are going to question the Daughters of the Moon. Bonita, you lucky girl, you get to stay here and wait until Duluth gets desperate enough to escape Brother Verber's counsel that he'll tell you why he came here."

"That's not fair," she shot back. "Sheriff Dorfer sent me down to investigate a murder, not baby-sit some pathetic drunk. I need it for my resume."

So she could get on with her life, while I grew zucchini and whittled balsa wood ducks that ultimately resembled toothpicks.

"I sympathize," I said, "but at this point he may be a suspect. He has no legitimate reason to be here. Once we rescue him from Brother Verber's suffocating holier-than-thou sentiments, maybe he'll talk to you. I'll make sure you receive credit in the report."

Bonita was not buying it. "Who do you think these women are more likely to open up to—you and me or Les and Corporal Robarts? They didn't take up this lifestyle because they're all that fond of men. Think about it, Chief Hanks," she concluded with the very faintest prick of sarcasm.

I could almost see her sitting on the bench, staring down lawyers with three-piece suits and paternalistic smirks. "Can we find this place without you?" I asked Corporal Robarts. "Please bear in mind that if you say we can't, and it turns out to be fairly simple, then Sheriff Dorfer will hear all about it. It isn't nice to lie to the head of the investigating team, you know."

Robarts's expression darkened, but he managed to keep his temper under control. "There's a dirt road not too far past the convenience store that goes into the backside of Camp Pearly Gates. The Beamers are living in two cabins at the top of the hill. Last I was there, laundry was hanging on a line and there was a garden. They don't know you, though. More likely than not, they won't talk to you."

"Oh, I think they will," I said grimly.

9

Hammet didn't much enjoy the evening in the closet, clamping his nose to hold in sneezes and trying not to squawk when a bug took to crawling up his pants. Jim Bob had stomped around for a long while, making it clear that he was real unhappy that Sonya and Tonya had left him high and dry. Not that he'd been dry, of course. From the way he kept popping open beer cans, Hammet figured Hizzhonor'd worked through a couple of six packs.

Finally, he'd gone to bed and Hammet had dashed outside to piss off the edge of the porch afore he exploded like a water balloon. Afterward, he'd crept back inside, opened the refrigerator, and taken a carton of orange juice back to the closet. The coats had made a soft bed, and he'd slept pretty well, considering where he was and what he was doing. His foster ma'd been reading the Bible to him most days, and he couldn't remember anything that said, "Thou shalt not sleep in thine enemy's coat closet."

Hammet didn't have a clue what time it was when he awoke to hear banging in the kitchen. Jim Bob cussed a blue streak when he couldn't find the orange juice, and just as much when he couldn't figure out how to operate the coffeepot. Hammet thought briefly about his foster pa, who always made breakfast on Sunday. It was kinda hard to know just what guys was supposed to be able to do, besides work on transmissions, untangle fishing line, and mow the yard. He had a feeling Jim Bob couldn't do none of that, neither.

Once the back door slammed, he eased open the door and listened real hard. The sound of a truck going down the driveway convinced him that the house was his, at least for the time being. It could be that Jim Bob was jest going to the supermarket to pick up a box of powdered dough-nuts and a cup of coffee, and that he'd be back in a matter of minutes. Or mebbe he'd gone to work and wouldn't be back for the rest of the day.

Hammet knew he was gonna hafta take some risks if he was to live in the closet for the week. He took the empty lasagna pan to the kitchen. Keeping an eye on the driveway, he crammed it into the back of a cabinet with other pans that looked sorta the same.

A nasty smell was following him like he'd brought home a baby skunk, and he finally decided he was the one stinkin' things up. When he was living up on the ridge, he hadn't ever noticed such things, but after having been forced to bathe on a regular basis, he'd forgotten what he used to smell like when his clothes were dirty and his hair was so sour it could have curdled milk.

He ate a couple of pieces of bread while he watched out the kitchen window. If Jim Bob was fixin' to come right back, he'd do it pretty damn quick. After fifteen minutes, Hammet decided, or at least hoped, that the house was safe for the rest of the day. He went upstairs and opened Jim Bob's closet. He took out a shirt but left the trousers, since there weren't no way he could keep them up. He found some underwear and socks in a drawer, then went into the bathroom and turned on the shower. If he got caught, then so be it. He'd put up a helluva fight, punch Jim Bob in the gut, and run down the stairs and out the back door, whoop-ing all the way like a wild Injun. Weren't no way anyone could catch him once he got to the grass and headed for the trees.

He leaned forward to peer at his face in the mirror. Yep,

that was definitely a whisker on his chin. Another week or two, and he'd have to shave it off.

✖

Bonita was quiet as we drove toward the cabins. I wasn't sure if she was feeling self-satisfied for having gotten her way, or alarmed because she had.

"Sheriff Dorfer seems to think you've got a career ahead of you," I said, sounding like my mother. If I didn't watch myself, I'd be asking if she had a boyfriend and what his parents did for a living.

"I'm saving my money for law school. I'll have to borrow and beg, and I don't know how long it'll take me to pay it back. But you just watch for me, Chief Hanks—I'll be a senator from Arkansas one of these days. Maybe the first woman vice-president. Maybe the first woman president. If that doesn't happen, I'll be putting on a robe with the rest of the Supreme Court justices."

"Not gonna mess around, huh?"

"We all have to start somewhere."

I might have been a bit worried about her sanity if she hadn't been so matter-of-fact. She, at twenty-three or so, knew exactly where she intended to go with the rest of her life. I was destined to be the Tomato Mama of Maggody.

"This ought to be it," I said as I turned onto a dirt road.

"According to the directions."

Feeling rather idiotic, I forced a smile as we bumped down a muddy road. "Now when we get there—"

"You're in charge. I understand that."

My smile tightened. "I was going to say that both of us need to tread carefully. I'll conduct the official questioning, but you watch for anyone who might want to confide in you. Take off that hat, Bonita, and undo the top button on your shirt. Admire their garden. Ask to see the schoolroom. Do your best to talk to the children."

"What do you think's going on, Chief Hanks?"

"I wish I knew. We're going to have to pressure them for an ID so that her next-of-kin can be notified. If she brought children with her, then it's going to be a bureaucratic nightmare. The law dictates that they'll have to go with social services until proper custody can be established. I can't leave them with their 'aunties,' no matter how moonstruck they may be. I doubt I'm going to be the Beamer poster-girl." I took a deep breath as I navigated down the road. "And call me Arly, okay? This is not a good time for formality."

I may have expected some small token of reciprocity, but she merely glanced at me and said, "Good idea. We don't want to come in like a couple of storm troopers."

The first cabin we came to was bleak, clearly uninhabited. The next two, however, had clotheslines as Corporal Robarts had predicted, along with picnic tables and well-tended gardens. Three children of indeterminate age spotted the station wagon and darted into the woods. A fourth, too young to do much of anything, eyed us as he sucked his finger, his discolored diaper threatening to slide off his hips.

"We're low-key," I said to Bonita.

"Oh, yeah," she said as I parked beside the cabin. "Maybe they'll think we're Avon ladies."

Bonita wasn't quite as cool when one of the women emerged from the cabin, her robe trailing in the mud. Shaved head, as I expected, along with a pasty white face and a serious lipstick addiction. It could have been Rachael, or the clone of the woman whose body we'd found the previous night. It could have been Mrs. Jim Bob, for that matter, had she been kidnapped and indoctrinated into the cult while I was at the PD in Dunkicker.

"Yes?" she said.

"I'm Arly," I said, flashing my badge, "and this is Bonita. We need to talk to you."

"And why would that be?"

"Because of what happened late yesterday afternoon," Bonita said before I could respond. "One of your group was found, and she was real dead."

"Anthony told us about Ruth," the woman replied levelly. "It was unfortunate."

"That she was found, or that she was dead?" I said. "We need some information about her. Are you Deborah?"

"Deborah is not here. I am Judith. There is very little I can tell you about that woman. Ruth arrived only a few weeks ago. She was assigned to assist at the hot-meal program at the church in Dunkicker in order to make her contribution, but she claimed to have migraines that kept her in bed almost every other day. While she complained incessantly, we fed her children, clothed them, and provided for them. I believe these days she'd be called a 'slacker.' This was not the right place for her. I doubt she would have been allowed to stay much longer. This is a religious community, not a shelter for the dysfunctional."

"You're sure that it was Ruth?"

"I know that everyone else was accounted for this morning. We're waiting for official confirmation before we tell her children."

"Can you give me her real name?" I asked.

Judith stared at me. "When a woman arrives here, she is given a new name, as are her children. We do what we can to eliminate the negative influences of the secular world in order to devote ourselves to observing the purity that is the Daughters of the Moon. Last night was stormy, obscured with savagery and malevolence, but tonight you can gaze in wonder at the moonlight on the lake. You will see God's fingers rippling the surface of the water. The sky will be filled with an infinite number of diamonds. All you have to do is look, Arly, with your eyes and with your heart."

"I most likely will," I said, "but in the meantime, I need to know what happened to Ruth."

Bonita whipped out the pad that was apt to have been issued to her in cop school. "Before she got rewarded with this new name, who was she?"

Judith's lips curled downward. "I have no idea. We do not demand passports."

"Why did she come here?" I asked.

"Again, I have no idea. Deborah could tell you more, but as I said, she's not here."

"How many women are living here?"

She paused. "Five as of yesterday. I suppose we're down to four now that Ruth is no longer with us. It's not much of a loss."

I was taken aback at her attitude. "She was murdered not too far from here. Doesn't that bother you?"

"I suppose it should, but all she did was whine and demand to be waited on. Everyone is expected to contribute. Some sisters work in town, others school the children, tend to the garden, and prepare meals. Once a month we make our own soap and herbal remedies."

"When the moon's full?"

Bonita edged around me, her pen poised as though she was hot on the trail of a late-breaking story for a tabloid. "Then Ruth brought children? How many and how old? Where are they now?"

"I don't think she ever specified. They're with the other children, all of whom are quite frightened by this intrusion. Naomi has taken them to the schoolhouse to study the Book of the Revelation in order to help them come to grips with what has happened. Under no circumstances can they be interrogated."

I bumped Bonita out of the way. "I need to examine whatever this woman called Ruth brought with her."

"You won't find anything. Her instructions were to dispose of any personal items that might identify her."

"Instructions from whom?" I demanded.

"Deborah, of course."

I wasn't sure if all this was silly, surreal, or supernatural. Most likely, all and none of the above. "Just show me her things, okay?"

"As you wish," Judith said, heading for the nearer cabin. "The women sleep here, and the children in the other cabin. Unlike most families these days, the older ones have learned to share responsibility for the younger ones."

I whispered at Bonita to locate the children, then went inside. The iron bunk beds were much the same as we'd found farther down the hill. Attempts had been made to create a cheerier decor, with potted plants on the windowsills and drawings taped to the walls.

"Quite a comedown from the lodge," I said. "You must have been annoyed when the church groups began to arrive."

"One might think that, but we celebrate all demonstrations of faith. We've accepted the fact we'll be living here until fall. After that, Deborah is confident we can return to the lodge, where we will be warm and dry."

"Mrs. Robarts said you do community service in Dunkicker in exchange for being allowed to live here."

Judith looked back at me. "Is that a question?"

It was a struggle not to imagine her with normal hair and makeup; she might have been a reasonably attractive fortyish woman, working as a real estate agent or moving up the corporate ladder at a bank. I glanced at her feet to make sure she wasn't wearing pantyhose beneath her robe.

"How long have you been here?" I asked.

"Since God called me to serve as a Daughter of the Moon. I have erased all memories of my former life, as have the other women. We have dedicated ourselves to prayer and good deeds. When the skies explode and the earth splits apart with fiery fissures, we shall be prepared to cast aside our physical shells and ascend to heaven."

"No men allowed, huh?"

"If one is to purify her soul, she must denounce all pleasures of the flesh and focus on her inner spirit." She produced a fleeting smile. "So, as you said, no men allowed."

"Corporal Robarts comes here."

"Anthony hardly qualifies, does he? Here is Ruth's bunk. Her possessions are in a suitcase under it. I will leave you now."

I waited until I had the cabin to myself. The suitcase contained nothing much more than dingy cotton underwear. Beneath that layer was a crumpled sundress and platform sandals, which she must have been wearing when she arrived. No purse or wallet, however, or so much as an envelope.

I took out everything to examine it more carefully. A few hairs on the dress indicated she'd been blonde before receiving her buzz cut, but the darker hue on one end suggested her coloring had come from the beauty aids aisle of a discount store.

I put it all back, replaced the suitcase, and pulled a similar bag from beneath the next bunk. It too held mostly underwear, but this Beamer had arrived in jeans and a faded T-shirt. I checked the pockets of the jeans. This time I did better, finding half a pack of flattened cigarettes and a matchbook from a glitzy bingo establishment just across the state line in Oklahoma. I found no other evidence that might help me identify the owner of the suitcase.

I was having no better luck with a third suitcase when Bonita came limping into the cabin. Her pants were torn and splattered with mud, and one elbow was bloodied. Dried leaves clung to her hair. Her face was scratched, her lower lip already swollen, her nostrils discolored with congealing blood. I could see she was going to have an impressive black eye within an hour.

"Are you all right?" I asked as I helped her to the nearest bunk. "What happened? Did they attack you?"

"Might as well have, the little shits. I finally found the so-called schoolhouse along a path behind the cabin just below us. I went on in. It's hard to say how many children were there. A few were in diapers, but most of them appeared to be between six and fifteen. All scruffy looking, with clothing that didn't fit well and bad haircuts."

"Take a guess at how many."

"I don't know—maybe a dozen. Naomi, who looks just like the other spooks, herded the smaller ones into a corner and somehow managed to keep them still. I told the older ones that I wanted to talk to them. They bolted out the door and into the woods. I was so pissed that I went after them, thinking I could catch at least one of them. Well, it seems like one of their homework assignments was to boobytrap the woods. Holes, hidden by twigs covered with leaves. Vines stretched between trees. Branches tied back with trip wires. I could hear them whooping every time I fell, which made me all the madder."

"And then you lost them. Stay here." I went into the bathroom and found a washcloth. I dampened it and took it back to her. "Police work's not as glamorous as they make it out to be in the movies."

"Where were you when I decided to enroll in the academy?"

"Start talking loudly if you see any of the Beamers heading this way. I doubt it'll do any good, but I might as well search the rest of the suitcases."

I found nothing more incriminating than a romance novel in one and a half-eaten chocolate bar in another. Deborah's dictum had been observed, with only a few misdemeanors.

I pushed the last suitcase back where I'd found it and stood up. The washcloth Bonita had been holding to her elbow was bright with blood. "We'd better get that seen to," I said. "Surely there's a local doctor who can put a few stitches in it."

"Don't rush off on my account. It's not like I'm bleeding to death."

"Poor choice of words," I said as I gestured to her to follow me out the door. I took her to the station wagon, put her in the passenger's side, and made her promise to stay there for a few more minutes.

Judith was observing this from the middle of a vegetable garden. "Would you like an herbal cream for her elbow? It'll fight off an infection."

"I don't think her health benefits would cover that. I'm going to take her into town to be treated by a doctor. Afterward, I'll go by the PD to find out if we've made any progress identifying the body. I can assure you that before the moon comes up tonight, I'll be back with arrest warrants and a social worker to take all the children into protective custody."

"You can't do that."

"I don't know if I can or can't, but I'll try—unless you and the other Beamers are willing to be candid with me. Will you promise to have them here, along with Ruth's children?"

"Rachael's working at the café, and Sarah is at a church, preparing hot meals to be delivered to the homebound. I have no way to go into Dunkicker and fetch them. Naomi and I will be here."

"What about Deborah?"

"I don't know."

I tried not to sound as frustrated as I felt. "Not much of a leader if she's never here. Maybe you all should take a vote and demote her."

Judith tossed aside a handful of weeds. "Naomi and I will be here, as well as the children. You should have no problem finding Rachael and Sarah in town. There's nothing else I can do, Arly, and little else we can tell you. Ruth never spoke about her former life. I don't know why Deborah considered her a likely candidate to become a Daughter of the Moon."

"Okay," I said. "I'll deal with Bonita, talk to Rachael and Sarah, and then come back here. As unpleasant as it may be, you're going to have to do better with the details of your former life. A woman has been murdered. I don't care if you want to play dress-up in the woods, but I will get to the bottom of this."

She crossed her arms and glared as I got into the station wagon and headed for Dunkicker. Bonita was sucking on her lip and doing her best to pretend her elbow wasn't giving her serious grief. A shadow below her left eye was already turning greenish-yellow; classic black and blue would appear shortly. She'd be lucky if she could get a straw through her lips to suck a milkshake.

"Those little pissants," she lisped as we reached the pavement. "As soon as I'm patched up, I'd like to go back and wallop all of them until they howl."

"You're out of commission for a few hours. Once you've been stitched up, I'll take you to the motel so you can lie down."

"I don't need special treatment."

"And you're not getting it."

"Would you treat Les or any other male deputy this way?"

I pulled into the lot outside the municipal building. "Please note that we are of the same sex, Bonita. I experienced all kinds of discrimination when I was at the academy, as I'm sure you did, too. The slope's a little steeper for us. Get over it."

I ordered her to stay in the car, went inside, and found Corporal Robarts, Les, and Brother Verber playing cards. "Is there a local doctor capable of patching up a deep cut?"

Corporal Robarts flushed with embarrassment. "Yeah, but he won't be in his office on Sunday morning. You want I should track him down?"

"That would be the idea," I said. "Brother Verber, did Duluth say anything?"

"He was disinclined to open his heart to me. Many a time I counseled him and Norella, but he was skeptical of the power of prayer. There were moments when I was obliged to rebuke him for his profane language. You'd think, in the house of the Lord, that he'd observe—"

I took Les aside. "Take Brother Verber to the lab in Little Rock to see if he can identify the body."

"You think it might be Duluth's wife?"

"This woman showed up at Camp Pearly Gates about the time Duluth said she left town. She brought children. Now she's dead and he was damn near drowning in a ditch. If nothing else, we can eliminate the possibility."

"What's wrong with Bonita?"

"She needs a few stitches and a pain pill. I'll take her back to the motel to sleep it off, and then Corporal Robarts and I are going to have a chat with the various members of Daughters of the Moon. I'm not putting up with any more bullshit from them."

"Maybe Anthony should take Brother Verber to Little Rock. You may need backup."

"Corporal Robarts knows more than he's telling," I said softly, "and, trust me, I'm not about to go scampering into the woods at the first sign of a softball bat. It's going to take some doing on your part to determine if Brother Verber can make the identification. He'll be wetting his pants before you open the door to the morgue. Stay with him, force him to focus on her features, have the lab people drape her head with a sheet to hide the baldness and make her look more normal. I think it's Norella, but we have to know."

"So Duluth killed her?"

"Let's make a positive ID before we jump to conclusions. Do the best you can with Brother Verber. Don't so much as turn your back on him to buy a candy bar out of a machine unless you want to chase him all the way back to Maggody. He's haunted by some personal demons from his childhood. Given the slightest opportunity, he'll take off." I took a deep breath. "Brother Verber, you need to go with Les. He should have you back here before too long."

"Go where?" he quavered, groping his pockets for a flask.

"Les will tell you the details. I should be here when you return. We'll go back to the lodge and find out if Ruby Bee's making chicken fried steak and cream gravy, or pot roast with potatoes and carrots. I think we can count on buttermilk biscuits in either case."

"Her biscuits are real light," he bleated as Les dragged him out the door.

Corporal Robarts hung up the phone. "Doc Schmidt will meet us at his office. He wasn't real happy about being interrupted on a Sunday morning."

"Then let's hope Bonita hasn't bled to death, therefore inconveniencing him for nothing," I said. "Your prisoner is secured?"

"Of course," said Corporal Robarts, strapping on his belt and holster in case Doc Schmidt turned unruly and needed a bullet between his eyes to get him back on task. "No prisoner has ever escaped under my watch."

I thought about asking him how many prisoners had ever been under his watch, sighed, and flipped off the light switch as we left the Dunkicker PD.

✠

"Say what?" croaked Earl Buchanon, gaping at his daughter-in-law. "You think you're moving in next door to the Beverly Hillbillies? That was nuthin' but a television show. Ain't nobody from Maggody buying a fancy mansion."

"Now, Earl," Eileen said as she passed him the hash-brown potatoes, "Dahlia's just talking about what might happen. She just thinks that because Kevvie Junior and Rose Marie are twins—"

"They ain't hardly identical."

"They most certainly are," Dahlia said as she forked open a biscuit and picked up the gravy boat. "They was born no more than three minutes apart."

Kevin twitched nervously. "They have the same adorable button noses and little pink toes. Kevvie Junior likes to kick his legs, while Rose Marie is fond of sucking on her fingers. But they're still twins."

Earl slammed a spoonful of potatoes onto his plate. "But they're not identical, fer chrissake!"

"I will not allow blasphemy on the Sabbath," Eileen said. "Just because we aren't going to church this morning doesn't mean that—"

"They're not identical," growled Earl. "Any idiot'd know that."

Dahlia put down the gravy ladle. "You callin' me an idiot? Kevin, I cain't believe you're gonna sit there and let your pa say that to me!"

"I'm sure he dint mean that, my lusty bunny. All he meant was that—"

Earl pushed back his chair and stood up, the napkin tucked under his chin flapping like a battle flag. "They ain't identical. Tell 'em, Eileen."

"Are, too," Dahlia said, standing up as well.

It occurred to Eileen that she could have agreed to chaperon the teenagers for their week at Camp Pearly Gates. She could be sitting in a rocking chair on the porch of the lodge, reading a book, crocheting, or just enjoying the breeze off the lake. Later, they'd toast marshmallows and sing about where all the flowers had gone and how Michael had rowed the boat ashore, hallelujah. Once nightfall came, she'd fall asleep listening to lovelorn whippoorwills calling to each other.

"Listen up," she said, "this is Sunday breakfast, not an amateur wrestling event. Shut up, sit down, and eat. Anyone with a problem about that can fix a plate and take it to the kitchen, the back porch, or out to the pasture, for all I care! I spent two hours fixing this meal, and I intend to eat it in peace. Kevin, please pass the grits."

"Are, too," Dahlia said as she sank down.

"Are not," Earl countered, then glanced at his wife and sat down.

Kevin didn't know what to say, but he had enough sense to keep his mouth shut and passed his ma the bowl of grits. The babies, in adjoining highchairs and happily stuffing bits of scrambled eggs up their adorable button noses, had the same rosy cheeks and rosebud mouths. Their little feet curled when they cried. Their diapers seemed to fill up at the same time, which was most of the time when he was caring for them so Dahlia could go visit her granny at the old folks' home. They both hated beets and loved applesauce. If that wasn't identical, what was?

Across the table, Dahlia stared at the gravy congealing on the biscuit. There was something she was gonna hafta tell Kevin afore too long.

10

Corporal Robarts and I sat in the waiting room while Doc Schmidt took care of Bonita. All the magazines involved blood sports and were dated from the previous decade. The weapons used to kill fish, fowl, and mammals were bigger and badder these days, but nothing else had changed: hook 'em, cook 'em, or mount 'em on the wall. The last of these was my least favorite. I was grateful that Doc Schmidt had not seen fit to adorn his walls with glassy-eyed heads of patients who had delayed treatment (or declined payment).

"I spoke to Judith," I said abruptly.

"She tell you anything?"

"Not really. According to her, the women are all victims of remarkably convenient amnesia. Previous identities have been wiped out; supposedly, not one of them could make her way back home, even with a map. I find that hard to swallow."

"I don't understand why they want to live that way," he said, "but it's no skin off my nose." He put on his hat, took it off, and looked at the prints of ducks captured in perpetuity as they winged their way across the walls. "How long you think it's going to take?"

"Shouldn't be much longer. Do the Beamers ever try to recruit local women?"

"That wouldn't sit real well with the townsfolk. Most everybody here's Baptist. We got a scattering of Seventh Day Adventists, one family that's Lutheran, and some old hippies in a cabin at the far end of Greasy Valley who claim they're Druids. This is a conservative town, but we get along with our neighbors, long as they don't flaunt themselves."

"Do you know anything about Deborah?"

"Only that she's kinda in charge."

"Have you met her?" I persisted.

"Once or twice," he said nervously. "I really don't have much contact with them, except for Rach and Sarah. Sometimes I give one or the other of them a ride home, but they always get out of the car before we get too near the cabins where they're staying. They say they do that to avoid upsetting the children. Same with Ester, who left a week ago or so. But, yeah, I've met Deborah. She looks just like the others. It ain't all that easy to tell them apart, as you might have noticed. I guess their mamas could, but no one else can."

I leaned back and crossed my legs. "Judith told me that Deborah wasn't at their site today. Could she be in Dunkicker?"

"I don't think so. To the best of my recollection, she's never had a job in town."

"But she somehow manages to send potential Beamers to Camp Pearly Gates. Where do you think she finds them?"

"How would I know?" He stood up. "Guess maybe I'll go by the Welcome Y'all and get a burger for the prisoner. After you've seen to Bonita, come to the PD and we'll figure out what we ought to do next. Les and Brother Verber won't be back for at least three, maybe four, hours."

"Okay," I said. "I shouldn't be more than half an hour."

After he'd gone, I stared blankly at the bleached prints and tried to organize what I knew. The four Beamers living in the cabins were Judith, Rachael, Sarah, and Naomi. Ruth had made five. Ester would have made six, but she was gone, as was someone named Leah.

If the body we'd found was indeed that of Norella Buchanon, how and why had she joined the Beamers and subjected herself to the bizarre makeover and less than luxurious lifestyle? If she'd been afraid of Duluth (and it seemed as though she might have had cause, after all), then why hadn't she found a third cousin twice removed to take her and the boys in until she could get a restraining order? Folks in Stump County have more cousins than they do dollars in the bank. Or common sense, for that matter.

It was clearly time for Duluth to crawl out of his hangover and do some explaining, I concluded.

I was beginning to get impatient when Bonita came into the waiting room, with Doc Schmidt holding on to her shoulder. He had shaggy white hair, bushy eyebrows, and shrewd blue eyes, the consummate personification of a country doctor—or a vet, which I hoped he wasn't. All creatures great and small did not include sheriff's department personnel.

"She's a little bit wobbly," he said apologetically. "I wanted to give her a local before I cleaned out the cut and did the stitches, but she wouldn't let me. I put a packet of pain pills in her shirt pocket. She needs to take two now, another in four hours, and get some rest. An ice pack should bring down the swelling in her lip; the black eye's gonna have to run its course. Bring her in tomorrow so that I can make sure there are no symptoms of infection."

"I'm perfectly fine," Bonita protested in a less than convincing squeak.

"Thanks," I said to Doc Schmidt. I took Bonita's uninjured arm and steadied her as her knees buckled like those of a newborn foal. "Send the bill to Chief Panknine and we'll sort it out later."

"No charge. Any chance you can tell me what happened out at Camp Pearly Gates last night?"

"What have you heard?"

"Nothing," he said, flushing. "Ol' Crank Nickle lives by the turnoff to the camp, and he said there was all kind of traffic coming and going in the wee hours, including the hearse from Tattersol's funeral home."

"We'll release information when the time comes. I need to get Bonita to bed," I said as I urged her into motion.

We drove down the road to the Woantell Motel, where the primary decor consisted of water stains on walls and a crusty shag carpet underfoot. I waited while Bonita put on a nightgown and washed her face, bullied her until she took a couple of pills, and made her swear to stay in bed until I returned to check on her.

She was still squeaking as I turned out the light and left, but I figured she'd be asleep in a matter of minutes. I drove back to the PD and parked beside Corporal Robarts's car. Duluth had been able to resist Brother Verber's pious reproaches and offers of redemption. No matter how daunting a man of the cloth might be, a woman of the badge, especially when deeply frustrated, was a whole 'nother ballgame.

Corporal Robarts met me at the door. "I was just coming to find you," he said. "The prisoner escaped."

"I'm not in the mood for jokes."

"I'm not, either. The cell door's open."

"And on your watch. Imagine that." I stomped down the short hallway, ascertained that Duluth was not cowering under a bunk, and returned to the front room. "So when did this happen?"

"He was here when you and Brother Verber arrived at about nine o'clock. I asked him if he wanted coffee and he spat at me, so I figured he could make do with the pisspot in the corner and the sink if he wanted water. After you and Bonita left to question the Beamers, Les, Brother Verber, and me went over to the café for breakfast. We weren't back five minutes when you got here. I didn't think to check before you and me took Bonita to Doc Schmidt's office. The key to the cell door's on a hook on the opposite wall. Maybe Brother Verber unlocked the cell door so's to pray with the prisoner, then failed to make sure it was locked when he came back out."

"So Duluth could have hightailed it as much as two hours ago? A possible suspect in a brutal murder, who may be hiding in the woods at Camp Pearly Gates, where ten teenagers and a scattering of adults are getting ready for Sunday dinner and planning to spend the afternoon at the softball field or fishing off the dock? Is this who we're talking about?"

"It wasn't my fault," he said in a surly voice.

"Then whose fault was it?"

"Like I said, Brother Verber most likely didn't lock the cell door."

"Did you lock the door of the PD?"

"We was just going across the road for breakfast. Chief Panknine never locks the door, even at night. The only time anyone's ever come in after hours was when Miz Neblett brought in her son and locked him in the cell after she caught him smoking dope. Chief Panknine gave him what for the next morning, and the boy upped and joined the army that very afternoon. Ain't never been back, far as I heard."

"All right," I said with great restraint, "here's what is going to happen. I'll call Sheriff Dorfer and ask him to put out an APB for Duluth, who may be in the area—or heading for Missouri, Oklahoma, Texas, Louisiana, or British Columbia, where he'll stow away on a freighter for Hong Kong."

"Hong Kong?" he echoed. "Isn't that where they make those karate movies?"

"Don't worry about it. We won't get a posse on horseback or bloodhounds, but the state troopers will be looking for him. Then I need to go back to the campgrounds and make sure the group from Maggody is taking precautions. All you're going to do is sit down, shut up, and take telephone messages. Got it?"

"What about the Beamers and their kids? If he knows karate—"

"Shit," I said as I tried to think. Bonita was snoring in the Woantell Motel, out of commission for at least a couple of hours. Les would not return with Brother Verber any time soon. "All right, I can deal with the group from Maggody and be back here in an hour. You go on down to the Beamer compound, tell them what's going on, keep everybody from straying too far, and sit on a picnic table until Les or I show up. If you see Duluth, shoot him in the leg."

"Just like that?"

"Yeah, Corporal Robarts, on the off-chance he does know karate. He may have killed a woman. The Beamers will not appreciate your presence, but we need to do what we can to ensure their safety."

"So I'm just supposed to sit on a picnic table while everybody else searches for this killer."

"That's right—park your butt and keep your eyes open." I waited until he stalked out of the PD, then reluctantly called Harve at home. Odds were good he'd already gone fishing, but it turned out he hadn't yet assembled his gear, which consisted primarily of a cooler and a picnic basket. Sunscreen was mandatory; bait was optional. After I'd finished telling him what had happened, I let him sputter for a moment, then added, "Thing is, we don't even know if the body is that of Norella Buchanon. Duluth may have just sobered up and decided to go home, presuming he had a vehicle parked somewhere. Why he showed up here is a bit of a mystery, though."

"Could he have been looking for you or Ruby Bee?"

This hadn't occurred to me. "I suppose so. He was in

charge of all the repairs to Ruby Bee's kitchen. Everybody in Maggody knew where we were going."

"So he drove down to show you paint samples, drank too much on the way, and ended up in a ditch on account of the thunder and lightning. Some folks are fearful of things, no matter how tough they pretend to be. I seem to recollect you let out a screech when a field mouse ran across your foot while we was pulling that body out of the reservoir last fall."

"It was a rat," I said stiffly. "You're saying Duluth came all this way to show us paint samples?"

"Or something along those lines. I'm not claiming he's an interior decorator. Like I said, I'll put out the APB, but you got no call to assume he's hiding in the woods with a softball bat."

"Somebody was," I pointed out.

Harve paused to light a cigar. "I can't argue with that. You need help? I'm not sure I can scare up anybody today, it being the weekend, but I can send somebody tomorrow."

Tomorrow was another day, I thought wearily. "I'll call you tonight and let you know. We should have an ID on the body; if it's not Norella, then . . . I don't know what to do. Maybe I can get some information from these damn Beamers."

"I hear the bass crooning my name," he said, then abruptly hung up, as if I'd been trying to sell him storm windows or his-and-her cemetery plots.

I checked the cell one last time to make sure Duluth wasn't hanging on to the light fixture, then drove back to Camp Pearly Gates. What I had to say would be tricky; I didn't want to alarm them, but I needed to make sure they were reasonably careful until the situation was resolved. And to explain the whereabouts of Brother Verber, which would require more tact than I felt capable of on a few hours of sleep and one forkful of pancakes.

I parked and went inside the lodge. Mrs. Jim Bob sat at

one of the tables in the dining room, muttering to herself. Her lipstick had been applied by an unsteady hand, and her hair was unkempt, as though she hadn't bothered to run a comb through it. I would have told her she looked like hell, but I had a feeling my comment would not sit well. I went into the kitchen. Ruby Bee was finishing up the breakfast dishes while Estelle put away food in the oversize refrigerator. The aroma of pot roast and garlicky potatoes perfumed the air, sweeter than wisteria blossoms. I reminded myself that I was going to have to tuck away something unless I wanted my blood sugar and insulin levels to engage in a high-spirited game of Ping Pong.

"Everybody okay?" I asked brightly.

Ruby Bee slammed down the dish towel. "Just where have you been? All you seem to do is come and go, Miss Revolving Door. Don't you think, as your mother, that I'm entitled to an explanation?"

"What's more," said Estelle, "you seem to think you can take my car whenever you want. Did it ever occur to you that I might have preferred to use it to drive Darla Jean to get her ankle seen to? I felt like a dang fool when we drove up in that awful excuse for a bus. Two nurses coming off duty asked me if I cleaned carpets."

"Do you?"

"You're about as funny as a flat tire."

I backed off. "So how's Darla Jean?"

"Nice of you to ask. Her ankle's sprained, and we're supposed to keep ice on it the rest of the day. I'm gonna be so worn out from going up and down those stairs that I won't have the strength to reel in a fish, presuming I get more than a nibble. Which I most likely won't, but that's beside the point."

"Do either of you know Norella Buchanon?" I asked.

Ruby Bee sat down at the kitchen table. "Is that who got herself killed?"

Estelle joined her. "That'd be Duluth's wife, right? I bleached her hair once or twice, but she was trash and we didn't much talk. She had a real mouth on her, though. She carried on so much about how she was forever being snubbed at the supermarket that I finally took to telling her I was booked up."

"Any chance of coffee?" I asked as I pulled up a chair.

Ruby Bee read me as only a mother can, then rose. "I'll put on a fresh pot. How about a sausage biscuit to go along with it?"

"Thanks, that would be nice. Part of the problem is that we don't know who was killed up by the softball field. Duluth showed up yesterday and was arrested for drunk and disorderly, or whatever they call it in Dunkicker. These Moonbeams all look alike. I don't remember ever encountering Norella, but even if I had, I wouldn't have been able to identify her."

"Moonbeams?" said Ruby Bee.

I was explaining when Mrs. Jim Bob came into the kitchen, wiping her nose with a wadded tissue and gurgling in a most disturbing way.

"Why don't you start again?" she said as she sat down. "I do not intend to be kept in the dark about this wicked cult—or, more likely, coven. Larry Joe Lambertino stuttered, stammered, cleared his throat, said virtually nothing, and then hustled the teenagers out the door before we could have a proper Sunday morning service. I am responsible for their well-being, as you know. Their parents entrusted them to my care. You, on the other hand, seem to have no interest in their safety, and now Brother Verber has disappeared. Do you have any idea where he is?"

"Actually, I do. He rode into Dunkicker with me and has gone to Little Rock with a deputy from the sheriff's office. He ought to be safe unless they encounter a chicken truck careening the wrong way down the interstate." When she swayed so violently that Estelle had to clutch her arm, I hastily added, "He's helping with the investigation, and will be back before too long."

Ruby Bee put a mug of coffee in front of me. "She's not gonna admit it, but she's worried," she whispered. "He upped and took off this morning without so much as a word of explanation."

I regretted my tactless joke. "He had breakfast at the café and has gone with the deputy to see if he can help us identify the body that was recovered last night. He's in good hands, Mrs. Jim Bob."

"Why didn't he say something to me? You'd think, after all these years, that he'd feel an obligation not to just disappear like that. He is the lighthouse shining throughout the dark night to save us from crashing against the rocks of iniquity and damnation, you know."

I told her what I knew. Once I'd finished, Ruby Bee set a sausage biscuit on the table and said, "So Duluth could be around here?"

I gulped down half a biscuit and took a swallow of coffee. "If Duluth did come after Norella, he'd have no reason not to head as far away from here as he can get before we find him."

"But if it wasn't Duluth—" said Estelle, then stopped.

Mrs. Jim Bob was beginning to perspire. "The way I see it, we need to load everybody in the bus and head right back for Maggody within the hour. Arly, you go up to the softball field and tell Larry Joe. I'll start packing my things. Ruby Bee, you and Estelle need to get Darla Jean out to the porch, then fetch whatever you brought."

"Wait a minute," I said. "As long as no one decides to go wandering off on his or her own, we should be fine. Whoever did this is apt to be long gone. I'll go up to the field, have Larry Joe and the kids bring down the tools and softball equipment and lock everything in the back of the

bus. They can stay in the yard until it's time for Sunday dinner. Maybe you can get them to sing a hymn or two."

"And then what?" Mrs. Jim Bob said shrilly. "If they're
not kept busy, who knows what sinful things they'll find to
do!"

I resisted the urge to throttle her into silence. "Larry Joe
will handle them. After dinner, he can escort the girls to
their cabin and wait—outside, of course—while they
change into bathing suits. The boys can take care of themselves as long as they stay together. The Sabbath is supposed to be a day of rest, isn't it? The dock is within sight
of the porch, so you can make sure there's no hanky-
panky."

"I still think we should leave."

I crammed the rest of the sausage biscuit into my
mouth. "Give me a few hours," I said indistinctly, trying
not to spew crumbs with each word. "Everybody's covered.
As soon as Brother Verber gets back, I'll send him down
here to thump invaders with his Bible. Why don't you take
a break and plan a sunset vespers service, Mrs. Jim Bob?"

Her eyes narrowed. "I don't like this. What are Ruby
Bee, Estelle, and me supposed to do if some maniac comes
screaming into the lodge?"

I pushed back my chair. "The three of you should be
able to take on a Mongol horde and win back the Holy Ro-
man Empire. I'm going up to the softball field. I'll stop back
by here before I go to Dunkicker."

Ruby Bee gave me a halfhearted hug. "We'll be just
fine."

"Of course we will," chimed in Estelle. "There's a whole
drawer full of butcher knives and cleavers. No maniac is
gonna have his way with us."

"His way with us?" said Mrs. Jim Bob. "You don't
think he'd . . . have his way with us, do you?"

"Not if he has the sense God gave a goose," I said

brusquely. "Keep the doors locked until Larry Joe gets here with the kids."

Ruby Bee looked over her shoulder at the back door. "I was thinking I'd hang the dish towels in the garden."

"Do it later," I said as I left the kitchen and went out the front door. Everybody was not covered, I realized. As far as I knew, Jacko was still at his campsite, blithely listening to classical music while he made futile attempts to catch fish. It was possible he might not hear anyone approaching through the thick brush until it was too late.

But first, Larry Joe and his charges. I took the path up to the field, where the boys were sawing planks and bolting them onto the frame of the bleachers, and the girls were sprawled in the grass, reading magazines.

I took Larry Joe aside. "Do you know Duluth and Norella Buchanon?"

"Why are you asking?"

"It's way complicated," I said. "Do you?"

"I reckon so. They used to show up for Sunday morning services at the Assembly Hall, but not on a regular basis." He paused to think. "They probably haven't come in the better part of two years. When Joyce and me had our fifteenth wedding anniversary a few years back, I let her pick out linoleum for the kitchen floor and Duluth installed it."

"Quite the romantic, aren't you?"

"She was real pleased. I was gonna get her a new lawn mower, but she wanted the linoleum instead. Duluth did a real fine job."

"That's good to hear, Larry Joe." I gave him a terse version of what had happened and told him to declare a day of rest, adding that I didn't want the kids to be out of his sight for even a few seconds.

"About yesterday," he said, scratching his head. "There's something I might ought to mention, although it most likely doesn't mean anything. After you left with

Heather, we put everything in the dugout and went down to the cabin. Mrs. Jim Bob would have a hissy fit if she knew, but I figured nobody was gonna do anything while I was with them. Big Mac turned on his radio, and most of them were playing cards when Jarvis told me he'd left his wallet up at the field. He said it was a birthday present from his ma and he was afraid it'd get wet."

"And?" I said.

"It was a good thirty minutes before he came back."

I glanced at Jarvis, who was busy with a cordless drill. "With his wallet?"

"Said he couldn't find it," admitted Larry Joe. "About then the storm hit and we headed for the lodge."

"Did he find it this morning?"

"I asked him. He said he must have left it at home."

Jarvis was by far the most mature boy in the group, at least a head taller than Big Mac, Parwell, and Billy Dick. He'd taken off his shirt, and his muscles were those of a beefy construction worker. He had a few postpubescent pimples on his back, but he undoubtedly shaved more often in a week than the others did in a month. Then again, he'd tried to filch a package of cookies, indicating he was far from wise beyond his years.

"So why did you bring this up?" I asked Larry Joe.

"It shouldn't have taken him more than five minutes to go there from the cabin and get back. I told him to hustle."

"Did he have an explanation?"

"No, and he was real twitchy, like he'd gone through a patch of chiggers. I was trying to pin him down when it started raining and we skedaddled to the lodge. The girls were shrieking about their hair getting ruined and screaming ever' time thunder boomed. It was all I could do to keep them moving. I guess I forgot about Jarvis."

"But he might have known Norella?"

"She was teaching their Sunday school class until Mrs.

Jim Bob found out that the topics most weeks were the same Old Testament stories I used to read under my covers with a flashlight. It drove my ma crazy, since I was reading the Bible like she wanted me to do. Once Mrs. Jim Bob caught wind of it, Norella was demoted to the nursery and drummed out of the Missionary Society. Not too long after that, her and Duluth got divorced. Neither of them's been back to church since then."

"Jarvis most likely detoured to smoke a joint," I said. "I want all the tools and softball equipment locked in the back of the bus." I expanded on the scenario for the rest of the afternoon, then added, "Unless we find whoever did this, I'm afraid everybody's going to have to sleep at the lodge again tonight."

"On a concrete floor," he said glumly.

"Mrs. Jim Bob thinks we ought to pack up and go back to Maggody, but I don't think it's that critical yet. If I haven't gotten anywhere by tomorrow afternoon, I suppose we can call it quits and go home. I wouldn't want you to have to take out a second mortgage to pay a chiropractor."

Larry Joe looked at the bleachers, which were progressing. "We take on the job, we finish it. That's my first rule in shop class. Well, the second one, anyway. The first has to do with not thinking you can get away with stealing tools. The shitheels managed to make off with a tablesaw last year. You know how much those things weigh?"

"Gee, not offhand," I said. "Just make sure that every one of the girls is within your eyesight, and that the boys don't go off unless they go together. They don't have to hold hands, but I don't want any of them on his own, not even to go behind a bush to pee."

"So Duluth killed Norella? What was she doing here, dressed in a robe with her head shaved?"

I stiffened. "Did you recognize her?"

"Hell, no. I wouldn't have recognized Joyce if she

looked like that. 'Course it was getting dark, but even so."

"We're still trying to get an ID. In the meantime, the kids won't object to an afternoon of sunbathing on the dock and swimming in the lake. I'm trusting you to keep them safe."

I left before he could ask more questions. I hurried by the lodge, ducking behind the bus and station wagon in hopes I wouldn't be spotted, and went on down the road. I stopped at the cabin and allowed myself a moment to regroup, then continued to the place where I'd fought through the brush to Jacko's campsite. Okay, brush is brush, but this time I heard an NPR pundit expounding on the latest setback in civilization.

He was seated on an aluminum folding chair, eating stew out of a can and regarding the fishing boats on the lake. His plaid shirt was of different hues, but his khakis and canvas hat were familiar.

"I was wondering when you'd come back," he said.

I caught my breath. "And why would you be doing that?"

"I thought you might have some questions."

I realized that I most certainly did.

11

Jacko held up a spoon. "Want some? The carrots are mushy and the beef's chewy, so it balances out: mush, chew, chew; mush, chew, chew. Sounds like a ballroom dance, doesn't it?"

"I don't think so," I said, staying where I was. "Not much of a fisherman, are you?"

"It's not much of a lake."

"Then why are you here?"

He grinned. "Just taking a break. I can listen to my music, dress up like the coverboy for *Field and Stream,* and fall asleep listening to the crickets and owls. No cellphone, laptop, or late-night television. This trip I've been rereading Henry James. You like him?"

"A break from what?" I asked. "Prison?"

"You overestimate me." He put down the can of stew but remained seated, which was for the best, since I didn't want to be obliged to whack him with the stick I had my eye on. "Merely an office job riddled with tedium and tacit despair. Several times a year I make a point of getting away."

"And where would this office be?"

"In a galaxy far, far away, at least for this week."

"I can run your license plate," I said, "and I will if you don't answer my questions. What are you really doing here?"

"Ah, yes, I heard you're a cop. You don't exactly dress like one, do you?"

"Heard from whom—the crickets and the owls?"

"And how well-educated you are, considering your profession. You recognized Vivaldi and had the sense to turn up your nose when I mentioned Henry James. Do you write poetry when you're not running a speed trap?"

"Yeah, but it doesn't rhyme. Why are you here?"

"Why are you worried about me?"

"Well, you're no fisherman, obviously. Even those clowns out on the lake are pulling up crappies. The best you seem to have caught is Dinty Moore."

"And that's a crime?"

"As I said, I'll run your plate. There was a homicide yesterday afternoon. It seems to have happened about the time you were taking a stroll, unaware of the thunderstorm. If I'd been you, I might have stayed by my tent."

He appraised me for a moment. "What if I said I'd hiked into Dunkicker for a hot meal at the café and been caught on the way back?"

"I'd say you were lying."

"Okay, so I'm not here to fish. That doesn't mean I killed anyone."

"Why are you here?" I repeated. "Is there something about the swarms of gnats and mosquitoes that appeals to you? Cold stew, poison ivy, the occasional cottonmouth dangling in the branches above your head? Aren't you too old to be working on a merit badge?"

"I'm, well—I guess you could say I'm along the lines of a private investigator."

I'd suspected as much, but I still wasn't sure how to respond. "So you're keeping tabs on the Beamers?"

"I was hired to look into things."

"By whom?"

"You know I won't tell you," he said with a wink meant to distract me, which it did, but only momentarily. "Privileged and all that shit. I'm just making sure the children are healthy for the time being. My employers will make the next call."

"No, I will. A woman was murdered yesterday, and you just happened to be walking down the road in a downpour. You must have seen the clouds gathering. Why on earth did you opt to walk to Dunkicker?"

"Exercise?"

"No, Jacko, or whatever your name is," I said. "We're grateful that you were there to bring Darla Jean to the lodge. No one's arguing with that. But if that's all you have to say, I'll have no choice but to have you taken into custody until you can produce a better explanation than a sudden urge to appreciate nature at its worst. The food in the Dunkicker jail is likely to be better than canned stew. The view, on the other hand, is not so picturesque."

"You've talked to these women, right? They brought their children and started preparing themselves for what they call the Rapture. The family that hired me is worried. They suspect their daughter might . . ."

"Harm the children?"

"Yeah," he said. "Can you blame them? Jonestown wasn't that long ago; it may have been an anomaly, or it could happen again."

"Which woman have you come to find?"

Jacko shook his head. "I have no information concerning the homicide yesterday. I walked to the gate, then realized the storm was moving in and headed back. I found the girl under a scrub oak and carried her to the lodge. That's pretty much all I have to say. Run my plate if it entertains you; you'll discover that I live in Springfield, Missouri, and have no outstanding warrants for felonies, misdemeanors, jaywalking, or overdue library books. I may be a lousy fisherman, but I am an upstanding citizen. I'd show you my plaque from the Jaycees if I hadn't left it at home."

"You are very annoying," I said.

"Any chance you'd like to crawl into my tent and let me really annoy you?"

"No, I would not," I said forcefully, if mendaciously. "Don't leave the area without telling me or Corporal Robarts."

"I'll be here for a few more days." He picked up the can of stew. "Sure I can't offer you lunch?"

I went back to the road and found his car. The license plate had been removed. The doors and trunk were locked, naturally. I contemplated letting the air out of his tires just to prove which of us could be more annoying, then virtuously headed for the lodge.

✹

Raz gazed sorrowfully at Marjorie. "I reckon you would have preferred a mule, but it was a real nice goat. Not pedigreed like you, a'course, but with fine flanks and big brown eyes. You and her could have got along jest fine, even been friends."

Marjorie looked away.

"Uncle Tilbert raised goats till his lactose intolerance got the best of him. He always said they wasn't the smartest animals, but they could find their way home come suppertime, which was more than his young'uns could do. I can't hardly keep from cacklin' when I recollect how his eldest boy upped and married that bearded lady named—"

Marjorie sniffled.

Raz realized he wasn't makin' no progress with goats. "Thing is, I can't just up and go over to Perkins's place, unless I want a load of buckshot in my backside. Even if I was to temporarily borrow Perkins's mule, it'd have to stay in the barn till things quieted down. What kind of companionship are you gonna git with a mule down in the barn? It ain't even air-conditioned."

It was clear from Marjorie's expression that she hadn't considered that.

"If you was to spend your time in the barn," he persisted, "you'd miss your favorite shows on the satellite channels. I'd say offhand that it's a matter of time afore Gilligan drags Ginger behind a coconut tree. What's more, any fool can see that Ozzie and Harriet are headin' for divorce court, with Judge Judy presiding." He paused, then went in for the kill. "But if you're down in the barn, as opposed to watching reruns and pay-for-view, then so be it. Don't think I'm going to bring down bags of microwave popcorn, 'cause I ain't. I'll be sittin' right here watchin' Xena's boobs bobble."

Marjorie's eyes watered and her snout began to drip on the new tangerine area rug.

Raz figgered he needed to reconsider his options. Arly was out of town, which was good. Perkins, on the other hand, had been mouthin' off at the barber shop about what all he might do iff'n anybody set foot on his place. It occurred to Raz that a quart of 'shine might help.

><

All was idyllic at the lodge. The kids were sitting on the lawn, the girls still involved with magazines, the boys with poking each other and making what I was sure were crude remarks. They were doing so quietly, however, since Mrs. Jim Bob was on the porch in a wicker throne, staring at them as though she would, if a profanity was spoken aloud, order Larry Joe to pull out the tools and start constructing a guillotine. She professed to being a devout Christian, but I'd always felt she preferred the Old Testament approach when faced with transgressions of both major and minor magnitude.

"Where's Larry Joe?" I asked.

"Calling his wife," said Amy Dee. "That is like so sweet. If I ever get married, I'd want my husband to call me every day."

Big Mac snickered. "I hear they have rules about how often you can make phone calls from the state pen."

Heather arched her eyebrows. "And you should know, considering how many of your kinfolk are there. I hear tell they have a whole wing set aside for Buchanons."

"Excuse me," came a voice from the porch.

"Not your side of the clan," Heather said hastily. "All I meant, you know, was like how maybe—"

"That will do," said Mrs. Jim Bob. "In case all of you have forgotten, this is the Sabbath. Put away your trashy magazines and gather on the porch steps. We will have a reading from the First Epistle of Paul the Apostle to the Corinthians, in which he expounds on the evils of sectarianism. There is enlightenment to be gleaned."

"Good work, Heather," Jarvis muttered as he rose.

I grabbed him. "I'll bring him back in a few minutes," I said to Mrs. Jim Bob, then dragged him behind the bus, ignoring the alarmed stares of the other kids.

Once we were out of sight, I said, "I need to ask you a few questions."

"About what? Cookies missing from the pantry?"

"Why? Did you steal some?"

Jarvis gave me a sly look. "Wanna frisk me?"

In that he was wearing a threadbare T-shirt and tight shorts, I was fairly certain he had not concealed much more than a cloverleaf on his person.

"Larry Joe said you went back to the softball field yesterday afternoon," I said.

"Yeah, I did. My ma gave me a wallet for my birthday last month. I thought I'd left it up there, but I was wrong. I must have left it at home."

"But you were up there for half an hour."

"Look, I didn't want to come here in the first place," he said. "It was my ma's idea. She ain't doing all that well these days, so I said I'd do it just to keep her happy. By the afternoon, I was getting real tired of all the whining and complaining. These girls carry on like they're in middle

school. Big Mac, Parwell, and Billy Dick don't stop brag-
ging about . . . well, you know. It's not my thing. I went to
the softball field, sat in the dugout for a few minutes, and
then went back to the cabin."

"You didn't hear anything?"

"Like what?"

"A loud conversation?" I suggested. "A scream?"

"Or someone getting whacked with a softball bat?"

I debated whether or not to tell him that it was possible
that Norella Buchanon had been the victim of the brutality.
Later, I decided, when we had some sort of confirmation.

"Okay," I said, "we can let this go for the moment. I'm
not satisfied with your story, but I'm willing to concede that
it makes sense. Don't go off by yourself anymore."

Jarvis returned to the lawn. It was possible that I was
not endearing myself to the teenagers, but I wasn't sure that
I'd ever had a snowball's chance of winning their confidence. I was, after all, not only a member of the adversarial
generation, but also a cop. In this case, two strikes and I
was out.

I waved at Mrs. Jim Bob, then drove away before she
could dethrone herself. As I reached the highway, I saw
what I supposed was Crank Nickle's farm at the intersec-
tion. The fences were in disrepair and the barn appeared to
be standing by only spit and a prayer. The house was a trib-
ute to tattered tar paper. Mangy hounds sprawled on the
porch barely opened their eyes as I drove by.

I hoped they had enjoyed the previous night's activity,
although I suspected it would have taken a presidential mo-
torcade and a slew of Secret Service agents to rouse them.

Ruth, when she'd been forced to get out of bed, had
worked with Sarah at the church. I decided to stop there,
then go by the café and speak to Rachael before I tackled
Judith again.

The Baptist church was situated between a body shop

and a seedy building with a portable sign that advertised a
flea market every other weekend. A few members of the
congregation were still conversing out front, but no one
openly gawked as I pulled around to the back.

Several pickup trucks with oversize tires were parked
near a door. I parked well away from them and went inside,
where I found myself in a kitchen. Three hulking boys,
neckless and most likely witless, were loading Styrofoam
containers onto cookie sheets under the instructions of a
Beamer with a noticeably sharp tongue. Same shaved head,
lack of eyebrows, and ghoulish lipstick, of course, but in
this case dressed in jeans and a white T-shirt beneath an
apron. She was shorter than Judith and broader than
Rachael, but those were the only differences I could detect.

"I've had it with you, Byron," she was saying. "You
miss one more stop and Chief Panknine's gonna have you
picking up litter alongside the highway until Christmas—if
you're lucky. Any questions about your deliveries?"

"No, ma'am," he mumbled.

She turned to the other two. "I'll make a point of visit-
ing with all of our patrons later today. If so much as one of
them is missing a green bean or a sliver of cake, you'll find
yourselves in orange jumpsuits, hoeing turnip fields at the
state prison. You should be back in an hour, with all the
names checked off your lists. Got that?"

After more mumbling, the hulks left with their loads. I
waited by the door for a moment, then advanced. "I'm Arly
Hanks," I said. "The sheriff asked me to investigate the
murder that took place yesterday afternoon."

"You mind if I start cleaning up while we talk? Once the
boys get back, I'd like to leave. I've been here for five hours,
preparing forty meals for shut-ins. My back's killing me."

Sarah may have assumed that I'd pitch in, but I sat
down on a stool.

"I'm here to ask you about Ruth," I said.

"She was useless, when she even showed up. She'd peel one carrot, then start gabbing about some soap opera. Do I look like someone who watched soap operas? I worked in a factory, second or third shift most days. I was a lot more concerned about the deductions on my paycheck than I was about a bunch of actors and actresses with capped teeth, perfect hair, and the morals of alley cats."

"Ruth hadn't been here long, right?"

Sarah began to fill the sink with steamy water. "I don't know why she was allowed to come here in the first place. We were all told what was expected, but she carried on like she'd thought she was coming to a fancy spa. Well, my knuckles are scabbed and my ankles are so puffy they look like bread dough. The masseuse ain't called to make an appointment."

"So Deborah warned you?" I asked.

"I knew what I was getting into. Nobody pressured me." She submerged a roasting pan and began to scour it. "I've got another three weeks here, then I'll start working at the motel. I pity the next Moonbeam that has to deal with those boys and a bunch of snivelers who want peas instead of beans, molded lime salad instead of cole slaw, biscuits instead of cornbread. It wouldn't hurt them to show a little gratitude every now and then, but all they do is bitch."

Somehow, we had moved away from the topic into volatile territory. I waited a moment, then said, "Did Ruth say anything about her background?"

"She didn't have one, any more than I do. It's part of the deal."

"You gave up your past because of your religious convictions?"

"Yeah, that's right. My children are being taught the fundamentals and learning the value of physical labor. They have chores in the garden, not time to waste on television and video games. My daughter is making a scrapbook of pressed wildflowers. My son likes sketching down by the creek. They complained at first, but they've adjusted real well."

"How about Ruth's children?"

Sarah looked over her shoulder at me. "I should know? I get up at dawn, take a cold sponge bath, and walk here to start preparing the meal. I'm usually ready to go back in the middle of the afternoon. If Anthony sees me, he'll give me a ride to the top of the road, but that doesn't happen very often. When I get there, I barely have the energy to deal with my own kids, much less worry about any of the others."

"So why are you doing this?" I asked, having noted a distinct lack of spirituality in her recitation. "You said you knew what you were getting into."

"Yeah, I did."

I waited for a moment, but she seemed more interested in scrubbing cake pans than elaborating. "Where were you recruited?"

"I'm not allowed to talk about that. My children are safe for the time being, and so am I. I ain't gonna say anything else about it."

"No, of course not," I murmured. "How did you and your children get to Dunkicker?"

"In a rusty white Honda Accord with a faulty transmission and a cracked windshield. Now I think you'd better leave. If Deborah finds out I've been talking to you—well, I need the Daughters of the Moon for my children's sake, and mine, too."

"How would Deborah know we'd been talking?"

"Just go on, please. I've got pots and pans to wash, and the oven needs cleaning. After that, I'll have to wipe down the counters, mop the floor, and put everything away so I can be ready to leave when the delivery boys get back."

I got off the stool, but paused by the door. "I have to ask this, Sarah. What about the father of your children?"

"We're divorced. He never paid child support, but always expected me to produce the children every other Friday evening so he could spend the weekend poisoning their minds. The last time he had them, my daughter came home and asked me if I was really a whore like Daddy said. Helluva guy, huh?"

"So you took your children and left?"

"I already told you that I don't want to talk to you anymore. Either grab the mop or let me work in peace."

✖

I drove to the PD. The door was unlocked, but the adage about barn doors and horses applied. We certainly didn't want to prevent Duluth from returning, should he find the urge to spend more quality time on a urine-stained mattress no thicker than a paperback novel.

It would have been a waste of time to try to call the state medical examiner's office. At best, I would have spent thirty minutes working my way through various option menus before I was left on hold while the kudzu vines slithered over the windowsills and choked the last breath out of me. Harve was on his johnboat, swilling beer, eating his wife's chocolate cake, and defying the fish to disturb him.

I poured myself a cup of coffee, then rooted through Captain Panknine's desk until I found a candy bar. I also found some evidence that he was less than loyal to Mrs. Panknine, who was driving to Little Rock every day to sit by his bedside and relate the latest local gossip.

That, however, was none of my business. Chief Panknine's chair was not as comfortably worn as mine, but I rocked back and propped my shoes on the corner of the desk, my preferred posture for thinking.

Sarah was hardly a devout Daughter of the Moon, and I doubted Norella had been, either (if, of course, she had been there, and I still wasn't sure). Both of them had gone through hostile divorces and squabbles over visitation. Duluth had claimed to have paid child support on a regular basis, but I had only his version. Sarah had offered me an abbreviated story; it could have been tainted with the animosity that usually accompanies divorce. My own had been bitter, but in that children had not been an issue, I'd been able to walk away with my dignity and the gawdawful crystal pickle dish Estelle had given me as a wedding present.

These days it serves as a depository for change and a few keys whose purpose eludes me.

The Welcome Ya'll Café was likely to be busy in the middle of the day, so Rachael would not be available for a private conversation. If she were inclined, which she most likely would not be. Sarah had not been frightened when Deborah's name came up in our conversation, but she had been uneasy. Judith had been less than forthcoming. Deputy Robarts had barely stopped short of fidgeting.

The only person I could think of who might be able to offer information was Willetta Robarts, august matriarch of Dunkicker and its environs, which might stretch as far as Greasy Valley. I decided to try to talk to her before I returned to the Beamers' campsite. How to find her was a problem, however. I found a slim telephone directory in Chief Panknine's bottom drawer, but an address on Robarts Road was of little help, since Dunkicker, like Maggody, had yet to find funding for street signs.

I was about to dial the number when I heard scratching from the back of the building.

There are moments when you just want to cast your fate to the wind. This was not one of them.

I was unarmed. I'd been trained in one-on-one combat at the academy. Supposedly, I could take on a Ninja warrior or a psychotic twirling without a baton. If Chief Panknine had a weapon, he'd had enough sense to keep it well out of Deputy Robarts's reach. I wondered how much damage I could do with a bad attitude and half a Snickers bar.

Not much.

I cautiously opened the door that led to the cell. The scratching sound intensified, but I couldn't identify the source. If I'd been back in Maggody, I most certainly would have found my gun and put one of my last three bullets in it. As it was, I was armed with a rolled-up copy of a magazine devoted to lake trout.

"Someone there?" I called.

"I reckon you be wantin' this feller."

I realized there was a door at the end of the short hall. "What feller?"

"The one what ran away this mornin'. You want him, come and take him. I got better things to do."

I opened the door with a certain amount of trepidation. Duluth Buchanon was being held upright by a citizen who looked and smelled worse than Raz Buchanon. His beard dribbled over his gut in strings so drenched in tobacco juice that they might have turned to amber. His pale eyes were entirely too intense.

"Found him hunkered in my barn," he said. "I ain't got time for the likes of him. You don't want him, I'll cart him down to the pond and put a bullet up his nose. The catfish will dispose of him afore too long."

Duluth gave me a panicky look, but had enough sense to keep his mouth shut.

"Are you Crank Nickle?" I asked.

"I ain't the queen of England."

"No, I suppose not," I said. "I would very much like to take this trespasser off your hands. Chief Panknine will appreciate how you did your civic duty."

"Dumbshit scared my cow."

"Perhaps you might enjoy participating in a firing squad later this afternoon," I said as I yanked Duluth inside. "Say about four?"

"And miss the last round of the PGA finals? You jest tell

Chief Panknine to keep his prisoners outta my barn." He stomped off before I could respond, assuming I could have.

I took Duluth to the front room, sat him down, and poured him a cup of coffee. He looked like hell, which was to be expected, considering the depth of his hangover. I gave him a moment, then said, "Well?"

"Well—what?" he growled.

"I'm hoping you have some innocuous reason for being in Dunkicker. Your great-aunt lives here, for instance, and needed you to plant pole beans and cucumbers. There's an orphanage somewhere down the road that has a leaky roof. You were ready to repaint Ruby Bee's kitchen, but you were torn between oyster shell and ivory. You tell me, Duluth."

"Norella."

"What about her?"

"Her mother finally got around to mentioning that she'd called a few days back. Said her and the boys was staying at an old church camp, and that she'd be moving on shortly. When folks in Maggody started buzzing about how the teenagers were going to a church camp, I figured it might be the one where Norella had taken the boys. Like I told you, she didn't have much cash, and her car leaks oil bad."

"So you followed the bus?"

"Right till it turned down the road. I decided I'd better wait till it was dark, so I parked my truck behind that old coot's barn. I'd brought a cooler with a couple or three six-packs, and after I finished those, I remembered I had a bottle of whiskey under the seat."

"And finished that, too, I assume. What were you doing staggering alongside the highway—looking for a liquor store?"

Duluth gave me a watery look that came from either embarrassment or a doozy of a headache. "I was real nervous about seeing Norella. More likely than not, she'd start screaming at me and trying to claw my face. One time she bit me on the ear so hard you can see the scar to this day. Look right here." He pulled his ear forward and waited until I produced a properly horrified frown. "I was gonna press charges for assault, but then I realized if she was locked up, her family might not be willin' to take care of the boys while I was working."

"Probably not," I said. "Then you never went down the road to the campgrounds?"

"Hell, no, I dun told you what I did. You seen Norella and the boys hanging out down there?"

I shook my head. "How do you think she came to find out about Camp Pearly Gates? Did she go there as a kid?"

"I about had to hogtie her to get her to church on Sundays. She always said everybody was real snooty, looking down their noses at her like they thought she bought her dresses at yard sales. Soon as we got home, she'd send the boys to their room and cuss up a storm. I got to where I dreaded Sunday mornings, knowing what I was in for the rest of the day. I'd just keep turnin' up the volume on the football game, but she didn't care even when the Cowboys was playin' Tampa Bay."

"Must have been tough, Duluth," I said, wondering what his sons had thought during the weekly ordeals. "One more question: How'd you get out of the cell?"

He rubbed his temples so hard I was afraid his head might shatter. "It don't make any sense, but I'll tell you. After Brother Verber left, I took a piss, then crawled back on the bunk. I must have dozed off, 'cause the next thing I saw was this . . . uh, this . . ."

"Alien?"

"Yeah, this alien unlocking the cell door. I pulled the blanket over my head, and when I finally got up the guts to look, it was gone. Putting up with Brother Verber's one thing, but I wasn't about to find myself being the subject of unnatural medical examinations in a flying saucer. I beat it back to my truck, but the damn thing wouldn't start. I decided to stay in the barn till it got dark, then find a pay phone and call my cousin Leroy to come get me."

"But Crank Nickle found you first."

"Reckon so. Any chance I can call Leroy from here? I'll leave fifty bucks to pay the fine. I mean, all I did was get drunk. That ain't much of a crime these days."

"No, I guess it's not," I said, "but you'll have to remain in custody for the time being."

"On account of being drunk?"

"It's a little bit more complicated than that." I gave him what remained of the candy bar and locked him in the cell. He didn't much like it, naturally, but I assured him that the aliens were on their way back to Alpha Centauri and I'd find him something more substantial to eat.

One of the Beamers had unlocked the cell door, for some reason. Willetta Robarts would have to wait until I could try to talk to them.

Or so I thought.

12

"Please, my dear, tell me what's going on," said Willetta Robarts as she came into the PD. She was dressed in a gray silk dress and the sort of hat more often seen at Ascot than at rural Baptist outposts. "I was chatting with Sister Silvester when I saw you drive behind the church. Everyone here in Dunkicker is aware of the crime, but no one knows what to think. Sister Silvester was literally dribbling with distress, but she hasn't quite been the same since her boy joined up with those heathens in Greasy Valley. You must tell me if you've made any progress."

"Not much," I said. "Would you like a cup of coffee?"

"I have a better idea! Why don't you come to my house for a nice Sunday dinner? Colleen is making fried chicken, mashed potatoes, creamed peas with onions, biscuits, and rhubarb pie for dessert. You do like rhubarb pie, don't you?"

I would never, ever, not for a second or even a nanosecond, have considered this if I hadn't needed to ask her some questions about her dealings with Deborah and the Daughters of the Moon. "I shouldn't," I said reluctantly, as if debating the wisdom of going to the prom with the captain of the football team—which is not to imply I'd gone to the prom, having instead spent the evening on the bank of Boone Creek with Masie Cockran, drinking cheap wine and plotting our escape from Maggody. According to Ruby Bee, who keeps a stranglehold on the grapevine, Masie's currently a weathergirl in Fort Worth and hasn't set foot in

Maggody since the day after our high-school graduation.

"There's a prisoner in the back room, and I need to feed him," I added.

"Then I'll have Colleen bring him his dinner. Come along, we don't want the biscuits to get cold."

My salivary glands kicked in like automatic sprinklers. I drove behind her to a three-story house of Victorian vintage set in the middle of a neglected pasture. Apparently the budget had gone for the structure and furnishings, with nothing left over for such petty concerns as landscaping. No one over the ensuing decades had seen fit to mitigate the starkness with so much as a shrub or clump of begonias. There were no other houses, or even mailboxes, along the road. The trees at the far side of the pasture seemed to be keeping their distance.

"Colleen is such a jewel," Mrs. Robarts said as she took me into a foyer paneled with mahogany parquet. She took off her hat and put it on a table with spindly legs. "I don't know how Anthony and I could get along without her."

I was more concerned with her culinary expertise. "What a lovely house," I said, my nose twitching like an intruder in Mr. McGregor's garden. I never read a Sherlock Holmes story in which he'd missed a meal, and Nero Wolfe had dined without fail on snail, quail, and other gourmet extravagances. Even Miss Marple had been served tea and scones on a regular basis. I had not had a decent meal since the fire at Ruby Bee's Bar & Grill, after which I'd been forced to survive on burritos from the Dairee Dee-Lishus and peanut butter sandwiches. And canned soup, of course; it's one of my basic food groups.

"This was my grandfather's study," Mrs. Robarts said, opening a door so that I could, had I been in the mood, have gaped in admiration at musty drapes, a globe that included India as part of the British Empire, and splintery spines of leather-bound books that had not been opened in fifty years. She gave me a moment, then went on. "My grandmother had a small library on the third floor where she dedicated her time to genealogy. As I may have told you, the family—"

"And this is the dining room?" I said as I moved down the hall.

"Why, yes, please go seat yourself. I need to freshen up, then I'll let Colleen know that we're here. Anthony and I often have guests for Sunday dinner, but I gather he's occupied elsewhere for the moment. Would you prefer your iced tea sweetened?"

"Unsweetened, if it's not a bother." I sat down at one end of a massive walnut table that could have easily accommodated sixteen, a few of whom might have been dukes and duchesses (of Hazard, anyway). The arrangement of dusty silk flowers in the middle of the table and a chandelier dripping with cobwebs suggested that Colleen's duties were limited to the kitchen.

Ten minutes later, Mrs. Robarts returned and sat down at the opposite end of the table. "Colleen will be serving shortly."

"This is very kind of you."

"I was concerned about your health when I first laid eyes on you. So many young women these days sacrifice their health in order to emulate models in fashion magazines. When Anthony marries, I want him to choose a solid, well-nourished wife who can bear children. Someone with the spirit of the pioneer women who settled the West, yet with the grace to move into proper society and uphold her position."

I tried desperately to keep my eyes from reflecting anything ranging from panic to petrification. "I hope you're not thinking that . . ."

"I've always felt he might do better with an older woman. The dear boy does his best, but he needs a firm hand to guide him. Last fall he fell prey to the advances of a teenaged trollop from a trailer park in Bugscuffle. I still cringe when I think of the diseases she might have exposed him to."

She might have been preparing to list them when a sullen young woman brought in a platter of fried chicken. Moments later, bowls of mashed potatoes, creamed peas, and gravy were banged on the table.

"Colleen," Mrs. Robarts warbled, "the proper way to serve is to offer each dish to our guest, and then to me. I thought I made this clear after Preacher Skinbalder graced us with his presence last Sunday after church."

Colleen looked like someone who wore a lot of makeup when she wasn't working. A whole lot of makeup, and not much else. I did not want to imagine what private body parts she'd had pierced. Her blonde hair was pulled back in a ponytail, but might well have exploded like a frizzy fright wig without the restraint of a rubber band.

"Soon as I get the biscuits," she muttered.

Mrs. Robarts smiled at me. "I'm still training her. It's so hard to get good help these days. My grandmother used to oversee a full staff, most of whom were indebted for her instruction. Many of them went on to find suitable employment in private homes and hotels in Little Rock and Hot Springs. The Robarts family was well-known for sending along the right sort."

I would have made rude remarks had the chicken not been so irresistible. I loaded up my plate, gratefully accepted a hot biscuit when Colleen returned from the kitchen, slathered it with butter and honey, and chowed down.

"You must be concerned about Anthony," she said.

I froze, a forkful of peas halfway to my mouth. "Why should I be concerned about Anthony?"

"Didn't you send him to the Daughters of the Moon

campsite, knowing there might be a vicious killer out there?"

"You've talked to him, then?"

"He called me on his way, since he knew I was expecting him for dinner. He's very considerate about things like that. I find that rather endearing, don't you?"

"Oh, yes." I resumed eating. "But I don't believe he's in any danger. Our prime suspect, who's also our only suspect, is locked in the cell."

"He's the one who killed poor Ruth?"

I put down my fork and took a swallow of tea. "It's hard to know until we have a positive identification of the victim. If she's who I think she is, then this man was her ex-husband. They weren't getting along."

"How would he have learned that she was here? The Daughters of the Moon are very closed-mouthed."

"So I've discovered," I said dryly. "The woman you knew as Ruth called her mother and said she was staying at an old church camp. The suspect had heard locals talking about the teenagers coming to Camp Pearly Gates, so he simply followed the bus. He arrived in Dunkicker when we did, which was about ten o'clock yesterday morning. The body was found at four. His story is that he parked his truck behind Crank Nickle's barn and proceeded to get drunk. I'm not sure what time Corporal Robarts—"

"Call him Anthony," she said with a coy smile, "and please call me Willetta. I'd always dreamed of having a daughter, but now all I can hope for is a daughter-in-law with whom I can share a warm relationship. I do pray that before I die, I will have grandchildren romping at my knees."

I took another swallow of tea, wishing it were something more potent. "As I was saying, I'm not sure what time the suspect was taken into custody, but it was after the storm came in. He had the better part of five hours to go to the grounds, lurk in the woods near the Beamers' cabins, and follow his ex-wife when she went for a walk." I paused as Colleen came out of the kitchen and put a piece of rhubarb pie in front of me. "You seem to have some idea about the Beamers. The ones I've spoken to are indeed closed-mouthed."

"But Ruth called her mother, you said. What precisely did she tell her?"

"Just where she was staying and that she'd be leaving in a few days. What I'd like to know is how she and the others came here in the first place. It's hard to see them reading ads in newspapers."

Willetta, as I'd been instructed to call her, took a small bite of pie and pushed her plate away. "Did Ruth not give her mother any hints?"

"Not from what I was told. What I'd really like to do is talk to the Beamer called Deborah. You negotiated free lodgings and utilities in exchange for community service. Was this with Deborah?"

"I believe so." She tinkled a crystal bell, and when Colleen appeared, said, "Wrap several pieces of chicken and biscuits in a dish towel and take it to the police department. There is a prisoner in the cell in the back room. Require him to remain on the cot while you put the food within his reach. Do not under any circumstances unlock the cell door. He very well could have murdered a woman yesterday."

"Yeah, Maddy Van told me about that last night. One of those creeps, huh?"

"That will do, Colleen," said Willetta. "After you return, you may finish cleaning up the kitchen and take the rest of the day off. Anthony and I will fend for ourselves at suppertime. Arly, I hope you'll join us. It will be a simple meal of cold chicken and salad, but we'd both love to hear more about you."

Colleen gave me an amused look, then went back to the kitchen.

"What can you tell me about Deborah?" I asked, ignoring the invitation. "Do you have any idea where she stays?"

"With the others, I assume."

I wished I'd taken a class in Fork Flinging 101. "How did she know to approach you about living in Camp Pearly Gates?"

"Let me try to recall." She blotted her lips with her napkin and gazed blankly at her tea glass for a full minute. "Why, yes, it's come back to me. Approximately two years ago, Anthony heard rumors that there were squatters in the cabins. He investigated, then reported back to me. My first impulse was to have them arrested for trespassing, but he persuaded me to meet with them and so I did. Because they were afraid to come into town, they were surviving on meager supplies. The children were all skin and bones, like little refugees. Anthony is far more warmhearted than he allows others to see. He suggested, since the lodge was not being used at the time, we allow them to stay there and arrange for a few of them to work here in town to earn enough money to feed the children."

"But you know nothing about them?"

"They are devout religious women with children. Anthony saw that right away. Are you a Baptist, Arly?"

I opted to miss the question. "And this was arranged with Deborah?"

Willetta's lips pursed. "I've already told you all that I can. They go about their business and cause no problems."

"You said earlier that Deborah comes to you for assistance when they need medicine for a sick child."

"She appears at the door when there is a problem she cannot resolve. Only a week ago, one of the children came down with a frightful cough. They lacked the resources to take the child to an emergency room, but Doc Schmidt donated his services."

"But what about Deborah?" I said stubbornly. "Why

did she bring her group here in the first place? Where does she find recruits? How can I find her?"

Willetta rang the bell, then chuckled. "Silly me, I forgot that I sent Colleen on an errand of mercy. I truly hope you'll join us for supper, Arly. Perhaps we'll play a game of Scrabble afterward. Anthony has an impressive vocabulary."

I gave up. "Thank you for the lovely meal. I'd better check on the prisoner and then go out to the Beamers' campsite to let Anthony know that he can leave."

"I'm sure the Beamers have taken great comfort from his presence."

I shrugged and left. If I'd been a Beamer, I would have been more worried that he might shoot himself in the foot than thwart an intruder. However, I had no desire to relieve him of his post until I felt more confident that Duluth was our perpetrator and the woods were filled with nothing more threatening than rabbits, squirrels, and ill-tempered polecats.

I looked at my watch as I drove back to the PD. Les and Brother Verber were surely on their way back by now, swilling sodas, munching on corn chips, and listening as some preacher on the radio harangued his audience about the perils of damnation. Ruby Bee and Estelle would be putting away the leftover pot roast and potatoes. Larry Joe would be the lifeguard on the dock, while Mrs. Jim Bob monitored morality from the porch. I envisioned her with binoculars and a bullhorn, the serenity of the scene shattered each time she spotted a male hand approaching any component of female anatomy.

A fine time was being had by all—with one exception.

✹

Hammet was having a fine time. He'd used a whole bottle of perfumed shampoo on his hair, slapped on cologne for good measure, and was dressed in a clean shirt that hung past his knees. The underwear was kinda baggy, but he'd used a safety pin to keep it from sliding down to his ankles whenever he moved.

Not that he was doing much moving. He'd made a thick meatloaf sandwich, poured himself a glass of milk, and was stretched out on the sofa watching a television program where assholes drove noisy cars around in a big circle. It wasn't like they was going anyplace, for pity's sake. If they was on a highway, headed for Disney World or someplace like that, it'd have made more sense—and been more exciting, what with all the eighteen-wheelers they'd have to pass. As it was, the most entertaining moment so far had been when one of the cars bounced off a wall and spun around like a headless chicken. Nobody'd been killed, but Hammet hadn't given up hope.

He was thinking about fixing another sandwich when he heard the kitchen door open. He used the clicker to turn off the TV, flung himself off the sofa, and wiggled into the space between it and the wall.

"Tonya? Sonya? You gals here?" called Jim Bob as he came into the living room. "I could smell your perfume all the way out in the kitchen." After a moment of silence, he plopped down on the sofa. "They could have waited," he added to himself in a churlish voice, "or at least told me they was coming over. Aw, hell, maybe I'm smelling whatever they had on last night."

The TV came on.

Hammet realized he was clutching his sandwich, but he'd left the glass of milk on the coffee table. It didn't seem likely that Jim Bob would think the two women had stopped by for milk and cookies. He crawled around the end of the sofa and peeked at Jim Bob, who was drinking a beer and watching the cars go in circles. If the sumbitch had noticed the glass, he hadn't said anything.

He stayed where he was as Jim Bob switched channels, pausing here and there to take a chug of beer. Basketball gave way to cartoons, shiny-toothed women selling diamond jewelry, and for a brief moment, some hairy-chested singer strutting around in clown makeup and black leather shorts.

Afore too long, Jim Bob belched and went back into the kitchen. Hammet grabbed the glass of milk and crept back behind the sofa. He 'sposed he could have made it to the closet, but in there it was dark and stinky.

Jim Bob came back and fell on the sofa. "Damn those prancy bitches," he said as he popped open another beer. "I might just ought to call Cherry Lucinda and see what all she's doing. Ain't no reason I should sit here like some pimply girl hoping some asshole's gonna call and ask her to the dance. Screw 'em!"

Hammet hoped he wouldn't, at least not on the sofa anyways.

✕

When I got back to the PD, I went to make sure Duluth had been fed. The cell was empty. This trend, if indeed that's what it was, was beginning to irritate me. Colleen did not seem a likely conspirator, but there were no traces of chicken bones and biscuit crumbs on the floor. There were three possible scenarios: Duluth had been gone when she arrived; he'd waited until she left and then taken his meal away for a picnic by the lake; or he'd kidnapped her (and good luck to him; her kin were more likely to show up with shotguns than ransom money).

But Duluth was once again at large, with Camp Pearly Gates as his playground. There was no point in driving out to Crank Nickle's place; Duluth was a Buchanon, but he wasn't brain dead. He was most likely hiding somewhere in town, waiting for a chance to call Leroy to come rescue him. Putting out an APB on Leroy would be difficult, since his name was pretty much all I knew and I doubted Harve would agree to a roadblock until we had a big-time blood-bath, with Beamers being splattered every which way and upstanding citizens like Willetta, Mrs. Panknine, and Doc Schmidt being seriously inconvenienced.

But, dammit, Duluth wasn't wily enough to keep escaping on his own. Earlier, when Willetta came into the PD, I'd been trying to think why one of the Beamers would have helped him. One of their own, no matter how unlikely a candidate for Miss Congeniality, had been murdered, and he was a suspect. Judith and Naomi had been at their campsite. Sarah had been preparing meals on four wheels, and Rachael had been at the café. Ruth was at the morgue.

Which left Deborah, who wasn't anywhere.

I realized it had been the better part of two hours since I'd dumped Bonita at the motel. I taped a note on the front door of the PD telling Les where I'd gone, then drove down the road and pulled up in front of the unit. The curtains were still drawn, a good omen. I subsequently found the door unlocked and the room empty, a distinctly bad one. If there were some way, I told myself, that I could just make everybody stay in place for even a fleeting moment or two, I might get somewhere. But, no, the aliens were clearly collecting them with the same exuberance Marjorie exhibited when confronted with a thick scattering of acorns.

Bonita was on foot, which helped. I went back outside and looked around, then drove slowly down the road, hoping she was not so addled by the pain pills that she had broken into Buttons and Bows to try on hats or into the body shop to, well, look for a body.

As I drove past the junkyard, I spotted Sarah walking alongside the road. I pulled over. "Want a ride?"

"Sure, thanks," she said as she got into the station wagon. "Far as I know, all forty meals were delivered. Those damn boys are so friggin' irresponsible that at times

I want to grab them and shake them until their pitiful brains dribble out their ears."

"They're not volunteers?"

"Hell no, they're slave labor, same as me. Petrie and Eustace were arrested for vandalizing a cemetery, and Byron burned down a church a few miles from here. Chief Panknine persuaded the judge to give 'em community service. I'd rather see them doing time at the prison farm."

I glanced at her. "Slave labor? Didn't you tell me that you knew what you were getting into?"

"Community service was part of the deal. I took over from Ester, and the next Beamer will take over from me."

"What happened to Ester?"

"Nothing, far as I know. She didn't whine all the time like Ruth, but she admitted herself she wasn't cut out to live like that. She trained the both of us to fix the meals, then started cleaning the Robarts's house. She didn't like it, but at least she was making minimum wage. Of course most of it went to the Daughters of the Moon, same as everybody else's. After she managed to save a little money, Anthony gave her a ride to the bus station in Starley City."

"Wouldn't she have looked . . . conspicuous?" I asked.

Sarah snickered. "She was so worried about that she bought herself a scarf at Buttons and Bows. Folks that noticed probably thought she'd been sick or something. And don't bother asking me where she went. Ruth was the only person she ever talked to. They used to sit out on the picnic table and whisper until Judith shooed them inside."

"What about Ester's children?"

"She said she'd send for them when she could. Before she left, she was acting like she expected to win the lottery and come back for them in a big white limousine. Now they're moping around and causing trouble."

I let it drop. "You want to stop at the café and have something to eat, or at least a glass of tea?"

"So you can keep trying to weasel information out of me?"

I parked in front of the Welcome Y'all Café. "Are you afraid Deborah might find out?"

Sarah's hand moved toward her forehead, as though she intended to push a lock of hair out of her eyes. Realizing the incongruity of the gesture, she managed a smile. "Old habits die hard, I guess. I'm not afraid of Deborah or anyone else. As long as I make my contribution, I'm free to do whatever I want. I'd probably go dancing over in Azure if I didn't look like something out of a cheap comic book. The good ol' boys might get the wrong ideas."

I put my hand on her arm. "Aren't you at all upset that Ruth was murdered yesterday?"

"Yeah, sure I am," she said. "She wasn't much help in the kitchen, but she was better than nothing. I hope you're paying, because I don't have a dime to my name."

We went inside. Most of the booths and half the tables were occupied; the buzz of voices faltered, then resumed. I reminded myself that Sarah was no more peculiar-looking than Rachael behind the counter. Several stools were uninhabited, one of which was conveniently situated next to Bonita, who was working on a cheeseburger that oozed mustard and catsup.

I let Sarah drift away and sat down. "I thought you were going to stay at the motel," I said in a low voice.

"The vending machine was out of peanut butter crackers."

"What if I'd needed you?"

Bonita wiped her chin with a paper napkin. "Then I guess you would have found me. It wasn't as if I was spending the afternoon at the library doing research. This is the only place open in the whole damn town, and believe me, I checked. No cars in front of the PD, no hustle and bustle at Buttons and Bows. I did learn something of interest while I

walked down here, though. If you're ready to climb off of
your high horse, I'll tell you."

I was tempted to pull rank and remind her that I was in
charge of the investigation, courtesy of the Stump County
sheriff, also known as her boss. However, I sighed and said,
"My heels are on the ground. What?"

"Well, I was thinking that these women and their rotten
children must have gotten here somehow."

"In a Honda Accord," I murmured, pointing discreetly
at Sarah, who was whispering to Rachael at the end of the
counter. "Norella had a car, too."

Bonita made me wait while she ate another bite. "Did
you notice the body shop next to the church?"

"Yes," I said. I had noticed, after all; I just hadn't noticed anything much about it.

"If you want to hide stolen cattle, you add them to a
herd. If you want to hide a car, you leave it parked with a
bunch of other cars." She took a scrap of paper out of her
shirt pocket. "I wrote down the license plate numbers of
four cars that weren't obvious candidates for body work.
Two have Arkansas tags, one Oklahoma, one Missouri.
One of them's a Honda Accord."

"Very good, Bonita," I said.

"I should have thought of it sooner, but the pain pills
dulled my thought process."

Fried chicken and creamed peas were having the same
effect on mine. "Stay here and keep an eye on Sarah and
Rachael," I said. "I need to call these in, but I can't see doing it from the pay phone by the restrooms."

"I already did."

"Oh."

"It may take time, it being Sunday, but we should know
something in an hour or two. Did you learn anything from
the prisoner at the PD?"

"He was convinced his ex-wife had brought his boys

here, but he claimed not to have gone to the campgrounds. Until we have an identification—"

"Les called me at the motel, since nobody was answering at the PD. Brother Verber wasn't the most coherent witness, but he was fairly sure the body at the lab was Norella Buchanon."

"Fairly sure?"

"That's what Les said." Bonita finished off her cheeseburger, licked mustard off her fingers, and looked at me. "Now what?"

13

"It seems pretty straightforward," I said. "She brought the boys here, so he came after her and killed her. Odds are good that he was drunk at the time and doesn't even remember doing it."

"Why kill her?"

I shrugged. "He has a temper. I've seen it in action."

"How did he know she'd be in the woods yesterday afternoon? What if another Beamer followed her?"

"None of them has anything resembling a motive. Ruth, or maybe I should say Norella, wasn't popular, but she told her mother she was leaving. I'd imagine the other Beamers would have cheerfully carried her suitcase and her boys to the road and left them to walk to her car. They may have been irritated with her, but I can't see them doing more than short-sheeting her bed and cutting off her nightly quota of herbal tea. Crushing someone's head requires blind rage."

"Divide and conquer?" suggested Bonita. "You take one of them and I'll take the other."

"Not just yet. These two are safe here, and Corporal Robarts is at their campsite, watching over the rest of them."

"Boy, that'd make me feel safer than a heifer in a barn with a coyote scratching at the door."

"Mrs. Robarts is in the market for a daughter-in-law with breeding potential. If I send you to her house for questioning, you're likely to end up on the sofa looking at Anthony's class photos and report cards."

"Okay, then what? I can't bear to just sit here when some poor woman's been killed like that."

"Did you bring your dental records? I'm sure Mrs. Robarts would like to examine them. Win any medals in high-school field and track? Swim team? Certificate from the health department that you're free of communicable diseases?"

Bonita floundered, then settled on self-righteous indignation. "Does Sheriff Dorfer know you carry on like this when you're in charge of a murder investigation?"

I stood up. "Beats me. I'm going to the PD to make a fresh pot of coffee, rock back in Chief Panknine's chair, and try to figure out how to proceed. You may come with me if you promise to keep your mouth closed. Your other options are to stay here and have a piece of pie, spend quality time with Willetta Robarts and amateur videos of Anthony stark-naked in a wading pool, or go back to the motel and watch pay-for-view porn movies on the TV."

"I could interrogate the witness."

"Not exactly."

"Surely he's sobered up by now."

I told Sarah to stay at the café until I returned, then beckoned Bonita to follow me. While we drove to the PD, I described Duluth's disinclination to remain in jail for any length of time, even under what I had to admit was my watch. She was not impressed.

Les's car was parked by the door. Brother Verber was splayed in a chair, mopping his neck with his handkerchief. Les was likely to be in the back, gawking at the empty cell. I could hardly wait to tell him the whole story.

"So finally you show up," Brother Verber said with his customary eye for technicalities. "I must say I was mightily surprised you weren't here to offer support when I got back from this terrible ordeal. The very minute I went into that cold room and they pulled out the metal drawer, the only thing that kept me from keeling over was my unflagging faith in the Good Lord. I put my hands together to pray like I'd never prayed before."

"But it wasn't Daisy," I said, ignoring Bonita's sudden intake of breath. "It was Norella, right?"

"I reckon so. Daisy had a big ol' scar on her chin from when she chased me with a shovel and tripped. As for Norella Buchanon, I couldn't help but notice during our counseling sessions that she had a well-endowed bosom."

"And that's what you based your ID on? Her bosom?"

Brother Verber dried his forehead. "Norella's nose was right perky. Perky's hard to miss."

Les came into the room. "You know Duluth's gone?" he asked me.

"Indeed I do. Why don't you and Bonita sniff around town while I take Brother Verber back to the lodge? Duluth may be trying to call someone to come get him. Try the motel lobby, the church office, the café, the convenience store, places like that. I'll meet you back here in forty-five minutes."

Bonita stopped me at the door. "Who's Daisy? Should we be looking for her?"

"She's been dead for forty years, so you'd better hope you don't have much luck." I raised my voice. "Let's go, Brother Verber."

Once we were driving toward the gate, he gave up trying to stanch the perspiration that trickled down his face. I'd always theorized that his brain, as well as his liver, were saturated sponges. Now I had hard evidence, if not proof.

He cleared his throat. "You spoken to Sister Barbara today?"

"All I told her was that you had gone into Dunkicker and then Little Rock to assist us in the investigation."

"That's all?" he said, sounding relieved.

"She wasn't very pleased about it."

"No, I don't 'spose she was," he said, then lapsed into gloomy silence.

I parked next to the blue bus. The girls, including Darla Jean, were stretched out on beach towels covering most of the dock. Big Mac was dog-paddling near the shore, splashing the girls and guffawing when they squealed. Parwell and Billy Dick were tossing a softball back and forth. Jarvis sat well away from the others, gazing moodily at the lake.

"Why, ain't that nice to see our fine upstanding young folks observing the Bible's stricture to rest on the Sabbath," said Brother Verber. "Instead of going to the lodge, mebbe I'll just join them. I might could offer a few words to further inspire them to meditate on the glories of creation. 'The earth is the Lord's and the fullness thereof; the world and they that dwell within.' That'd be the Twenty-fourth Psalm, which ain't as famous as the Twenty-third."

"She's watching from the porch," I commented without turning my head. "You head for the dock, you can bend over and kiss your lily-white ass goodbye."

He may have wanted to object to my choice of words, but he could hardly dispute the sentiment. "I meant later," he said huffily, then got out of the car and trudged toward the porch, his hands clutched behind his back. I was mildly surprised he didn't fall to his knees and crawl the last twenty feet like a supplicant approaching a shrine.

I waited by the car until I saw Larry Joe emerge from a path that probably led to the boys' cabin. In that he was struggling with his zipper, I had a good idea what he'd been doing. I leaned against the hood until he joined me.

"Everything okay now?" he asked.

"Not yet. About all I've learned is that the victim was Norella Buchanon—and no, we don't know for sure who killed her. Keep up the good work."

Before he could protest, I went across the lawn to the porch. Mrs. Jim Bob sat on the wicker chair as though it

were the first pew in the Assembly Hall. I was pretty sure
which one of us had elected herself to cast the first stone.

Her eyes narrowed as I came up the steps. "Have you
anything to tell us?"

"We're still investigating. Brother Verber was a big help,
by the way. I brought him back so he could rest after the
long ride to Little Rock and back."

"What's this about Norella Buchanon? I just happened
to be standing outside the kitchen when I heard Estelle and
Ruby Bee discussing her. You should have come to me. I
could have told you a great deal more than they can about
her tawdry behavior. She was the first woman asked to re-
sign from the Missionary Society since Elspeth Caskell took
to wearing miniskirts to church."

"But surely, as a compassionate and forgiving Christian,
you'll be praying for her—and Elspeth, too."

"Well, of course I will," she said, her lips so tightly com-
pressed that she could barely get out the words. "It's too late
to save her soul, but I never abandon hope that a black sheep
can be cleansed of sin and be brought back into the flock."

I left her to her ovine beneficence and went into the
kitchen. Ruby Bee was flattening dough on a cookie sheet.

"Pizza," she said in response to what would have been
my next question. "You found Duluth yet?"

"No, but the victim was Norella. He's probably hitching
back to Maggody."

"Unless he's thinking to hang around until he can snatch
the boys," said Estelle as she came in from the back patio.

"That may be. I wish there were a way to rattle those
damn Beamers into talking. They might as well be aliens.
The irony is that I'm the one saying, 'Take me to your
leader.'" I sat and watched Ruby Bee start on a second
pizza crust. "Just how much food did you bring? Did you
loot the SuperSaver on your way out of town? Is the Na-
tional Guard going to be there when I get back?"

"I had a lot in the freezer, and it's a good thing I did. Once I saw what was going on, I told Mrs. Jim Bob in no uncertain terms that I was taking charge of the kitchen. I could tell from the look on her face that she wanted to argue with me, but she finally just stalked off, saving me the trouble of whacking her with a spatula. It still may happen before the week's out."

"Ruby Bee," I said, "how about you let Estelle finish that so you can do me a favor? You'll be back in time to sprinkle on the cheese and put them in the oven."

"What kind of favor?" she said suspiciously.

"A small kind of favor. It shouldn't take more than a couple of hours." I gave her my most beseeching look. "I really need your help."

Estelle butted in, as she's been known to do on more than one occasion. "I don't reckon I heard myself being consulted. What if I was aiming to get in some fishing this afternoon?"

Ruby Bee took off her apron and dropped it on the table. "All you have to do is finish patting down the other crusts. Cover 'em with damp dish towels and go fish your heart out. Maybe you can win a tournament and be named the reigning Miss Crappie."

"Better than being Miss Crabby," she retorted.

"Somebody must have baited your hook with a sourball," Ruby Bee said with a sniff of disdain. "Come on, Arly. I can always make another batch of dough later."

When we were in the dining room, I looked her over. She was wearing a skirt and a pink blouse. Instead of the support hose and orthopedic shoes she usually wore at the Bar & Grill, her legs were bare and she had on sneakers.

"What're you staring at?" she asked. "I got a bug in my hair or something?"

"I'll explain in the car. Let's go."

I gave Mrs. Jim Bob a vague smile as we went across the

porch and out to Estelle's station wagon. Larry Joe scratched his head as he watched us from the edge of the water. Of the kids, only Jarvis bothered to look over his shoulder as we drove away.

"You planning to tell me what we're doing?" said Ruby Bee as she yanked the rearview mirror around so she could inspect her hair. "If this is nothing but a wild goose chase, I'd just as soon go fishing with Estelle. I'm getting too old for tomfoolery."

"No, you're not."

She returned the mirror to an approximation of its previous position, and leaned back. "I was thinking I ought to get myself a job as a cook in one of those smarmy retirement homes. That way, they'll feel obliged to take me in when my mind goes and I can't tell the difference between a teaspoon and a tablespoon. Just this morning, I came close to dumping cinnamon 'stead of black pepper in the gravy. The day before the fire, I made half a dozen apple pies and left out the sugar. When Roy Stiver took a bite, he puckered up like I'd used green persimmons instead of perfectly good Granny Smiths."

"Everybody has lapses now and then," I said comfortingly. "Last week I left a load in the washing machine at the Suds of Fun for four days."

"Elsie McMay calls them 'senior moments.' She said she heard it on one of those afternoon talk shows. I'm surprised she remembered the phrase. She's still looking for her upper plate."

"Let's worry about that later," I said. "Now listen up so I can tell you what I want you to do."

✄

"Dahlia, my dearest, I brung you a little present," called Kevin as he came into the house. He paused, bumfuzzled, when he saw her sitting in the darkened living room, the blinds all closed like a dead man's eyes. "Is something wrong, my lusty warrior princess?"

"The babies is napping," she muttered as she sucked on a can of grape Nehi. "I been up since dawn, dressing 'em, feeding 'em, burping 'em, and changing their diapers. Then your pa has to go and insult me like I ain't any smarter than a mess of collard greens. First, he goes saying that Kevvie Junior and Rose Marie ain't identical—"

Kevin sat down beside her on the couch. "You know how Pa can be. Most mornings Ma makes him eat his breakfast on the back porch so she don't have to listen to him. Doncha want to know what I brought you?"

"What?" she growled.

"A great big ol' gallon of fat-free frozen yogurt. You want I should fix you a bowl?"

"Your pa just doesn't understand about twins," she said, refusing to be distracted. "I carried them in my belly, side by side like ying and yang, or whatever they call it."

He tried to stroke said belly, but she batted his hand away. Scooting down the couch, he said, "How's little Earl doing today?"

"Or Earlette," she said, glaring in case he attempted another move on her. "The doctor ain't told me if it's a boy or a girl. After what your pa said to me today, I ain't so sure I want to name this baby after him. Maybe we ought to name him after my grandpa Eckzemma."

"You think?" said Kevin.

Dahlia squinted at him with a real unfriendly expression. "You got a problem with that?"

"Whatever you want, my lotus blossom." He put the frozen yogurt into the freezer and came back to the living room. "There is something I ought should tell you, though. When I stopped at the supermarket to buy the yogurt, I happened to mention to Idalupino about the ad you saw for child models."

"You went talking to Idalupino about our private business?"

Kevin braced himself. "She said her cousin Charo saw the very same ad and called the number. Turns out it was a motel room down by the airport. Charo made an appointment and showed up real promptly, thinking she'd come away with a modeling contract. What happened was she found herself obliged to write a check for more than four hundred dollars just so this feller would take a bunch of pictures of her baby for what he said was a portfolio. When she gets the photographs in the mail, she's supposed to submit them herself to advertising agencies in California and New York."

"Identical twins are different," said Dahlia.

Kevin had to work on this one for a minute. He had a gut feeling that no matter what he said, it wouldn't sit well.

He was saved when Dahlia continued. "Babies are cute enough, most of them, anyway, but identical twins are special."

"Kevvie Junior and Rose Marie are real special," he said diplomatically, "but that don't mean this feller in a motel room can guarantee they'll be making a million dollars this time next year. We've only got six hundred dollars in our account, and we need to be saving up for the blessed arrival of"—he gulped—"little Eckzemma. We're gonna need another crib and more diapers. The washing machine's likely to explode any day now."

Dahlia didn't have the heart to tell him that they didn't have six hundred dollars in the account, but more like twenty dollars and seventy-three cents—and that the washing machine had spewed water on the floor before it had burped one final time and died.

✄

"I ain't much of an actress," said Ruby Bee as she, Bonita, and I got out of the station wagon at the Beamers' campsite. "I was the tooth decay fairy in a play in third grade, but all I had to do was leer at the audience. I disremember having any lines. If I did, I most likely flubbed 'em."

I squeezed her hand. "Do you recollect when that snippety woman from the health department tried to issue you a citation for the mouse droppings in the pantry? You squared your shoulders and told her that you weren't taking any guff from her. That's all I want you to do. You don't have to initiate any exchanges, but just make it clear that you're the authority figure. Remind yourself of that morning when you caught me crawling in the window and damn near blistered my skin with your stare. I'll do the rest."

"You think they'll fall for this?" asked Bonita.

"As long as you back me up, they will," I said with such confidence I almost fooled myself. "Ruby Bee, you are now Mrs. Coldwater from the Department of Family Services. You are empowered by the state to remove these children and place them in shelters until foster care can be arranged."

"I don't know anything about foster care," she protested, getting antsier than an understudy peering from behind the curtain on a Broadway stage.

"Keep repeating this to yourself," I said. " 'I am empowered by the state to remove these children and place them in shelters until foster care can be arranged.' That's all you have to say."

"But what if they agree? You intending to load the children in the back of the station wagon and take them back to the lodge?"

I shook my head resolutely. "They won't agree."

"Five bucks says they do," murmured Bonita.

"Then what a high time you'll have tonight at the Woantell Motel," I said. "Wait till Harve runs that bill by the quorum court. You may find yourself wearing his badge before you expected."

Judith appeared from inside the cabin, her face furrowed with displeasure. Ruby Bee's less-than-subtle gasp reminded me that she had yet to encounter a Beamer. "Stay calm," I warned her as we halted by the clothesline.

"You're back," said Judith.

"Got that right. Where's Deputy Robarts?"

"At the schoolhouse with Naomi and the children. Every Sunday they spend the afternoon studying the Bible and memorizing verses. At supper, we give an award for the best achievement."

I elbowed Ruby Bee, who squawked, "I'm from the Department of Family Services."

"Oh, really?" drawled Judith. "You look as though you got lost on your way home from the bowling alley."

As I'd hoped, Ruby Bee turned ornery. Jabbing her finger at Judith, she said, "Now you listen here, you tacky tabloid centerfold, I don't have to put up with any lip from the likes of you! If you don't cooperate, we'll have the children in shelters in Little Rock afore you can pluck another hair from your eyebrows. I want to see them right this minute. Where are they?"

"I'll take you," Bonita said.

"Send Naomi back here," I said, wondering how Judith would respond. "Then you and Mrs. Coldwater need to get names and home addresses."

"They will not cooperate," Judith said, sounding a bit uneasy. "You have to understand that this does not mean they're neglected or abused. We see to their physical, emotional, and spiritual needs. The only things they've been deprived of are violent video games and R-rated movies. Their lives are structured. Any punishment that is meted out is done only after a community meeting, and then with reluctance and restraint."

I sent Ruby Bee and Bonita down the path. "But they're allowed to run free in the campgrounds? Yesterday one of my girls chased a four-year-old all over the woods, losing him when the storm came in."

"Damon is seven, but small for his age," she said. "He told me about it later. All of them are curious when we're invaded by outsiders."

"Was Ruth curious, too? Is that why she went down by the softball field?"

Judith sat down on the bench of the picnic table. "She went to look for Damon, or so she told me."

"You wouldn't go looking for your child?"

"I adopted my sister's girls after she died. They're eleven and thirteen."

I looked around. "And they're content to live among the squirrels and rabbits and memorize Bible verses on Sunday? No mall time, no MTV? They don't sound like typical teenagers."

"It's been hard on them," she admitted, "but they agreed to come here."

"At what age do you shave their heads?" I asked bluntly.

"It won't come to that."

"Then you won't be staying, either? The woman named Leah is history. Ester left a week ago. Ruth called her mother a few days ago and said she would be leaving shortly."

"That's absurd. We have no access to telephones, and even if we did, we all swore not to make any calls to friends or family members. Calls can be traced to their origin. Ruth made no calls to anyone."

I wandered over to the garden. "Did Ruth say why she came here in the first place?"

"Our conversations were limited to the schedule and assignment of duties."

I was sadly lacking in women friends in Maggody these days, but I remembered what it had been like in Manhattan when I'd gone to lunch and swilled white wine all afternoon at whichever café was trendiest at the moment. Ruby

Bee and Estelle talked incessantly over sherry, often long past closing; Elsie and Eula may have claimed all they ever drank was tea, but we knew better. Millicent poured out her heart whenever she had a permanent, and Dahlia came by the PD every now and then to tell me about Kevin's latest boneheaded remark. Even Mrs. Jim Bob's confidential sessions with Brother Verber qualified in their own perverse way.

Unlike Judith, I had eyebrows to raise. "The Daughters of the Moon never talked to each other? Here you all are, stuck in the middle of nowhere, scrubbing clothes in the creek and making soap, all in total silence? Nobody had a life before she submitted to bad hair? Nobody had a bozo of a boyfriend or a husband who limited his conversation to grunts and drank himself into a stupor on the sofa every night? Nobody wanted to sit out here on the picnic table at night and talk about whatever sent her here? Were you all brainwashed? This is beyond preposterous, Judith—or whatever your name is!"

"We abide by the rules," said a voice from the path.

I turned around. "You're Naomi?"

I would have offered a description, except she looked like the others. Pale skin, shaved head, dark lipstick, draped in a white robe that hid any physical idiosyncrasies. At best, she qualified as "ditto."

"And you are?" she countered.

"Take a guess," I said, still simmering with frustration. "You are aware that Ruth was found murdered yesterday, aren't you? I realize communication skills aren't what they might be around here, but surely this was mentioned to you."

"So you're the cop," she said as she sat down next to Judith. "There's nothing I can tell you about Ruth."

Surprise, surprise. "All right, then," I said, "tell me about yourself."

"My name is Naomi. I tend to the children and help Judith with meal preparation. When it becomes feasible, I'll have a job in Dunkicker."

"What would make it feasible?"

"We're short-handed at the moment," said Judith. "Two of us are needed here to handle domestic concerns. We rely on Rachael to earn enough to purchase staples, and on Sarah to bring back leftovers when she can. Preacher Skinbalder often slips her a few dollars from the collection plate, which helps."

"And how does Deborah make her contribution? Does she prowl homeless shelters and bus stations, looking for recruits?"

Judith's eyes shifted away. "In a manner of speaking."

I gave her a moment to elaborate, then said, "We found your cars behind the body shop, by the way. We're running the plates right now, and should hear back by late this afternoon. Two from Arkansas, one from Oklahoma, and one from . . . Missouri. Either of you ready to volunteer a hometown?"

"We have no hometowns," Judith insisted, but without her earlier conviction.

"Well, I'm sure Mrs. Coldwater can persuade the children to cooperate. She can be very grandmotherly when it suits her. I don't enjoy allowing children to be manipulated, but I'll do so unless you work with me. What's more, local police will be knocking on doors this evening, and questioning neighbors if necessary. If you don't want your families to know where you are, you'd better start explaining."

"None of us committed any crimes," Naomi said sulkily. "This isn't one of those cults where the children are starved or beaten. There's no fat white guy making all the women have sex with him. The only weapons around here are homemade bows and arrows. You have no right to interfere with us."

I shook my head. "I'm sorry to say that I have. One of
your members was murdered not more than half a mile
from here. Someone committed a crime, and a serious one
at that."

Naomi looked at Judith. "Do we have to tell her where
we're from?"

"Eventually, although the information may not be as
clear-cut as she hopes. I, for one, did not drive a car to Dunkicker, and neither did Rachael."

"Then how did you get here?" I asked her.

"Deborah arranged transportation."

"From where?"

Judith gave me a pitying smile. "Why are you bothering
to ask?"

I dug my fingernails into the palm of my hand. "And
what about you, Naomi? Is your memory any better now
that you know we'll have your name and address in an
hour?"

"Not just yet," she said, visibly disturbed. "Maybe I
ought to go back to be with the children. The little ones
aren't comfortable with strangers. They've been around
Anthony every now and then, but this Mrs. Coldwater is
likely to have them all poopin' in their pants."

"So, are you the Beamer from Springfield, or the one
with the fondness for bingo?"

She made it to her feet, took a step, and collapsed. It
might have held more dramatic effect had she not gone
facedown in a muddy bed of asparagus.

14

Judith, Bonita, and I stared, mesmerized by this unanticipated belly flop. If we'd been required to hold up scorecards, I would have given Naomi at least a six for style. Maybe a six-point-four.

Bonita came to the end of the picnic table. "Is she all right?"

"Shouldn't we do something?" said Judith. "It looks uncomfortable."

"Feel free," I said. "She's your loony sister, after all. Maybe Rachael or Sarah can toss the robe in the machine at the laundromat tomorrow. So she's from Springfield?"

"I don't know."

"Get off it," I said, going over to the supine figure to make sure she wasn't snuffling mud. "One of the cars behind the body shop must belong to Naomi, and another to Sarah. That leaves one for Ruth, and one for whom—Ester?"

"Ester left by bus," Judith said. "I presume she arrived that way, too. Deputy Robarts brought her out here, and when she said she wanted to leave, he came and picked up her suitcase while she waited at the PD. She told him she'd break down if she had to say goodbye to her children."

"That leaves Deborah, unless there are other Beamers you haven't mentioned." I nudged Naomi with my foot. "She's starting to come to her senses. One of you needs to help me haul her up—and stop gawking like she fell into a pile of hog manure."

Judith began to pick at a blister on her thumb. "We use organic fertilizer. Anthony buys it for us from a chicken producer in Azure. We have more than a dozen mouths to feed, you know, and the soil here is thin. We need to put up a lot of vegetables to get through the winter months."

"Chicken shit," said Bonita, her nostrils flaring. "You're saying she plopped in chicken shit. She's your suspect, Chief Hanks."

I doubted that I could pull rank on her with any success. "Supreme Court justices wade through shit every day. Consider this practice."

Judith stared at me. "Supreme Court justices? Do you think I'm Sandra Day O'Connor in disguise?"

"I wish I knew just who you were," I said irritably. "Naomi's a fellow Beamer."

"She'll get up when she's ready," Judith said, crossing her arms. "Is Mrs. Coldwater intending to take away the children?"

"Ruth's children can't stay here, and neither can Ester's. They'll have to go to a shelter until legal guardians can be located."

"This is all they have right now. They've had upheavals in their lives, and a strange environment will only traumatize them all the more. Can't you let them stay here for another day or two so I can talk to them?"

"If I could trust you," I said, "I could delay the paperwork. As things stand, we don't even know their names. We may have to take all the children until we can sort them out."

"All of them?"

"I warned you this might happen," I said without sympathy. "You, Naomi, Sarah, and Rachael may wallow in the chicken shit to your hearts' content. The children will be returned to civilization, where they will thrive on sitcoms and hot dogs until the DFS sorts through all this."

"You have no right to take away my children," protested Naomi as she sat up. She flicked a brownish clump off her nose and glared at me.

"I have every right to take them into protective custody," I said, unsure if I did but damn sure Mrs. Coldwater didn't. "You are potential suspects in a murder investigation. You've refused to provide me with your names and background information. I don't know what's going on here, but it smells like—like chicken shit!"

"My goodness, Arly," said the purported Mrs. Coldwater as she came up the path. "I never thought I'd live to see the day when you was carrying on like that."

"What did you learn?" I asked her, pulling her aside before she ventured into telltale familial territory. "Have you documented the children?"

"Not hardly. The little ones were right friendly, but those older ones were too terrified to speak to me, even when I invited them to the dock for a pizza party this evening. You'd have thought they'd been threatened with rubber hoses and thumbscrews if they so much as opened their mouths. I couldn't get a first name out of any of them."

Anthony came stumbling around the corner of the cabin. "I just had a call on my cellphone from Les. He's got Duluth Buchanon back in custody. He wants to know what he should do."

"Tell him to handcuff Duluth to the bunk," I said. I turned to Judith and Naomi. "I'll allow the children to stay tonight, but Corporal Robarts is going to remain here to make sure you don't attempt to leave."

"That's not fair," he said, pouting. "I was here all afternoon. Can't Bonita take the next shift?"

"No, she can't. Once everyone's asleep, you can sit in your car, but keep the windows down and try not to snore."

"But Duluth's in custody. Can't I at least go back to town and have a decent meal?"

I was quite the center of attention as I debated his request. Bonita clearly wanted him to dine on grubs and toadstools. Ruby Bee, who would be serving pie and refilling iced tea glasses at her own funeral, was likely to invite him to the lodge for pizza. Judith and Naomi would have preferred that we leave once and for all.

To everyone's surprise, I said, "Okay, Corporal Robarts, follow me in your car. I'll drop Bonita and Mrs. Coldwater at the PD and then we can go to your house. Your mother invited me for supper. I'd pick up a bottle of wine if I could, but it's Sunday."

"Sunday in Dunkicker," said Judith. "What could be finer?"

I didn't have the nerve to ask her what she meant.

✻

Raz left Marjorie in the front seat of the truck and made his way through the woods and under a barbed-wire fence to the back of Perkins's pond. He squatted and remained motionless, jest as he always did when revenooers was creeping around Cotter's Ridge. Bugs was drifting over the scummy green water and grasshoppers was whirrin' in the tall weeds. And, as luck would have it, Perkins's mule was chomping away near the fence.

"Mulie, mulie, mulie," crooned Raz, whose grandpappy had been a renowned mule charmer back in the days of the Great Depression. "Look what I got for you. Come on, mulie, mulie, mulie. It's real good, nigh onto two hundred proof of the county's finest white lightning."

The mule's ears quivered.

Raz made sure Perkins hadn't come out to the porch, then crept closer and took the lid off the jar. "You just mosey down this way and I'll give you a li'l taste to wet your whistle."

The mule moved away, its eyes wary.

Raz took a mouthful of 'shine and smacked his lips. "Reckon you don't know what yer missin, mulie. It's pure as mother's milk and jest as sweet. I'll bet that sumbitch Perkins makes you drink pond water. This here stuff's so clear you can see right through it and it sure as hell don't stink of dead fish. No sirree, this is good."

The one thing you shouldn't do to a mule is rush him, Grandpappy had always said. You had to take your time and give him a chance to get used to your voice, to figger out if you was friend or foe. Raz took another swallow, then put the lid back on and slithered under the fence.

Sooner or later, he thought, that ol' mule was goin'ta amble over and stick his snout in the jar. When the time came, Raz was plannin' to have a pair of wire cutters pokin' out of his back pocket.

✖

Corporal Robarts, Ruby Bee, Bonita, and I went into the PD. Les, who'd found something to amuse himself, crammed the magazine back into the bottom drawer of Chief Panknine's desk and stood up.

"I caught the suspect trying to break into the hardware store down the street," he said.

"Very good," I murmured. "I need you to take Bonita back to the motel and Ruby Bee out to the lodge."

"Mrs. Coldwater's staying at the lodge?" said Corporal Robarts. "That seems kinda strange."

"Stranger than fiction," I agreed.

Bonita sat down. "There's nothing wrong with me."

Ruby Bee clucked under her breath. "You might ought to take a look at yourself in a mirror. If you'd been brawlin' at the bar, I'd have to think you were on the losing side. Why doncha come along to the lodge and have a nice hot piece of pizza? Afterward, you can sit on the porch with Estelle and me and tell us all about yourself. A nice girl like you shouldn't be sporting a black eye and a fat lip. Now Arly here—"

"Enough," I said. "Maybe you should go with her, Bonita. When I get there, I can bring you back to the motel. You may be feeling okay at the moment, but you'll be needing another pain pill before too long."

Reverting to his John Wayne mode, Corporal Robarts slapped his weapon. "I'll stay here to guard the prisoner."

"You'll stay in this room while I talk to him," I said. "Go on, Les. You deserve pizza, too."

"And a bowl of cherry cobbler," said Ruby Bee, the siren of Stump County.

I waited until they left, then turned to Corporal Robarts. "As soon as I've had a few words with Duluth, we'll go have supper at your house."

"Shouldn't I call my mother and tell her we're coming?"

"You can call and tell her you've decided to shave your head and dance by the light of the moon. I'll be back in a few minutes."

I went down the hallway and stopped in front of the cell. Duluth sat on the edge of the bunk, glowering. His complexion was less greenish than it had been earlier, and his eyes were more yellow than red, which I assumed was a sign of recovery in the Buchanon clan.

"So, another alien visitor?" I said.

"I oughta be selling my story to one of those cable shows, but I'd just as soon go home and forget about it. Fer chrissake, Arly, all I did was get drunk. Even Sheriff Dorfer turns me loose after twelve hours."

I realized I hadn't told him what had happened the previous day. "Norella was found dead. It's pretty hard to ignore the fact that you came here looking for her."

"Dead? You sure?"

"Somebody went after her with a bat. Her body was left in a creek behind the softball field."

"What about my boys?"

"They're fine," I said, hoping they were. Judith and Naomi were far from Mary Poppins material, but I could not imagine either of them harming a child. "Why should I believe you never went to Camp Pearly Gates yesterday afternoon?"

"'Cause I didn't, dammit! I already told you that I sat in my truck and got drunk. If you'd known Norella, you'd understand. You ever run across a rabid dog, foaming at the mouth and jerking ever' which way? Norella could get like that, 'specially when she was high on meth. I'd take the boys to her ma's house, then go to the Dew Drop to shoot some pool till I figured it was safe to go home."

I did my best to look sympathetic. "Must have been tough, Duluth. Let's talk about the call Norella made to her mother. A few days ago, you said?"

"That's when I heard about it. Do you think you can take off this damn cuff? I don't fancy pissing in my pants, but I'm gonna have no choice afore too long."

"You'll have to take your best shot at the sink. What exactly did Norella say to her mother?"

He made it clear I wasn't winning him over with my winsome smile. "Aw, hell, I don't know. She said she knew where to get enough money so's she could leave with the boys."

"Get money from where?"

"You wanna talk to Norella's mother, you call her. Any chance of getting a six-pack?"

"You drove over the River Styx on your way here," I said. "Live with it."

He was grousing as I went back into the office. Corporal Robarts looked no more genial than the prisoner, but I presumed he wasn't worried about wetting his pants.

"Is your mother expecting us?" I asked.

"Yeah, she's pleased as punch. You planning to scrape the shit off your shoes before we go?"

He was a boy whom only his mother could love. "What a charming idea," I gushed. "Willetta and I had a most intriguing conversation over fried chicken earlier today. She thinks you need a firm hand."

His face turned pink. "She didn't start on that, did she?"

"On what?" I asked. When he was unable to respond, I said, "Let's go, shall we?"

We took separate vehicles to his house. Willetta was in the foyer, her hands intertwined as if she'd been offering a prayer.

"How lovely of you to join us, Arly," she said. "Don't you agree, Anthony?"

"Yeah, right." He stomped upstairs; moments later, a door slammed.

"Anthony is so sensitive," she said as she took me to the dining room. "He was inconsolable when his puppy died last year."

She did not seem to realize the incongruity of her remark. I smiled and sat midway down the table. Beaming at me, she prattled on as though we were discussing brands of potting soil or the price of begonias. "May I assume you've solved this grisly crime? Dunkicker has always been a quiet little community. We've never had any violence of this sort."

"I wanted to ask you about Ester," I said.

"Ester?" she echoed.

"She cleaned for you, right?"

"Yes, but she was unsatisfactory. It's my understanding that she's gone. Ruth was the name of the woman who was killed yesterday. Why would you ask about Ester?"

"Why was she unsatisfactory?"

Willetta poured a glass of iced tea and put it by me. "Ester was a nice enough girl, reasonably attractive, soft-spoken, and really quite pleasant in her own way, but . . ."

Anthony came into the dining room and sat down. "Just

tell her, Mother. It's not like she's gonna sue you for bad-mouthin' her."

Willetta winced. "I offered Ester the opportunity to clean and cook, despite her lack of domestic skills. Within a week I began to notice things missing. At first, it was nothing more than change from my handbag or a trinket from my jewelry box. I tried to sit down with her, but she was defiant and angry. Then, well, sadly, the telephone bill came. Ester had made several long-distance calls that were charged to our account."

"Who did she call?" I asked.

"She'd made half a dozen calls to a number in Florida," Anthony said as he chomped down on a drumstick. "When we confronted her, she broke down and admitted it. She wouldn't say why, though, so Mother had no choice but to fire her. I guess I should have saved the bill but I thought the matter was resolved."

"Did you report this to Deborah?" I asked.

Willetta shook her head. "I didn't want to further embarrass the girl. We didn't know anything about her background, so maybe this was an habitual thing, like shoplifting or kleptomania. I even gave her a week's salary as severance pay, although I would have been well within my rights to demand that she make reparations. I still feel bad about it. If I could have helped her, I would have. She was very unhappy."

"But she decided to forsake her commitment to the Daughters of the Moon and abandon her children?"

Anthony stared at me over the remains of the gnawed drumstick. "Three days later she asked me to take her to the bus station in Starley City. She cried all the way and said she'd send for her children when she could afford it. What was I supposed to do—tell her to walk?"

"Did you go into the bus station with her?"

"She told me to drop her off out front. I was wearing my uniform, so I guess she didn't want to be seen with me. She said she had enough money for a ticket. I took her suitcase out of the trunk and set it on the sidewalk, then drove off."

"Well, she didn't exactly blend in, even with a scarf around her head," I said. "I'll have the sheriff send a deputy there tomorrow to see if anyone remembers which bus she took. We ought to be able to trace her all the way to Florida, if that's where she went."

"Why bother?" he asked, grabbing another piece of chicken. "She's probably found a job and is saving up to arrange for her children to join her. She was convinced that she could do it in a few weeks."

"I'd like to know if she has any idea who might have been stalking Ruth."

"Stalking Ruth?" said Willetta. "Don't you have her ex-husband in custody? Shouldn't you be starting with him?"

"He's the most likely," I admitted, "but he keeps swearing he never went out to Camp Pearly Gates. Ruth said that she was going to look for her son just as the storm hit, but I don't see how her ex-husband would have known this. It seems more likely that she had arranged to . . ."

"Meet somebody?" suggested Willetta.

"Yes," I said, "and I can almost put a name to it. This has been lovely, but I need to go now."

She put down her glass. "Now, Arly, I realize you're used to having free run in Maggody, but we do things differently in Dunkicker."

"Why don't you drop by the lodge and share your grievances with Mrs. Jim Bob? She seems to think I need to consult her every time I issue a speeding ticket. Corporal Robarts, stop by the café and drive Sarah back to the Beamers' site with you. You're under orders to spend the night there. I'll ask Les to stay at the PD and read a bedtime story to the prisoner. I have a feeling they'll enjoy the illustrations."

I left before either of them could sputter.

Everything seemed peaceful at the lodge. Les had removed the visible vestiges of his profession and was flinging a Frisbee with Parwell, Big Mac, Billy Dick, and Larry Joe. The girls had flopped over to maximize tanning. Bonita had taken off her shoes and socks and was wading along the edge of the lake; I could see from her expression that she shared Darla Jean's theory about perfidious minnows.

On one end of the porch, Mrs. Jim Bob appeared to be dozing, although it may have been a ruse. Brother Verber sat on the opposite end, an open Bible in his lap and a notebook nearby in case he stumbled across inspiration.

I gestured at Larry Joe to join me. "Where's Jarvis?" I asked him.

"He went ballistic when Big Mac splashed him. I sent him to the cabin to put on dry clothes and cool off. Yeah, I know you said to keep 'em together, but Jarvis can take care of himself. Wish I could say the same about Big Mac. One of these days that boy's gonna smart off to a gorilla on a Harley and end up walking bow-legged the rest of his life."

"I'm going to talk to Jarvis," I said. "Don't let anyone else go to the cabin."

I walked down the path and along the shore of the lake until I found the cabin. Jarvis was perched on a picnic table out front, throwing bits of gravel into the water.

I sat down beside him. "There's something I have to ask you."

"About Norella?"

"How'd you find out?"

"Mrs. Jim Bob started bawling out Brother Verber, then he got all pathetic about how he was forced to go to the morgue in Little Rock to identify her body. A couple of the girls had gone into the lodge and were scared to go back out to the porch, so they heard it all."

"Norella taught your Sunday school class, didn't she?"

"For a couple of months. She thought she could impress us by talking about Sodom and Gomorrah, Jezebel, Job, biblical stories like that. Kind of pathetic, if you ask me, but more entertaining than Elsie McMay. She thought we should be able to detect secret recipes in the New Testament if we'd put our minds to it."

"This isn't time for jokes. Did you see Norella outside of church?"

Jarvis gave me a smirky smile. "You mean, did I drop by her house when Duluth was gone and the boys were napping? Yeah, Chief Hanks, I did. Four or five times, I mowed her yard. Once she'd cleaned out closets and wanted me to take some boxes of old clothes over to the church for the next rummage sale. Billy Dick came along on account of having his pa's pickup. Another time I pruned her apple trees and hauled off the branches. Norella was okay, kinda crude at times."

"Then you and she weren't . . .?"

"Hell, no. I've been dating my second cousin's best friend over in Emmett for more than a year. The only reason I did those things for Norella was that she paid me good money. Sometimes she wanted to talk, so we'd sit on the porch steps and drink lemonade while she told me what a jerk her husband was. I wasn't sure I believed half of it. Duluth always seemed like a good ol' boy. He came over last fall and helped me put a new roof on the house. He didn't charge anything, and I suspected the shingles he brought were from another job. I didn't ask. Things have been tight lately. My pa wasn't laid off. He's earning fifteen cents an hour in the laundry at the prison and my ma needs treatment at the hospital every few days. Folks like us don't have health insurance."

"So why did Norella call you a few days ago?" I asked.

"Who said she called me?"

"For starters, I did," I pointed out flatly. "I don't know why else you would have gone to the softball field to meet with her yesterday afternoon."

"I already told you I went to look for my wallet."

"And maybe I should have told you that I didn't just get off the turnip truck. Mr. Lambertino didn't buy your story, and neither did I. You could be in serious trouble, Jarvis. Norella's body was found an hour after you came back here."

"Yeah, Darla Jean told us. You sure it wasn't a Klingon?"

I wanted to shake him, but managed to control myself—for the moment, anyway. "Just tell me the truth. I know it's hard to believe, but I'm on your side."

"Even if I killed her?"

I resisted the urge to scoot down to the far end of the table. He was several inches taller and a good twenty pounds heavier. Then again, I'd had five sessions of self-defense at the academy and could fend off a chipmunk and perhaps a squirrel. "Did you?"

"No, 'course I didn't. Why would I? She was just some broad that was bored with her life and liked to cry on my shoulder from time to time. Long as she paid me twenty bucks to mow her yard or clean out the gutters, it was fine with me."

"Was that why she called you—to cry on your shoulder once again?"

Jarvis stared out at the lake. "She needed money. She'd heard that the teenagers from Maggody were coming, and guessed I'd be in the group. I told her I could loan her fifty dollars. She wasn't real happy, but said she'd take it so she could get out of here, and once she did, she'd be able to pay me back and cover my ma's cancer treatments. I knew that was hogwash and I'd never see one penny, but I told her we were scheduled to work at the softball field. She was supposed to wait in the woods."

"But you couldn't slip away."

"Mr. Lambertino kept a real sharp eye on us till we packed up for the day. I went back, but I couldn't find her."

"Then you didn't go behind the field?" I asked, trying to keep my voice steady.

His head sank. "No, I just sat in the dugout, thinking she could see I was on my own. I finally decided she'd gone back to wherever she was staying. When you said a woman had been killed, I figured it was her. Maybe I could have prevented it if I'd gone looking for her, but I didn't. Reckon I should have felt more sympathy for her all along."

I considered his story. "Okay, Jarvis, I'm going to believe you for now. Tell me about her call."

"Tell you what? She called and told me what to do. I wasn't happy about it, but I said I would."

"Where did she call you from?"

"How would I know?" he said, getting jittery. He threw another piece of gravel at a chipmunk. "She just called. It was damn lucky my ma didn't answer the phone. She didn't care for Norella or any of her kinfolk." He made a noise under his breath. "Like we should have been settin' a place at the table for the governor."

"Think, Jarvis," I persisted. "Did you hear anything in the background?"

He sat for a moment. "Yeah, voices, country music of a sort. Norella was whispering most of the time, like she was afraid somebody'd overhear her. We didn't talk for long, and all I said was that I'd do what I could."

"Did you know she'd left town with her children?"

"I may have heard something," he said, "but it weren't none of my business. Shouldn't we be heading back to the lodge?"

"You go on," I said distractedly. "I need to think things over. I'll catch up in a few minutes."

"What if Mr. Lambertino decides I've attacked you, too?"

I sighed. "Tell him to put on tights and a cape, and come bounding to my rescue. It's not going to help, but it might improve my spirits."

He hesitated. "I feel real bad about Norella."

"I know you do, Jarvis. She had no business involving you in this."

"In this what?"

"I wish I knew," I said. "Go on back and stay with the others. Ruby Bee's making pizza for supper."

He shot me a bitter—or perhaps bittersweet—smile, then went up the path. For a stunned second, I thought I heard him whistling, then realized it was nothing more than a boat across the lake.

15

Hammet was beginning to think he'd made one of those "sinful decisions" he kept hearing about in Sunday school every damn week. Some sinful decisions were like drinking water from the creek or stealing candy. Either way, there'd be hell to pay.

Crammed as he was on the floor behind the sofa, tired of Jim Bob's grumblin', Hammet decided he was gonna hafta do something if he didn't want to end up crippled. Jim Bob hadn't so much as gone to pee in over an hour, and seemed real intent on watching some stupid movie with folks gropin' each other and moanin' like their bellies was aching.

He'd watched for awhiles, thinking maybe monsters might come clawin' out, but the folks jest kept right on grabbin' each other and panting. He was about to do something desperate when Sonya and Tonya came clattering through the kitchen.

"Mister Mayor," they trilled in unison.

Jim Bob's beer splashed on the carpet under the coffee table. "I didn't think you two was comin' back," he said.

"Now why wouldn't we come back?" cooed one of them. "Husky man like you, with all kinds of stamina to take care of girls like us?"

"You want something to drink?"

"A little splash of bourbon might be nice," said one of them, plunking herself down next to him. "You been working all day?"

"Well, yeah," said Jim Bob, sounding as if he had no idea what he'd been doing. "Why doncha make yourselves comfortable while I get a bottle and some glasses? This here movie's been givin' me all kinds of ideas." He came darn close to whimpering, but managed to stop himself. "I reckon you girls have seen movies like this before."

"We didn't come all this way to watch a movie," purred Sonya, or Tonya. "We came to make one, starring you. Later, we'll snuggle down and watch it right here."

"Make a movie?" Jim Bob said uneasily. "Like tape it?"

"Now you just go get that bottle of bourbon and sit right here. We'll all three relax and enjoy what's on the screen. Later, if you want, we can go upstairs and have some fun—or Tonya and I can leave. It's up to you, Mister Mayor."

✳

I sat down on the grass at the lake's edge and waited until Bonita joined me. "Let's go back to Dunkicker," I said. "I'd like to know if the department's heard back about the license plates."

"You planning to dump me in the motel room?"

"If I thought you'd stay put."

"Don't count on it," she said dryly. "My ass is the only part of me that doesn't ache, and I'm not about to rest on it. What'd you say to that boy? When he came back, he looked like he was ready to cry."

"I'll tell you on the way back to town." While she put on her socks and shoes, I stood up and gestured at Les, who took a final fling of the Frisbee and came across the road.

"You're going to have to spend the night at the PD," I told him. "Corporal Robarts has gone back to the Beamers' campsite, and Bonita's going to crash before too long. Need to swing by the motel and pick up your teddy bear?"

"I knew I'd forgotten something," he said. "Any chance

I can grab a meal at the café before I settle in for the night?"

Voices and country music. "You go on to the PD. I'll get something for you and Duluth, presuming he hasn't been liberated by aliens again."

"So who do you think's been letting him loose? I can't see Brother Verber unlocking the cell in the first place, and, from what you said, nobody should have been there while you were having Sunday dinner with Mrs. Robarts."

I sank back down on the grass. "From what Duluth said, it must have been a Beamer. It doesn't make any sense, though. Why would any of them do him a favor?"

"To keep him from being questioned?" suggested Bonita as she sat down beside me.

"But why?"

"Until you talked to him, you thought he was the obvious suspect," she countered in a complacent voice that would serve her well after she'd joined the bar, or even bellied up to one. "Once he gave you his boogerwoods story about being drunk, you started having doubts. Maybe the Beamers would just as soon let you go on assuming he went crazy and killed Norella. If he'd been found facedown in a pond, the whole thing would have been written off as another abusive man going after his ex-wife."

Les stared at her. "Are you saying that one of the Beamers killed her? You prepared to pick one?"

"Well," she said, giving it serious consideration, "Judith and Naomi were at the campsite. I don't know about Rachael and Sarah, but they could have been there, too."

"Rachael was working at the café," I said. "I think I would have noticed if she'd been soaking wet when I came looking for Corporal Robarts. Sarah seems to finish up by the middle of the afternoon, though. I suppose it could have been one of them."

"Or Duluth," said Les.

"Or some maniac wandering around the woods." I got

to my feet. "Les, I've changed my mind. It'll be better if you stay here tonight. Everybody sleeps in the lodge again."

"What about you?"

"I'll stay at the PD to keep an eye on Duluth. Don't sleep too soundly; the kids may seem innocent, but they can be devious when their postpubescent urges kick in."

"Yeah, right." Grumbling, he went to rejoin the Frisbee game.

I told Bonita to wait and went into the lodge, managing to ignore both Mrs. Jim Bob's dark look and Brother Verber's piteous one. In the kitchen, Ruby Bee was regaling Estelle with her adventures as Mrs. Coldwater, implying that she'd alphabetized the children by name and packed them all off to some sort of mysterious shelter where they would be saved from brutal hardship and the influences of bald-headed women with smart mouths.

As reluctant as I was to interrupt a truly fanciful narrative, I said, "Bonita and I are leaving. I'll be back in the morning. Les is going to stay here."

"Then you don't think it's safe?" demanded Estelle, getting so agitated her beehive hair wobbled and several bobby pins clattered on the floor. "We still could be murdered in our beds? Mercy me, Arly! I didn't like the looks of this place since we first laid eyes on it, but I never in all my born days thought—"

"Feel free to sleep in the living room with ten teenagers, Les, Larry Joe, and Mrs. Jim Bob. Sleep with Brother Verber if you prefer, or out on the dock so you can enjoy the moonlight."

Ruby Bee caught my arm. "And just where are you planning to sleep?"

"I'll be at the PD. Les has the telephone number if you need me." I snatched up two squares of hot pizza and left before she could pepper (or even pepperoni) me with more questions, most of which I couldn't answer.

Bonita was in the station wagon. This time not even Jarvis looked up as we drove away. I tried to count up how many times I'd driven from the Camp Pearly Gates lodge to Dunkicker and back again since our arrival. The gas gauge indicated I could not continue to do so too many more times, but I had no cash to speak of.

"Do you have a county credit card?" I asked as I braked for a rabbit.

"What do you think?" muttered Bonita, sounding as though her stitches and bruises were catching up with her. "You want the rest of the pizza?"

"Toss it out the window. Do you want to lie down on the backseat?"

"And vomit? I don't think so, Chief Hanks."

"I told you to call me Arly."

"When we were interrogating the Beamers. You've made it real clear who's in charge." She leaned her head against the back of the seat and closed her eyes.

As we went into the PD, I heard clattering and curses from the hallway in back. "Call the sheriff's office about the license plates," I said to Bonita, then went to see what was happening. Duluth's cell door was open, but he was having a hard time dragging out the iron bunk. "What do you think you're doing?" I said, exasperated. "Should I add attempted theft to the charges? Get back in there! I don't even want to talk about it."

"This looks like the kind of town that could rally a lynch mob. I ain't about to—"

"Just shut up." I waited until he was back inside the cell, slammed the door, and locked it. "I'll keep the keys with me. If you're sitting there quietly when I get back, you can have something to eat. If you're not, I'm going to deputize Crank Nickle and issue him a license to kill. You want to end up as catfish food, Duluth?"

Tears filled his eyes. "I wanna go home."

Bonita was on the phone when I returned to the office. She glanced up, nodded, and resumed scribbling in her notebook. Although I was dying to peer over her shoulder at her notes, I started a fresh pot of coffee and kept a civil distance until she hung up.

"Got it?" I asked.

"All four of them, but I can't see how it's going to do much good. One of the cars was registered to Norella Buchanon. The other three are just names and addresses. Some guy in Cave Springs, another in Muskogee, Oklahoma, and a woman in Springfield, Missouri. You want me to try to send deputies to question whoever might be home?"

"Do your best," I said. "I'm going to take a look at the cars, then stop by the café and get Duluth something to eat."

"You don't think I could read license plates?"

"Bonita," I said warningly, "don't make me hold you down and cram half a dozen pain pills in your mouth. I worked for a vet one summer, and I know how to coerce unwilling patients into taking medicine."

She picked up the receiver.

I drove to the body shop. The building itself was dark, as was to be expected, but I was surprised when my headlights shone on a ten-foot chainlink fence that prevented me from continuing around back. I parked and got out, glumly noted the padlock on the gate, and then walked along the perimeter, avoiding foul-smelling batteries, rusty cans, and other obscure automotive debris. A utility pole cast enough light for me to see the four pertinent cars parked along the back of the building. Examining them more closely was a problem, however.

I'd about given up when I saw a pile of splintered wooden crates. I rattled the fence to make sure guard dogs were not on the prowl, then clambered up the boxes and grabbed the top of the fence, trying to recall when I'd last had a tetanus shot.

I was dripping with sweat when I at last scrambled over the fence and dropped to the ground. Dogs within a mile radius were barking, but the only sound in my proximity was the scurrying of rodents that had been interrupted while gnawing upholstery.

One of the cars was the white Honda Accord that Sarah had acknowledged; in the dim light it was more of a dingy gray. The plate was from Oklahoma. The one from Missouri was a red Camaro with a headlight affixed with duct tape. I'd never asked Duluth about Norella's car, so I had no idea which of the remaining two was hers. One was the sort of behemoth that Elsie McMay drove, the other a subcompact that did not seem large enough to be allowed on a highway.

Being a professional and all, I ascertained that the windows were rolled up and the doors locked. I was trying to see what might have been left on the seat of the behemoth when I noticed a pungent smell. I squatted down and peered under the car, assuming that some vital fluid had leaked out of the engine.

Darkness was a factor. I stood up, took a last look inside the car, and had turned to examine the subcompact when I heard a blood-chilling sound along the lines of a shotgun being cocked.

"What the hell you think yer doin'?" said a voice from outside the fence.

I finally located the figure on the far side of the gate. "Conducting police business. Does your mama know you go prowling with a shotgun, Crank?"

"I ain't prowlin'. Lester pays me ten dollars a week to make sure the local boys don't come scroungin' for parts for their trucks. Preacher Skinbalder pays me the same to walk around the church and watch for broken windows. Not more than a month ago, the little assholes made off with three televisions and a VCR. Miz Rutledge says she's gonna hire me if her watermelons start disappearing like they did the last two summers." He poked the barrel through a gap in the fence. "How do I know you ain't lookin' for an exhaust pipe."

"I don't smoke," I said curtly. "Do you have a key to the gate?"

"Ain't locked." He dragged it open and motioned at me to come out. "If you're a cop, where's your badge?"

"At home in a drawer. You saw me earlier at the PD, for pity's sake."

He lowered the shotgun. "Mebbe I did, but that don't mean you shouldn't pay a fine for trespassin', same as ever'-body else. I'll let you go this time for five dollars, but it'll be ten if I catch you again."

"Quite a little racket you have going," I said. "I hope you're not behind the thefts. You wouldn't have three televisions and a VCR in your barn, would you? Was that why you were so upset when you caught Duluth in there?"

"If you know what's good for you, you'll be about your business."

I make it a policy never to argue with those packing shotguns, rifles, handguns, crossbows, or even spatulas. I got into the station wagon and drove out of the lot before he decided for reasons of his own to blast out the rear windshield. Estelle would not take it well, and Harve most likely wouldn't pay for it.

The café was brightly lit, but the parking lot was again uncrowded. Hoping that Chief Panknine had a charge account, I went in and sat down on a stool. The threesome in the corner might have been the ones I'd seen the day before, or Sunday pinch-hitters. Two teenaged boys eyed me, scattered change on the tabletop, and left. I did not warn them that Crank Nickle, aka 005, was on patrol.

Rachael came out of the kitchen. "I heard it was Ruth who was killed," she said in a low voice. "We were damn scared when Anthony came out to tell us what happened. It could have been any of us."

"Any of you?" I said curiously. "The popular theory is that Ruth's ex-husband killed her. Why would he have hurt someone else?"

She turned around to pour a cup of coffee, then set it down in front of me. "I didn't mean him. It's just that we're women and children living in isolated cabins in the woods. The lodge was safer because we could lock the doors at night, but the cabins are wide open. Three days ago I took the afternoon off and went for a picnic with my kids down by the lake. It was getting dark before I could convince them to get out of the water and put on their shoes. I still get nervous sometimes."

"Shouldn't you find moonlight comforting?"

"I don't think moonlight's going to help much if some psycho comes charging out of the bushes with a baseball bat. We're used to drunks driving by, hollering and tossing beer cans all over the road."

"When you and your children were at the lake, did you notice anybody else?"

She thought for a moment. "A couple of geezers in a boat. They didn't look like they were having much luck. Then again, how would I recognize luck? I keep hoping someone's going to leave me a lottery ticket for a tip, and all of a sudden I'll have fifty million dollars in the bank. At the moment, I have twelve dollars in my pocket, and Judith will take most of it for bread and milk."

"So Judith's in charge," I said as I took a sip of coffee. "I thought Deborah was."

Rachael began to fiddle with the metal napkin holder. "We're not supposed to talk about her. I can't tell you how to get in touch with her because I don't know. There's no point in asking me any more questions. Ruth's dead and there's not a thing I can tell you!" She clamped down her lip until she regained her composure, then said, "You want to take a burger to the prisoner?"

"You may have twelve dollars," I said in an effort to regain whatever smidgen of trust I'd begun to establish, "but I don't even have twelve cents. Maybe Corporal Robarts has access to a petty cash box."

"Forget about it. The cook's gone on home, so I'll have to fix it. Wait here."

I wasn't tempted to join those in the corner booth for a debate about dawgs and hawgs. I wandered over to the jukebox and ran my finger down the glass, noticing the selections were disturbingly similar to those found on the jukebox at Ruby Bee's Bar & Grill. A cardboard sign thumbtacked to the wall directed me to the restrooms in a short corridor next to the end of the counter. I took advantage of the opportunity to use the facilities, wash my hands, and inspect my face in a mottled mirror. I was operating on very little sleep, I reminded myself as I splashed water on my puffy eyes, and I wasn't going to make amends in a chair at the PD.

I was back on a stool when Rachael emerged from the kitchen. She put down a brown bag and said, "Anything else?"

Before I could answer, the pay phone rang. "Hold on," she said, then went around the corner and picked up the receiver. After a terse conversation, she came back. "Merle, that was your daughter. She said if you don't get home in fifteen minutes, she's gonna bury your *Penthouse* magazines in the compost pile. She might just do it this time."

Merle shuffled to his feet, nodded at us, and hurried outside. After a minute, his compatriots followed.

Rachael sighed. "I'm ready to lock up. Francine's used to cleaning up that particular booth when she comes in every morning. She's welcome to the fifteen-cent tip they leave."

"I'll drive you to the campsite," I said.

"You don't have to do that. I can walk, you know. I do it all the time, even when it's cold and wet."

"But you don't have any reason to this evening. We'll have to swing by the PD to drop off the burger on the way." When she hesitated, I said, "I promise I won't ask you anything more about Deborah, okay?"

"Yeah, okay." She took my coffee cup into the kitchen, turned off all the lights, and waited until I was outside to lock the door. "I didn't mean to sound rude. I guess I'm jumpy because of Ruth. I hope that ex-husband of hers spends the rest of his life in prison."

I parked at the PD and asked her to wait. Bonita was nodding off, her face looking more and more as though she'd been hit by a freight train. Duluth, she told me, had been bellowing about how his civil rights were being violated, then calmed down. I gave her the bag and reminded her that Les had the key to the handcuffs and I had the key to the cell, so there wasn't a damn thing she could do even if a delegation from Amnesty International came through the door.

"I'm going to run Rachael out to their cabins and make sure Anthony is there. As soon as I get back, you're headed for the torturous confines of Woantell Motel. You can write your own letter to Amnesty International in the morning."

Rachael had pulled off her sandals and was massaging her feet as I got back into the car. "You'd think I'd be used to it by now," she said with a self-deprecatory laugh. "I was a third-grade teacher for fourteen years, so I spent a lot of the day standing in front of a blackboard."

"And now you're a waitress."

"I considered joining the army, but I don't look good in khaki."

I did not mention that her present appearance wasn't all that alluring. "I promised that we wouldn't talk about Deborah, but I'm a little bit puzzled about some of Ruth's actions. Are you going to fling yourself out of the car if I ask you?"

"There's not much I can tell you. Ruth was a bitch. Maybe it wasn't her fault, but it wasn't ours, either, and we're the ones who had to put up with her. That's why I didn't say anything when . . ."

"When she made a couple of telephone calls from the café?"

"Making calls was against the rules. We knew it before we ever arrived here. Sure, I've been tempted to call my mother and let her know we're safe."

"Safe from what?"

"The big bad world. We have adequate shelter and meals. The children are keeping up with their schoolwork. Before I started at the café, I sat down with Naomi and we individualized lesson plans for every child. I thought you wanted to know about Ruth."

"So she broke the rule?"

"Tuesday or Wednesday, I think. She came by late in the afternoon, asked for iced tea, then ducked around the corner. Guess she thought I wouldn't notice—or if I did, I wouldn't say anything to Judith."

I knew the answer, but I asked anyway. "Who'd she call?"

"Her mother, for one. About all she said was that she was all right and would be leaving shortly. Then she called somebody else and asked him to bring her some cash. It couldn't have been her ex-husband, could it? He'd be the last person she'd call."

"You didn't hear any details?"

"No, Merle put a quarter in the jukebox, then Anthony came out of the men's room and said the toilet was backed up again, and Francine started screaming because she saw a mouse run behind the refrigerator. One of these days she's going to set out the garbage and have a heart attack when she sees rats the size of raccoons."

"Did you know that Ester made long-distance calls while she was working for Willetta Robarts?"

She looked down at the floorboard. "A while back, whenever, Anthony came by the café and offered me a ride home. He told me Ester'd called a number in Florida several times, and he wanted to know if she'd said anything to me about having friends down there. I said that Ester and I never talked about anything personal, but he might do better if he asked Ruth. I also pointed out that all he had to do was call his long-distance carrier and dispute the bill."

"Refuse to pay it, you mean?"

"No," she said as if speaking to a third-grader destined for social promotion, "simply demand to know who was called. My ex-husband used to do that with every long-distance call I made. It took him years to learn that my brother lives in Boise and my roommate from college in Memphis. He even had trouble with the weekly calls to his own mother. He may able to raise bail, but he's never going to raise his IQ."

"Do you think she might have gone to Florida?"

"As far as I'm concerned, she went to hell in a handbasket."

We drove in silence the rest of the way. I parked behind Corporal Robarts's car and was climbing out of the station wagon when Naomi and Judith dashed up.

"Thank gawd you're here," said Naomi, gulping for breath. "Anthony's been trying to call you!"

"This is serious," added Judith.

Rachael stared at them. "Did someone else get killed?"

Naomi collapsed in the mud and began to sob. Judith put a steadying hand on her shoulder and said, "No one's been killed. It's just that, well, that Naomi's children have disappeared."

16

Corporal Robarts appeared from between the cabins. He wasn't panting, but his shirt was sticking to his body and his deodorant was less than effective at fifteen feet. At three feet, I wanted to cover my nose and mouth, but, as Ruby Bee was fond of reminding me, I wasn't raised in a barn. I didn't know anybody who had been, for that matter.

"Glad you're finally here, Chief Hanks," he said between gasps. "I called the PD and Bonita said you were on your way. I just came back from the lodge. Les is gonna check along the road that leads to the lake, and some teacher fellow agreed to search the cabins where your group's been staying. You think I ought to call Sheriff Dorfer? I got my cellphone right here. We might could call the state police as well."

"Let's calm down. Naomi, pull yourself together and tell me how old your children are and how long they've been gone."

She dried her face on her sleeve, leaving a smear the color of dried blood. "Adam's eight and Lizzie is five, and I don't know for sure how long. After Mrs. Coldwater left, I dismissed all of them until suppertime. Judith's girls agreed to watch the little ones in the schoolhouse."

"What about Damon?" demanded Rachael. "Is he at the schoolhouse, too?"

"He's in the children's cabin, reading, as are the rest of them. My children are the only ones we can't find."

I looked at Judith. "You implied that the children were permitted to play in the woods."

"Usually they are, but after what happened yesterday, they were all told to stay within sight."

"We left about two hours ago," I said. "No one's seen them since then? Are you sure they're not sitting in the kitchen of the lodge, having pizza and cherry cobbler?"

Corporal Robarts jerked around. "You don't think I made sure of that? I looked in every room and closet, under beds, and in the shed out in the garden. I went down to the basement, even though the steps were covered with an inch of dust and spiderwebs were getting in my hair. I'm not stupid, you know."

Naomi collapsed into Judith's arms. "How are we gonna find them? It's so dark, and there are paths all over the place. What if they went down to the lake and—"

Judith gave her a shake. "They're safe," she said firmly. "You stay here while the rest of us fan out. Your children are old enough to realize they might be taken away by Mrs. Coldwater. The obvious explanation is that they ran away and are hiding in one of the uninhabited cabins." She shot me a dirty look. "I told you that they were fragile. If you weren't so enamored of your role as an egotistical, authoritarian—"

"Stop it!" wailed Naomi. "Just find my kids. They're liable to be terrified. I used to make them sleep in my bed. I walked them to school and waited in the playground until they were let out. One time I agreed to have them sleep over at my sister Letitia's house, but I knew they'd start crying so I went and picked them up. I thought I'd protected them by bringing them here, but now—"

The wails were getting progressively louder and downright eerie; if Brother Verber could have heard them, he would have been scurrying down the road toward the gate, a handkerchief in one hand and a bottle of sacramental wine in the other. "Take her inside before she frightens all the children," I said to Judith. "Rachael, get Sarah and stay with the other children. Corporal Robarts and I will find these other cabins. If the children aren't there, I'll call in backup."

"Not dogs!" Naomi screeched as though she was being dive-bombed by bats instead of a scattering of moths. "If they hear dogs, I don't know what they'll do. I've always taught them that dogs are filthy and dangerous. When I caught Adam and Lizzie petting a puppy in the yard, I took a belt to them. The slobber was disgusting! Who knows what kind of diseases they were exposed to?"

Judith looked past me at Rachael. "Her medication's in a plastic bag in the flour canister."

"I'll get it and meet you in the cabin."

Sarah, who'd been hovering in the shadows, stepped forward. "I'll be with the children."

Corporal Robarts looked as if he thought he ought to whip out his weapon and shoot whatever slobbery, diseased puppy strayed into view to wag its satanic tail. "Maybe I should wait here."

"Sorry," I said, "but you're more familiar with these woods than I am. Do you still have the flashlight?"

"In the car."

"Then go get it," I said with admirable patience, having spent the last several years dealing with Kevin Buchanon and his kinfolk. "We'll spend an hour searching for the children. If we don't find them, I'll have to call Harve."

"It's awful dark."

"That's pretty much the way it is after sundown."

He licked his lips. "But what if we come across, you know, something—like, you know—"

I helped him out. "Snakes? Bears? Polecats? A tribe of cannibals living in a cave?"

"I was thinking more along the lines of the person who murdered Ruth," he said.

"The flashlight," I repeated. While he was rooting through his trunk, I told Judith that it might be best for the children and adults to stay together until we returned. She nodded, then grasped Naomi and headed her toward the cabin.

Corporal Robarts and I went around the garden and started down what had once been a road. Weeds sprouted in the middle like a bad Mohawk haircut.

"What can you tell me about Naomi?" I asked.

"I haven't had much to do with her. I brought them here and introduced the other Beamers. I don't recollect her being in town since then."

"You said you brought them here. Does that mean you told her where to leave her car when she arrived in Dunkicker?"

"That's not what I said. They showed up at the PD one afternoon and said Deborah had told them that I would drive them to Camp Pearly Gates. I didn't ask any questions."

"Bonita found their cars earlier this afternoon. The sheriff's department put enough pressure on the DMV to open its files on a Sunday. Four cars, four names, and four home addresses. Sarah's the one who came from Muskogee. Norella, or Ruth, if you prefer, had a car registered in her own name. I'd bet that Naomi's from Springfield. You know who that leaves, Corporal Robarts?"

"Hold on," he said. "There's a cabin behind those trees. We'd better stay quiet."

We might not have gone undetected by cannibals, but we reached the cabin without much ado. He eased open the door and swung the beam of light around. "Kids?" he whispered. "You hiding in here?"

I took the flashlight out of his hand and went around him. A minute later, I returned. "They're not here, and it doesn't look as if anyone else has been in here for the better part of a decade. Where's the next cabin?"

"Over that way," he said, pointing. "The ones away from the lodge tend to be clustered in groups of two or three, sometimes four." He retrieved the flashlight. "You want me to show you?"

I fell into step behind him, wishing he'd slow down so I could see the path. "I think the remaining car belonged to Ester."

"Why do you think that?"

I tripped over a stump and had to grab a vine to steady myself. Catching a whiff of him was more effective than sticking my nose over a bottle of smelling salts. "Well, Judith told me that she and Rachael didn't get here by car, that Deborah made arrangements. She wouldn't elaborate, but now they're panicky. Even if we find Naomi's children and return them safely, the others are going to talk to me. A missing child is every mother's worst fear. I hope Naomi's medication, whatever it is, is industrial strength and not some herbal concoction."

"Two hours is a long time." He stopped and shined the light at yet another cabin. "You want me to look this time, or are you too high and mighty to trust a good ol' country boy like me?"

"Whatever," I said, restraining myself from suggesting he soak his head while he was at it—or even take a quick shower. Two children, aged eight and five, were somewhere in the wooded acres. Corporal Robarts's unexpected outburst of petulance wasn't helping. "I'll sit out here and wait."

He looked back at me. "You don't want to give me detailed instructions on how to search a cabin? Didn't you have a course at the police academy on proper procedure?"

"I'm sure you can handle it," I said mildly. I bit my tongue before I could add that he needed to open the stalls in the bathroom.

A minute later, he came outside. "All clear. Ready for the next one?"

"Let's rest for a minute. What I was going to say earlier was that I'm pretty sure Ester's car is parked behind the body shop. You said you took her to the bus station in Starley City, though."

He leaned against the side of the cabin. "And that's what I did. She told me she'd tried to start her car that morning, but it was dead. Lester even came out and tried to jump the battery. Mind if I smoke?"

"Why, Anthony," I said inadvertently using his given name, "I didn't realize you have secret vices. Do you keep a bottle of whiskey under your pillow?"

"Yeah, and I pilfer pennies from the collection plate on Sundays."

"Your mother must be very proud of you."

I could see his smile as he flicked a lighter and took a draw on the cigarette between his lips. "She's not, though," he said. "My father was a banker. He invested in the stock market, bought up repossessed properties, and had a couple of car dealerships. I barely got through high school. If I'd had a different last name, I never would have graduated. Hell, I'd probably still be repeating the eighth grade."

I waited until he'd finished the cigarette and ground it under his heel. "I guess we'd better keep searching. Did you think to look in the dugout at the softball field?"

"The only place I went was the lodge. I can see that they might have gone over to the field, but why would they stay in the dugout?"

"They might have seen the teenagers working on the bleachers and found it entertaining—or they might have been there later when Jarvis went to meet Norella."

"I know Norella was Ruth's real name, but who's Jarvis? Shouldn't you have brought him in for questioning if he was at the field?"

"Jarvis is one of the boys," I said. "Norella called him a few days ago and asked him to bring her enough money to get away from the Daughters of the Moon. I talked to him about it. He could have been lying through his teeth, but I couldn't discern any reason why he might have attacked Norella. He agreed to give her what he could, but if he didn't want to, all he had to do was stay away."

"Maybe they had something going. A boy's brain is located between his legs. Could she have threatened him with blackmail?"

I stood up. "Let's get going. And slow down, okay? I'm partial to my knees, skin and all."

"Sorry," he muttered. We retraced our way to the road. "I still say you should have taken this Jarvis into custody."

"Even if she had been sleeping with him back in Maggody, nobody would care. Mrs. Jim Bob might have turned sanctimonious and fanned the gossip, and Brother Verber might have rumbled from the pulpit for a few weeks. I don't know what all goes on in Dunkicker, but we've seen worse in Maggody." I stopped to brush a bug out of my face. "Did you ever find out who Ester called in Florida?"

He stopped. "I told you I threw away the bill because I didn't see why it mattered. It was probably a relative. Now that I think about it, some man called for her after she'd left for the day. A cousin, he said. I told him not to call back."

"But you didn't take Rachael's advice and contact your long-distance company?"

"I didn't care what her cousin's name was."

"Well, I do," I said as I nudged him into motion, then allowed him a few steps. "First thing tomorrow, I'll get a locksmith so we can examine the interior of Ester's car. She may have left an address book or some letters. It'll help us track her down in Florida, if that's where she went."

He wheeled around. "Why are you so obsessed with Ester? The only crime she committed was making long-distance calls from our house, and that's hardly worth bothering with. You want to look in the cabin over there?"

"You do it," I said. "I'll wait here." There was no convenient picnic bench this time, so I settled for an unpleasantly damp log. Ester had not been a happy camper, although she had come of her own free will. Could she really have fathomed what she was getting into when Deborah invited her to join the cult? The Daughters of the Moon had provided her with an austere existence and the opportunity to clean bathrooms and fry chicken in someone else's house. She'd implied that she knew how to come into serious money, and it wouldn't be from pawning Willetta Robarts's odd bits of jewelry. Had her cousin found her a job at Disney World? Did Snow White have a dwarf named Baldy?

"All clear," Corporal Robarts said as he pushed his way past a scrub oak. "On to the softball field?"

"Good idea." I brushed off my butt and followed him. "I think I'll check on those numbers Ester called, just in case we don't find anything in her car. You may have tossed the bill, but the long-distance company will have records. Aren't you surprised that Norella made calls, too?"

"They go about their business, and I go about mine."

"But you came out of the men's room while she was using the pay telephone at the café. That must have startled her."

"I don't think she even saw me."

I slowed down, hoping to remain upwind from him. "She was talking to Jarvis. Did you hear her arrange to meet him?"

"I didn't pay any attention. You gonna stand there all night?"

"You knew she was meeting him yesterday afternoon. No one else, including her ex-husband, had any reason to think she'd be by the creek. Not Rachael, or Sarah, or Naomi, or Judith, or even Deborah—unless I need to take a closer look at Merle. It'd be a stretch, but odder things have happened in dear old Dunkicker in the last thirty-six hours."

"What is this shit?"

"Later in the day, did you go home to have supper with your mother, or to shower and dispose of your bloody clothes?"

"The way you're carrying on, the next thing you'll be accusing me of is putting on lipstick and prancing in the woods. I didn't especially like Ruth, or Ester, for that matter. Then again, I don't like Crank Nickle and I'm not overly fond of Chief Panknine's wife. You want to use my cellphone to make sure I didn't sneak away this morning to suffocate them in their beds?"

"Ester's not in Florida, is she?"

"How the hell would I know?"

I was beginning to feel like a lame-brained heroine who'd gone up to the attic to investigate. "I think Norella figured out what had happened. She was probably suspicious when she saw Ester's car behind the body shop. Quite the ironic place to stash a body, don't you agree? New and used parts, all of that."

"You want to explain?"

I wanted to grab his gun, but I demurely put my hands into my pockets. "The trunk will be opened tomorrow, Anthony," I said, this time using his given name deliberately. "You're the one who's going to have to explain why you lied about taking her to the bus station, why she did something so threatening that you killed her."

"Go on." He would have sounded more menacing if his voice hadn't cracked.

"There is something about Florida that not everybody knows. Most people think of the theme parks, the beaches, even the hurricanes. I think of all that, but I also think of tabloids. Most of them are located in Lantana. Was Ester planning to sell her Beamer story to one of them? They'd eat it up. These women didn't come here for religious sanctuary; they came to get away from abusive ex-husbands. Norella must have heard about it when she turned away from the battered women's shelter and went to the community outreach program, desperate for money to buy gas and feed her children. Most towns in the area have similar agencies. That's where Deborah recruited them, didn't she? She must have convinced a few good-hearted volunteers that this was the last refuge for women and their children, perhaps even arranged for transportation. The rules didn't sound so awful. Their shaved heads convinced the locals that they were members of a wacky cult, not fugitives. What they didn't realize was that they'd never put aside enough cash to leave. Not exactly slave labor, but close to it. First, mandatory community service, and then a low-paying job and an obligation to contribute most of their earnings to the grocery demands."

"They can leave whenever they want," he said sullenly. "Deborah never told them otherwise."

"Leave and go where? They wouldn't have come in the first place if they'd felt they had options. They sincerely believe they're protecting their children and themselves by going underground. Most of them, anyway. Norella's motivation seems to have been pure spite."

Corporal Robarts's hands were trembling as he lit another cigarette. "So your story is that I killed Ester to stop her from selling her story to a tabloid, and then killed Norella because of—what? Boredom?"

"Ester told Norella. When Norella figured out what had happened, she decided that there was nothing stopping her from doing the same thing. All she needed was enough money for a tank of gas and a cheap motel with a telephone, then stay low and wait for the tabloid boys to arrive. It would have made quite a cover story."

"So the Beamers are exposed and Norella makes out like a bandit. What if I said that Ester begged me to say I took her to the bus station?"

"Why would she do that?"

The cigarette bobbled as he worked on it. "She was afraid to get her car before it was dark. Rachael and Sarah might have seen her leaving and done something to stop her. They wouldn't have wanted their faces in a tabloid if they were hiding from ex-husbands."

"Not bad, Anthony," I said, "but we'll be comparing fingerprints in the morning. We may find some on both the outside and the inside of the trunk."

He flicked the cigarette into the brush. "You may not be doing anything in the morning, Chief Hanks. The whole town may think Duluth came to kill his wife, but they might just change their minds if your body's found out here. What's more, he isn't the only crazy coot roaming the woods these days. We've got druggies, war veterans, and most of Crank Nickle's kinfolk, who took off to wait for a Second Coming. Last I heard, they was perched in trees up in Greasy Valley, pestering the hippies, but you never know."

Lame-brained heroines always survived, I told myself. "You don't think the Beamers might have a problem with that? They saw us leave together."

"I'll just say you sent me to check the cabins on the other side of the lodge. More efficient, you'd said. No reason to stay together when the killer's already locked up. I wasn't real comfortable, but you were in charge of the investigation, as you kept telling everybody."

"At least let me have a cigarette," I countered, listening intently for the Mounties to come thundering up the creekbed.

"Yeah, I suppose so."

He handed me one and held out his lighter. As soon as the flame licked up, I jammed it in his face and took off on the sorry excuse for a road. He had the flashlight, but I had the adrenaline advantage. I leaped over logs like a damn gazelle, not always with success. Down would lead to the road that ran between the gate and the lodge. He couldn't risk shooting me: Bullets, like fingerprints, were too easily traced.

He seemed to have something in mind, though, and I was not eager to find out what it might be. I could hear him behind me, thudding along, heaving, and taking the occasional sprawl. His mother would be appalled at his language, if I lived to tattle on him. It seemed like a good idea to me.

I finally had to duck under a cedar and catch my breath. He stopped, too, although I had no sense of how far behind me he was. Not far, alas, and he'd finally remembered that he had the flashlight in his hand.

The beam began sweeping across the ruts and coming closer. If I stayed where I was, he would find me, and if I scrambled into the woods, he would hear me. I found a rock and threw it across the road, waited until he took a few steps in that direction, and took off running again.

"Hey!" he shouted.

It did not seem like the time to stop and inquire if I could do anything for him. The ground was getting steeper, which I dearly hoped meant I was getting closer to the road. I caught my foot on a root, but somehow managed to keep my balance as I slithered down the bank into a puddle of water.

As I climbed out of it, I was startled to see a car coming

toward me, its headlights off. I stood in the middle of the road and waved my arms as if I were directing a jet to its gate. It stopped with inches to spare.

"Need a lift?" Jacko asked softly.

"What I need is a little help. He has a gun, and by now he may be crazy enough to use it. When I yell, turn on your headlights and I'll take it from there."

"Shouldn't I get out and punch him in the nose or something gallant like that? Of course I don't know who he is, but I'm sure he's a villain."

"Stay in the car and"—I glanced at his backseat—"protect your children."

I stepped back into the middle of the road as I heard Corporal Robarts coming. As he reached the bank, I yelled, "Here I am, asshole!"

As he jumped over the ditch and landed on the road, the headlights caught him in the face. I took the opportunity to grab the gun out of his hand and send him sprawling backward. He went down with a splash.

"Very impressive," Jacko commented. "I didn't realize you were quite so aggressive. Is this typical of your behavior?"

"I need another favor. Will you go back to the lodge and tell the deputy that I need his assistance?"

He paused. "That may complicate things for me."

"Such as being charged with kidnapping?"

He shushed the children and got out of the car. "I have full custody. My ex-wife was given only supervised visitation, but she took the children while they were playing in the yard. It's taken me two months to find them."

"Then you didn't kidnap them," I said as I went over to Robarts and planted my foot on his back. He said something I hoped the children could not hear.

"I'm concerned that they might be taken into protective custody while this is sorted out. She'll start up again with how I was neglecting and abusing them. Her lawyers and mine will be back to having lunch at the country club and haggling on the back nine."

"I can't stand here all night, Jacko."

"You have his gun."

"He's not going to let that bother him, and I'm reluctant to shoot him. There's already been enough suffering at Camp Pearly Gates."

"I'll go find this deputy for you. Would you mind if I called you in a few weeks?"

"Try the Maggody PD. I don't keep tidy office hours, but I'm usually around. I appreciate this."

"And you ought to," he said as he got into the car and began to back down the road toward the lodge.

17

"You went and did what?" Raz said, gaping at Dahlia. She might have been kin, but she sure as hell wasn't acting like it.

"I took the mule," she repeated.

"Now why should I believe that?"

"I don't care if you do."

"Does Perkins know?"

"Maybe, maybe not." Dahlia sat down on the edge of the porch. "You and your sow might ought to decide what you want to do. I can wait if you want to crawl on your belly to the pasture and take a look. All I'm tellin' you is I took the mule."

"Where? It ain't all that easy to up and take a mule, you know. It requires a certain talent."

She jiggled the double-stroller with her foot and gave the babies a sober look. They stared back, just like they knew they wouldn't be getting braces if she didn't hold her ground. "Your grandpappy weren't the only mule charmer in Stump County."

Raz had to sit back and think this over. For one thing, the mule might be in Perkins's shed. Or dead, if it got to that. He'd been watching the last day or two, and the mule hadn't been anywhere to be seen in the pasture.

"Are you claiming to be a mule charmer?" he asked.

"I didn't say that," Dahlia replied. "All I said was I took the mule."

"And did what with it?"

"I don't recollect, right offhand. Why should you care? Go find another mule."

Raz spat on the yellowed patch of grass. "Mules are mules, but, well . . . Marjorie's taken a fancy, and . . ."

"Then here's what you're gonna do," she said. "There's a man staying at the Airport Arms Motel, in number three. He's greasy, worse than rancid bacon. You explain real nicely that Marjorie is going to chew off his foot unless he gives you the check I wrote. Once you hand it over to me, I'll tell you what I did with Perkins's mule."

"That's all?"

Dahlia smiled sweetly. "Give me a holler when you get back to town and we'll finish our business. Don't go thinkin' you'll tell folks about this. Sows can be charmed, too."

"Why, look who's here," said Estelle as I came walking down the dock. "Maybe we ought to call Brother Verber to come offer a blessing. He ain't had much else to do since Mrs. Jim Bob went through his bag and poured his wine out the second-floor window. He was sitting out here earlier today, looking like he was trying to figure out how to turn water into wine, but the Almighty wasn't cooperating."

Ruby Bee kept her eyes on the plastic ball drifting in the water. "About time you showed your face."

I sat down beside her. "So what's been happening?"

"Why do you care? You upped and vanished more than two days ago, like it weren't none of our business. I'm just your mother, after all. No reason why I should care, or even notice. We had ham and beans for supper last night. The cornbread was burnt on the bottom, but I'm not used to the oven just yet."

Estelle handed me a plastic bottle. "Better put some of this on your nose," she said. "The girls are still moaning about their sunburns. Larry Joe got so fed up with hearing it that he told them to stay in their cabin. He sez the bleachers will be finished this afternoon. I reckon we ought to go up there and have a look."

"I can't hardly wait," said Ruby Bee, still refusing to look at me.

I slathered my nose with sunblock, then wiped my hand on my shirttail and poked her shoulder. "You want to hear about it?"

"None of my concern."

Estelle scooted closer. "Well, I do. What on earth led Anthony Robarts to kill those two women? Where are the rest of them? I walked up that way yesterday, and it was clear they'd all left. It seemed real sad, the bunks all stripped and the garden already losing to the weeds. All I found was a diaper lying in the weeds and a notebook with drawings of the lodge and the lake. Whoever drew them might consider another career."

I made a tactical decision to ignore my mother for the time being. "Corporal Robarts did what he thought was the only way to protect his mother."

"His mother?" gasped Estelle. "Mrs. Jim Bob kept telling us about the charity and the sick little children and how they could frolic on the softball field and—"

"I know," I said, "but Willetta Robarts was the one who convinced volunteers at the community service agencies to screen potential recruits. She wanted women who felt trapped in unbearable situations and had nowhere else to turn. They were told they could have a safe place to live and the chance to earn enough money so they could move on. They never knew she owned the company store, in a manner of speaking, or that she was Deborah. She wears a wig, you know. She could transform herself in a matter of seconds from an aristocrat to . . . something more sinister. It took me a long time to realize she kept going into the police department to help Duluth escape so I'd assume he was guilty. It's hard to know if she ordered the killings or if Anthony did it to protect her reputation. The county prosecutor was leaning both ways."

"Why did she make the others go and shave their heads?" asked Estelle, always a cosmetologist at heart.

"So they'd be too intimidated to leave," I said, wishing Ruby Bee would at least acknowledge that she was listening. "That's how you create a subservient class, by isolating them and making them feel conspicuous. She would have fit well into the landed gentry two hundred years ago."

Estelle sucked on her lip for a moment. "I reckon I'd stay in my house if I looked like that. Ruby Bee, do you recollect when Elsie McMay gave herself a home permanent and burned her hair so bad she looked like she'd been caught in a forest fire? She pretended she was staying with her third cousin over in Jonesboro, but she had to come out for groceries and—"

"Just let Arly get on with it, will you?" said Ruby Bee, more than a little bit peevish.

Estelle patted her beehive as if to assure herself that it was still intact in all its towering grandeur. "So where are they now?"

"In Farberville." I sighed as I remembered the paperwork and interminable sessions with Harve, the county prosecutor, and a pair of FBI agents who'd been brought in because of the interstate factor. "The women and the children are being taken care of until it's sorted out. Anthony Robarts is in jail. His mother's hired a high-priced lawyer from Little Rock, but even he can't explain the fingerprints on the inside of Ester's trunk—or on the piece of pipe found alongside the body."

Ruby Bee reeled in her line, then cast the bobber back into the water. "Can't see why he left her in the car like that," she said, pretending she was talking to herself. "Myself, I would have driven the car to the end of a logging road and buried the body."

"Is that from personal experience?" I waited for her to smile, and when she didn't so much as twitch her lips, added, "Corporal Robarts bungled it. When he put Ester's body in the trunk, he didn't realize she had her car key in her hand. I suppose he thought he could deal with the situation later."

"Did the tabloids get the story?" asked Estelle.

I nodded. "Harve's not real happy to have his face on racks by the checkout lines in every grocery store across the country, but that's the price of fame, I suppose. He was elbowing aside the county prosecutor on the courthouse steps and smirking like a possum in a persimmon tree."

"Glad to hear someone's having a right good time," muttered Ruby Bee, yanking up her line to ascertain that some fragment of a decidedly deceased worm still dangled on the hook.

It wasn't tantalizing, but I wasn't a crappie or a perch. For once, I wasn't even hungry, having pigged out on a cherry limeade and tamales from the Dairee Dee-Lishus on the drive back from Maggody. "I talked to Duluth, by the way. He said he'll be done by Saturday, presuming the plumber sobers up. The health department inspectors will be by on Monday. One of them is his second cousin, so there shouldn't be any problem."

Estelle glanced at her compatriot. "You saying Ruby Bee can reopen next week?"

"If she wants to," I said.

"And what if I don't?" growled the proprietor of Ruby Bee's Bar & Grill, flicking her rod to plop the bobber back into the lake.

"You can probably get a decent deal if you sell the bar and the motel. It won't pay for a condo on a beach in

Florida, but you can buy a nice double-wide and park it in the Pot O' Gold. There's a vacant spot now that Norella's trailer is parked behind her mother's house. Duluth and his boys are living there for the time being."

Estelle swallowed. "Ruby Bee's Bar & Grill can't be sold to some stranger who'll turn it into a used-car lot."

"The guy who owns the Dew Drop Inn was by the other day," I said. "He's thinking about starting a franchise. He says he'll call his next establishment the Dew Drop Inn Too."

Ruby Bee flinched. "Well, he can just think about something else, like poking himself in the eye. I ain't selling to anyone, including the likes of him!"

"Whatever," I said as I gazed across the lake. "Looks like we've got nice weather for the next few days."

"Maybe," said Ruby Bee. "At least we got pork chops and fried okra for supper."

"And applesauce," added Estelle. "Lots and lots of applesauce."

><

"Now listen here, you schemin' pissant bastard," Jim Bob sputtered, repeating himself for the umpteenth time and getting redder each time. "If you don't give me that videotape, I'm gonna wring your scrawny neck and bury your body in a flowerbed."

Hammet didn't bother to look away from the television set. "Won't get you the tape, though. I hid it real good, but someplace where it'll get found afore too long if it stays there. I reckon folks around here are gonna have theirselves a real belly laugh when they watch it. You was squealing like a stuck pig when you got all tangled in your shorts trying to scramble out of bed to git away from—what was their names? Sam and Tim? Sumpthin' like that. It's a good thing you chased 'em all the way out to the driveway. Otherwise, I couldn't have taken the tape."

Jim Bob's eyes narrowed. "And done what with it?"

"I don't likely recollect, but iff'n you bring me another sandwich and a glass of milk, I'll stew on it. And I was thinkin' about doughnuts with powdered sugar for dessert. Long as you're goin' to the store, get some grape sodas and a box of vanilla sandwich cookies. I've had a hankerin' all day."

"I might could tie a concrete block to your foot and throw you in Boone Creek."

"And have some 'splaining to do when ever'body gets back to town," Hammet said coolly as he switched channels to some dumbass show with men running around in short pants, whacking at a ball.

Jim Bob tried again. "Ain't you scared of going to prison, you pint-sized sumbitch?"

"Not near as scared as you are of what's gonna happen when your prissy wife gets home. You gonna stand there and goggle like a bullfrog all afternoon?"

PROSPECT FREE LIBRARY
915 Trenton Falls St.
Prospect, New York 13435
(315)896-2736

MEMBER
MID-YORK LIBRARY SYSTEM
Utica, N.Y. 13502